S0-BHW-566

Also available by M. E. Hilliard

The Greer Hogan Mysteries

Shadow in the Glass

The Unkindness of Ravens

THREE
CAN KEEP
A SECRET

THREE CAN KEEP A SECRET

A Greer Hogan Mystery

M. E. HILLIARD

CROOKED
LANE

NEW YORK

This is a work of fiction. All of the names, characters, organizations, places and events portrayed in this novel are either products of the author's imagination or are used fictitiously. Any resemblance to real or actual events, locales, or persons, living or dead, is entirely coincidental.

Copyright © 2023 by Macaire Hill

All rights reserved.

Published in the United States by Crooked Lane Books, an imprint of The Quick Brown Fox & Company LLC.

Crooked Lane Books and its logo are trademarks of The Quick Brown Fox & Company LLC.

Library of Congress Catalog-in-Publication data available upon request.

ISBN (hardcover): 978-1-63910-236-5
ISBN (ebook): 978-1-63910-237-2

Cover design by Alan Ayers

Printed in the United States.

www.crookedlanebooks.com

Crooked Lane Books
34 West 27th St., 10th Floor
New York, NY 10001

First Edition: February 2023

10 9 8 7 6 5 4 3 2 1

For library staff everywhere

Chapter One

❧

Raven Hill Manor was silhouetted against a blazing scarlet sky. I stood in the shadow cast by the gothic pile of stone and wood, admiring the irregular outline and odd angles— the peaks and valleys of the slate roof; the false fronts and dormered windows; and the unexpected, octagonal tower jutting from one corner. Clouds moved across the setting sun, and red reflections flickered across the upper windows.

"'Last night I dreamt I went to Manderley again.'" I quoted the opening line of *Rebecca* as I pocketed my car keys. I'd always been a sucker for a creepy old house, with or without a creepy old housekeeper. Raven Hill Manor fit the bill, though after a year of working at the library it housed, I found it more quirky than creepy. The manor was far from sharing all its secrets with me, but I had reached the point where its creaks and groans and sighs, its odd artifacts, and its overlooked nooks were a familiar part of my day. The Raven Hill Library was a busy, cheerful place in spite of its brooding exterior. If it kept itself to itself after business hours—well, that was fine with me.

I was reaching for the back door of the building when it opened.

"Oops, sorry, Greer!" It was Felicity James, president of the Friends of the Library. The annual book and bake sale, the group's biggest fundraiser, was only five days away, and several of the volunteers had gathered to work out some final details. In spite of her recent widowhood, or perhaps because of it, Felicity had stepped up to finish out someone else's term as president and had thrown herself into the book sale organization. A few other members of the group were right behind her. We stepped to one side.

"So, any last-minute issues?" I asked Felicity.

"A couple of minor things—some confusion about schedules and who's doing what for the preview sale, but other than that, we're in good shape. As long as the weather's nice, I think it will be a success." Felicity looked toward the parking lot. Even in the fading light, large puddles and fallen leaves and branches were visible. We'd had a heavy rain that afternoon, but the clouds had given way to a brisk autumn breeze. Random gusts still set the trees thrashing in the fading light, but the forecast was for crisp, sunny weather through the weekend. I told her as much.

"Well, let's hope that holds," she said. "What brings you back?"

"I forgot something," I said. "I'm off tomorrow since I'm working this weekend, so I decided to come back and get it. I needed a couple things from the Market on Main anyway."

We chatted for a few more minutes, and then Felicity went on her way and I headed for my office. I moved a few files on my desk and found what I was after—a portable battery I could use to power or charge my phone or tablet. The battery was a gift from Ian Cameron, my one-time love, current friend, and future who knew? Since he was currently in Kuala Lumpur on a work project of several months' duration, I could think about that later. He'd sent a present to mark my one-year anniversary of working for the Raven Hill Library. The perfect gift considering how often we lost power. He'd included a headlamp as well. It was lightweight and on thick elastic. I had laughed, but I kept it in my desk drawer next to a flashlight. You never knew when you'd need to go hands-free. I had big flashlights at home and in my car, but the battery was something I'd never thought of, and now that winter was approaching, I liked to keep it handy. An icy November storm could knock out the electricity all over town. Besides, it made me smile. Ian was a techie, a gadget guy, and this was his idea of a perfect gift. Some men never thought past flowers.

I decided to see if we had a copy of Hitchcock's *Rebecca* checked in. I had the DVD of Christie's *Hallowe'en Party* at home but decided to save that until the following weekend. The sky over the manor as I arrived had put me in a gothic state of mind. As I walked down the hall toward the reading room, I noticed a light on in the director's office. Helene Montague, our director, had been off today after working the weekend, so I decided to take a look. Very little in the manor was kept locked, and with a small staff in the evenings it was easy for people to end up in places they shouldn't be. I was surprised it didn't happen more often. I poked my head into the office and immediately regretted it.

Anita Hunzeker, who chaired the library board of trustees, was looking for something in a portable file box that she'd placed on a chair. Thankfully, she had her back to me. My relief was short-lived. As I began to ease back out the door, she spotted my reflection in the window and turned.

"Oh, Greer, it's you. You're not closing tonight, are you?" she asked, eyeing my jeans and sweater with disapproval. Anita was wearing her usual uniform of dressy slacks, blazer, silk blouse, and colorful scarf. If she owned anything denim, I had yet to see it.

"No, I was here earlier. I came back for something I forgot," I said. "I saw the light and thought I'd check and see who was in here. I know Helene is off."

"Yes," she said. "I've been using her office. Board business, and then the Friends meeting. I wanted to make sure they had things in hand. Felicity had to step in rather late in the process. And now I've misplaced my new glasses. I'm supposed to use them for driving at night. Of course I can manage without them, but I'd rather not."

"Would you like some help?" I asked. It was the last thing I wanted to do. Anita Hunzeker was regularly referred to as "Attila the Hunzeker" by the library staff, the volunteers, and most of the rest of the residents of Raven Hill. She was ruthlessly efficient, had boundless energy, and was completely lacking in sensitivity. Though she had been involved in hiring me, I had fallen out of favor while investigating a murder on the manor grounds the previous spring. My stock had gone up when I solved it, leaving the library with no legal liability, but Anita still felt I had a tendency to stick my nose into things. This was true, so in general I tried to avoid her.

"Well, if you wouldn't mind checking to see if they're on the floor somewhere. Richard dropped off some files for me and knocked over my bag—men are so careless. I was sure he picked everything up, but he might have missed them. They're not in here—let me check my handbag again."

I heaved a mental sigh and knelt down. Helene had a little table and some chairs on one side of her office for smaller meetings. This was where Anita had been working. I looked around, feeling along the shadowed area by the baseboards. I heard Anita yawn. Odd, she was usually the Energizer bunny.

"Long day?" I said, as I backed up and then moved toward the radiator. It was too dark to see underneath it.

"An early appointment and several meetings. The historical society cannot wrap their minds around the need for a better facility. The proposed library would be ideal, but they're very territorial. Combining our archives and their collection makes perfect sense. Why let everything molder away in the dark when you can house it all in a bright, new research center?"

"Better climate control would certainly help. Some of those documents are fragile," I said, giving myself points for diplomacy. I liked working in the manor and would be happy to see the library stay there. Anita was determined that her legacy to the town she grew up in would be a new, state-of-the-art library and archive. She'd already picked out the location. She had a point about accessibility, air quality, and light—but she ignored tradition and history. The village was pretty evenly split on new versus old, and the preliminary discussions had been going on for nearly a year. I didn't see it getting any better. Add to that the terms of the Ravenscroft Trust and the deeding of the manor to the village for use as a library, and the whole thing got even messier. But Anita was determined.

"Exactly, Greer," Anita went on as I completed my search beneath the radiator. She was unusually chatty this evening, possibly happy to have an audience who seemed to agree with her. I moved to do one last check under the table as her phone rang.

"Richard!" she said. Her husband. She turned and walked to the office doorway, stepping into the small vestibule outside. I heard her ask about her glasses. I'd found nothing under the table but the portable file box Anita had placed there. I glanced up. She still had her back to me. I took a quick look at the files. Typical Anita—everything was neatly labeled except a couple of folders that had penciled names on the tabs. The labels were what I would expect—"New Building," "Historical Society," "Grants," "Book Sale." The penciled ones were harder to read—I'd need a closer look. Anita was still talking. I caught "wine—that new white I like" and "gift." I pulled the box toward me. I could make out "Millicent/Ames Family," "Margaret Emerson," "JP Walters," "Sean Harris," "J Bean," and something that looked like "Ravenscroft Deeds." It sounded like Anita was winding up her call. I could clearly hear "in my car? I'll look, I'm leaving shortly," so I backed out from under the table. I was standing, dusting myself off, when she turned around.

"Sorry, Anita, I've come up empty," I said.

"Well, thank you for helping," she said. "I guess I'll have to make do."

"Could they be in your car? Maybe they fell between the seats or something?"

"I guess it's possible, but I could swear I had them when I walked in. I picked up the new prescription this morning. Well, I'd better be going. It appears I still have things to do. Good night, Greer."

"Good night," I said.

I left Anita gathering her bags and boxes and headed to the reading room for my DVD. I saw Millicent Ames, our archivist, going out the front door as I went into the hall. She often parked in the old lot near the front of the building. Staff usually only used it when we were expecting a big crowd for programs or meetings, but Millicent had been parking there for decades and said she often did it by habit. The reading room was quiet. There were a few patrons browsing, a page shelving in the new book section, and two other staff members. David, an older gentleman who had retired from his regular job, gotten bored, and come to work for the library part-time, was at the circulation desk. Jillian Bean, our Youth Services librarian, was at Reference, her attention on some papers in front of her. It was a peaceful scene.

"Hi, Jilly," I said.

She jumped. "Oh, hi, Greer. What brings you back?"

"Forgot something and then decided to pick up a DVD as long as I was here. I ran into Anita. She was remarkably chatty."

Jilly frowned. "I thought she'd left," she said, her tone flat.

"Packing up. Couldn't find her glasses. She should be gone by the time you close up." I looked at the clock. "I'd better get moving."

I waved to David and went to the videos. I was pretty sure *Rebecca* would be checked in—the book wasn't usually assigned until later in the school year, so those who wanted to either skip it entirely or see how the film stacked up wouldn't be asking for it yet. I hadn't liked the novel when I'd read it in high school. The nameless heroine had been, in my opinion, also spineless and therefore irritating. It wasn't until I was older and heard a lecture on Du Maurier that I started to come around. According to the speaker, the author had been disappointed when her critics and readers saw the book as a gothic romance rather than a story about a man who had power and a woman who had none, which is what she'd intended. That, and the fact that I was older and wiser, had made me revise my opinion. Revisiting many of the things I'd read and judged in my teens and early twenties would undoubtedly be edifying. The view from forty is different. There are some things that never change, though. Tonight, I wanted junk food and Hitchcock. I plucked the movie from the shelf, checked it out, and went home.

Chapter Two

～

I woke for the first time at four AM on Tuesday when my phone chirped. It was a text from Officer Jennie Webber, my friend and workout buddy.

Can't make our run. Working accident scene all night. Call you later.

Calling it a run was kind of her. The part she did with me was more of a brisk walk/slow jog combo. I knew that after we were done, or sometimes before, she did a couple miles at a faster pace. She never missed a workout, whereas I would use any excuse. I squinted at the screen, turned off my alarm, rolled over, and went back to sleep.

I was awakened for the second time at a little after eight. It was Helene's ringtone.

"Greer, I'm sorry to disturb you. I know it's your day off. I'm afraid I have some bad news."

I sat up. "No problem. What's going on?"

"It's Anita. She's been in a car accident. She apparently died at the scene."

"Last night," I said, thinking of Jennie's text.

"Yes, after she left here. She was on her way home. You know she lives down that winding road. I'm not sure exactly what happened, but it sounds like she skidded and went into the trees. I really don't know much. Sam O'Donnell called me. He said they'd have some questions. Routine, according to Sam. I'll have more information after I speak to him."

We'd have more information, but only what Lieutenant Sam O'Donnell wanted us to have. He was a small-town cop, but he was a good one.

"Wow, that's awful. Hard to believe, even. She always seemed indestructible," I said.

"True," Helene said. "Anyway, the library will be open as usual, and the book sale will go on. It's what she would have wanted."

That phrase so often sounded trite, or convenient, but in this case it was absolutely true. Anita would never have let the death of a board member, volunteer, or even employee get in the way of a fundraiser.

"Yes, it is," I said. "Listen, it's probably not important, but I did see Anita last night before she left the building."

I explained about my late errand back to the manor and seeing the light in Helene's office. She agreed that my conversation with Anita probably had no bearing on anything, but said she'd let Sam know, and then hesitated a moment before saying, "I hate to impose, but would you be able to take care of a couple things today? I'm not going to be able to leave the office. I was supposed to be picking up some brochures from the printer and dropping them off at a few places around the village. After the book sale, I'll be able to give you a few hours of comp time."

"Sure," I said. "I'm out running errands today anyway."

"Thank you," said Helene. "That's such a help. I'll email you everything you need in a few minutes. It shouldn't take too long. I really appreciate it."

We hung up. I got out of bed and made coffee, mentally reviewing my conversation with Anita the night before. Maybe she *had* needed those glasses more than she let on. For someone nearing seventy, Anita had been in great shape and proud of it. Her entire family, she said, had always had "iron constitutions." It was an old-fashioned phrase, but it suited. She had recently mentioned a little arthritis in her knees but stated that it would not keep her from skiing this coming winter. She'd wanted some information on different kinds of pain relievers, both prescription and homeopathic, and I'd helped her find good sources. She must have taken the issue with her vision as a personal insult. The only glasses I'd ever seen her in were sunglasses. Could she really have gone off the road in the dark?

I'd had a little more trouble seeing things at night lately. Or far away. Did I need glasses? I covered one eye, then another, trying to make out things across the room. Meh. Then I tried to read washing instructions on the little labels on my clothes as I got dressed. Hmph. I scribbled "make appt. eye doctor" at the bottom of my day's to-do list. No harm in checking. Squinting created crow's feet, after all.

I had a busy week ahead and a lengthy list of errands now that I was handling some things for Helene. Since I'd missed my workout that morning, I decided to group anything in the village into the afternoon and walk. I'd visit only my more far-flung locations—grocery store, printer, historical society—by car. I was adding them to my list when I got a text from Jennie.

Questions about Anita. Java Joint later?

It looked like Helene had mentioned my conversation with Anita to Lieutenant Sam O'Donnell, Jennie's boss. I texted back, and we confirmed a time. After making a few calls and putting away my clean laundry, I set out. I stopped first at the printer, picking up a couple of boxes of brochures and handouts. Groceries next. I liked to use the Market on Main whenever possible, both because they were local and because they had a great selection of prepared foods. I wasn't much of a cook, and Raven Hill's takeout options were limited. For paper goods and pantry staples, I used the bigger chain supermarket in the next town. As I drove, I mentally reviewed all the stops I had to make that day, and wondered if there would be much talk of Anita's accident. I didn't have to wait long to find out. I was walking into the store when I ran into Dory Hutchinson on her way out. Dory was a circulation assistant at the library and a walking repository of village gossip. She was a lifelong resident of Raven Hill. That, and the fact that she had relatives scattered all over the Albany area, made her a great source of information as long as you took the time to sort out fact from salacious speculation.

"Greer! I'm so glad I ran into you. I suppose you've heard about Anita?" Dory steered her cart out of the lane to the door. She was ready to settle in for a gossip. I stepped over to her.

"Yes, Helene called me this morning," I said.

"Well, did she tell you that Anita was run off the road? Deliberately!" Dory said, looking not at all distressed. Dory had never liked Anita.

"She did mention the police weren't sure what happened, and they'd have some questions for us. Sam O'Donnell told her it was routine," I said.

Dory rolled her eyes. "Not likely. Bill went by Winding Ridge Road this morning. He had an early job out that way—burst pipe. He said the local police were there, but so were some state troopers. And you know what that means. They think something's fishy."

She was probably right. Raven Hill shared a police department with several other towns and villages in the area, but the force was small. Traffic accidents were one thing, but if anything required more sophisticated forensics, they'd need some help.

"So what's the theory? That road has some treacherous curves, doesn't it?" I asked. I'd only driven on it a few times, but the "winding" in the name was an understatement.

"It does, but she went off it along one of the straightaways," Dory said. "Bill had to go right by it. The police were directing traffic—it was down to just the one lane—and he had to wait for a few minutes while a car came the other way. He said she went down the bank *before* that hairpin turn, right where it's so steep and rocky. I think she was forced off the road right there."

"That *is* strange. It's still hard to believe."

Dory snorted. "The only thing hard to believe is that no one did it sooner. The police have their work cut out for them, that's for sure. Although . . ."

Dory paused. I knew my cue. I raised my eyebrows. Dory looked around. Satisfied that there was no one near enough to hear her, she leaned closer.

"Well, you know about Anita's feud with Cynthia Baker, right?"

I shook my head.

"Cynthia is president of the Raven Hill Historical Society. Has been for years. Her family has lived in the area forever. She and Anita went to high school together, and they've never gotten along. Started out fighting over who would edit the yearbook and moved on to the PTA and then every other committee in town."

"And you think that after all these years she snapped?"

"Sort of," Dory said. "Anita finally did something that pushed her over the edge."

"What?"

"I'm not exactly sure," Dory said. "But my cousin Angela was there at the last meeting—Monday afternoon it was—and she told me that afterward Anita and Cynthia had a closed-door meeting"—Dory put little air quotes around the last bit—"and that she heard them yelling at each other. Well, as much as you can hear anything through the doors of that place. Solid oak, every single one. Those Victorians knew how to build to last. Anyway, Angela said Anita sailed out, saying something like 'We'll see about that,' and that Cynthia was fuming." Dory gave a little nod. "And Cynthia lives up the same way that Anita does. Not the same road, but near it."

"So, she stewed all afternoon and then went after Anita that night?" I said. "How did she know when Anita would be on the road? I don't know, Dory."

"Well, listen to this. Angela was at the historical society building for a couple of hours after the meeting. She volunteers there doing office work, and they're closed to the public Mondays so that's her day. Anyway, she said that Cynthia stomped around for a while, and then went into her office. She made a few calls—Angela couldn't hear—but then she seemed to calm down. Right as Angela was getting ready to leave, she heard Cynthia shout 'hah!' or something like that. Angela looked into the office as she was walking out, and asked Cynthia if everything was okay. And Cynthia said, 'Everything's fine. Anita Hunzeker is in for a surprise. I'll teach her a lesson.' Something like that. And I'm sure she knew Anita would be at the library for the meeting—she was always going on about how busy she is." Dory rolled her eyes.

"It does sound suspicious," I said. "But I still think the timing would be tricky."

"True," Dory conceded. "But Cynthia has hated Anita for a long time. Of course, she's not the only one."

We paused while Dory greeted someone she knew. A natural salesperson, Dory threw in a pitch for the library book sale. "And we always have a wonderful bake sale at the same time," she said. Hard to go wrong with that.

Once the woman had left, we went back to our conversation.

"Who else is on your suspect list?" I asked Dory.

"I'm glad you asked," she said, "because I'm sure if you and I work together we can figure this out. Of course, since you and Jennie Webber are friendly, you may get inside information." She gave me a pointed look.

I shrugged. "Not likely. She's very tight-lipped about work, you know." Which was mostly true, but if Jennie did tell me something, I wasn't going to share it with Dory. She was the closest thing Raven Hill had to a town crier.

"Hmm," Dory said. "Then it's even more important that the two of us put our heads together." She went on to rattle off a list of names, followed by her theories on how likely a suspect each one was. A few names were familiar, but many weren't. According to Dory, Anita had alienated most of the town.

"Of course," she said, "there's always Richard and Sloane. They say it's usually the husband, don't they? Although I know Sloane and her mother never really got along. Still, I don't see either one of them having the nerve to stand up to her, let alone kill her."

"A cornered animal will attack to defend itself," I said.

Dory considered this. "That's true, Greer. But Richard never seemed to have any issue letting Anita run the show, and Sloane has a family of her own now and lives in the next county. I don't think they see each other that much. Of course, Richard spends a lot of time with his grandson now that he's retired, but Anita is always too busy. Well, we'll just have to keep our ears open, won't we? See you tomorrow?"

I told her I would and said goodbye. I ran through all Dory's theories as I pushed my cart around. I wasn't familiar enough with the Winding Ridge Road to argue with her, but the fact that Jennie wanted to meet and ask me some questions about Anita suggested that her car accident was being treated as suspicious. Dory was right in her assessment of Anita—she had alienated a lot of people. I knew that after only a year of living in Raven Hill. When people found out I worked at the library, the discussion inevitably turned to Anita and her plans for a new building. Whether for or against the idea itself, the comments on Anita's approach were uniformly negative. But were any of these people upset enough to kill?

Richard Hunzeker and his daughter merited a closer look. Years of proximity to an abusive personality could breed the kind of rage it took to commit murder, even in the most mild mannered. And then there was Cynthia Baker. I'd met her once or twice, but I couldn't say I had a good read on her. I hadn't known about the longstanding feud, but I'd bet anyone who'd lived here for any length of time did. Jennie probably didn't, so I'd mention it when I saw her. And since I was stopping to drop off brochures at the historical society, I'd drop Anita's accident into the conversation. If someone wanted to talk, I was always willing to listen.

Chapter Three

The building that housed the historical society was, as Dory said, a solid old Victorian a little removed from downtown Raven Hill. It didn't have the gothic vibe that the manor did, but I could see it more as an old-style funeral parlor than a family home. When I arrived, a silver-haired gentleman wearing a volunteer badge was showing some maps to a small group of visitors. I mouthed "library brochures" when he looked up, and he waved me toward the back. I wasn't sure where I was going, but followed the center hall until I came to one of those red velvet ropes and a sign that read "Staff Only." At this point the main hallway narrowed and continued toward the back of the house, and another hall branched off to the right. I stepped over the rope and looked around. Ahead of me was a swinging door—kitchen, probably. I could hear someone speaking somewhere down the hall on the right, so I turned. There was light spilling into the dim hallway from a door at the end, and as I got closer, I realized I was hearing one side of a phone call.

"Yes, this is Cynthia Baker, Raven Hill Historical Society. I need to speak to him urgently—do you know when he'll be back in the office?"

I paused, not wanting to interrupt. Also, curious. *Who did she need to speak to so urgently?*

"Thursday? Will he call in for messages? Yes, I've sent an email, but—all right, yes. A meeting that morning? Fine, if I haven't heard from him by midday, I'll call again. Let me give you my cell number as well."

Cynthia rattled it off, repeated that it was urgent, and hung up. I waited a few seconds and then strolled in. Cynthia was staring out the window, drumming her fingers on her desk. I knocked on the door frame to get her attention. She whipped her head around.

"Hi, Ms. Baker. Greer Hogan, from the library. It's been a while since we've met. I'm dropping off some things, and the gentleman out front told me to come back to the offices. I hope I'm not disturbing you." I gave her a big smile and waved the package of flyers.

She looked at me blankly for a second, blinked, and said, "The library? Oh, of course." She stood and came around the desk. "I'm sorry—I was distracted. Call me Cynthia. Yes, I do remember meeting you. You're the full-time reference librarian, aren't you? Come right in."

I stepped in and handed her the package from the print shop.

"Helene asked me to drop them off. She would have come herself, but she's been tied up at the library. With what happened to Anita . . ." I trailed off, hoping Cynthia would fill the void.

"Yes," she said. "Yes, I'm sure she has been. This has thrown a lot of things into . . . disarray."

Disarray? I raised an eyebrow.

"What I mean is—" Cynthia seemed to be reaching for the words. "What I mean is, Anita was involved in so many things. It's hard to pick up all the pieces."

"True," I said. "The two of you have worked together here for some time, haven't you? And I think she's been involved with the library nearly as long. I've only lived here for a year, so I could be wrong."

Playing the "new girl in town" card often elicited quite a bit of information. People loved to gossip about anything going on in the village, complete with history going back years or, in some cases, decades. They thought of it as "filling me in" or "bringing me up to speed." Unfortunately, Cynthia didn't seem inclined to go that route.

"Oh, Anita and I have known each other forever," she said. "We didn't always see eye to eye, but we got along well enough to get things done. Her contributions will be missed."

But Anita wouldn't. Everyone would miss the time and effort she put in, but the woman herself? Not so much.

"I'm sure they will," I agreed. "I know we're scrambling at the library—our book sale is this weekend, and we've had to do a lot of rearranging to cover the things she was involved in."

This was not technically true. The Friends had things well in hand—Anita had inserted herself into the process for the sake of checking up on everyone. They could run it well enough without her, but the fact of her death was sucking up a lot of time—both volunteer and staff. That's what had everyone scrambling.

"I'm trying to piece together quite a few things here as well," Cynthia said. She paused, looked at me, looked down at her computer, and looked up again. She opened her mouth to speak, then stopped.

I waited, doing my best to look pleasant and helpful, and not saying a word. Whatever Cynthia was trying to say was clearly important, to her at least. Otherwise, she wouldn't be having such a hard time getting it out. She drew a deep breath, squared her shoulders, and pasted on a fake smile.

"You know, I think you might be able to help with one of those . . . missing pieces. Anita was—well, both of us actually—were working on some research. For a project. I think she may have left all her notes at the library. She said she was waiting for something to come in too. Perhaps from another library? Could you take a look around, do you think?"

"It's possible there's something," I said. "Anita was a very good researcher."

"Yes, she certainly was. A real stickler for facts, no matter how minor." That last bit came out through clenched teeth. I wondered why.

"It would help to know a little more about what she was researching," I said.

"Oh, of course. It had to do with the Revolutionary War. Some prominent local citizens were involved early on. We think."

"Names?" I said. "Or is it the usual suspects? Ravenscroft, Schuyler, . . .?"

"Ah, well, we were casting rather a wide net. It was very hush-hush at the time. We were following up on a couple of letters that were donated recently. Amazing what people find tucked away in the attic. The whole thing only just came to light. I think Anita said she found some original scholarship on it somewhere. I'd love to see it."

So would I. Cynthia Baker was a terrible liar. Whatever Anita had been after, Cynthia wanted it badly. Which meant I wanted a look at it, and depending on what it was, the police might too. Since the whole concept of patron confidentiality had obviously not occurred to her, I decided to play along.

"I'll take a look around. Do you happen to know who authored this original scholarship? And what form it took?"

"Form? A thesis, I think. And the author would be—let me see . . .," she moved some papers on her desk, pretending to look for something. "Ah, here it is. James Walters. I'll write it down for you." She took out a business card and wrote on the back. Then she added something.

"Here you go. I've added my home number and my cell. Don't hesitate to call if you find anything."

"I'll do my best," I said, "but things are a little busy right now. Though I could ask someone to help me."

"Oh no, please. I don't want to make a fuss."

Of course you don't, I thought, *because you're up to something.*

"All right, then. I'll see what I can do."

"Thank you so much," she said. "I really appreciate it."

"I'm happy to help," I said. "And if Anita didn't start your research project, you can request the items yourself. I'll give you a call and let you know what I find. Bye now." I gave a little finger wave and smiled. Cynthia smiled back and watched me go. I glanced back as I turned the corner, and spotted her peeking out the door of her office. She ducked back in as I turned my head. She was wound tight. If Anita hadn't started looking for this thesis, I would.

By the time I arrived at the Java Joint, Jennie was already seated at her favorite table, with food, her notebook, and an enormous cup of coffee in front of her. I ordered and joined her. It was late for lunch and early for dinner, so we had the place to ourselves. Jennie didn't waste time getting to the point.

"Can you think of anyone who would want to kill Anita Hunzeker?"

"I can't think of anyone who wouldn't," I said.

Jennie sighed. "That's what Sam said. I was hoping you knew of something recent."

"Like someone threatening to do her in at last week's board meeting?" I asked. "The question is, *which* board meeting? Anita was involved in just about everything in and around the village."

"So I've heard. How did she get put in charge of so much if no one could stand her?"

I paused. I'd wondered about that myself at first, but after seeing Anita in action for a while, I'd begun to understand.

"You know that saying, 'If you want something done, ask a busy person to do it?'" I said.

Jennie nodded.

"I think it's because Anita was the type who got things done, and everyone knew it. She was willing to do the grunt work. There are a lot of jobs—volunteer jobs—that no one wants, but that need to get done to keep communities running. Anita would either do them or corral someone else into doing them. Pretty often, she'd come up with a better way to do them. Sometimes she was right, sometimes not. No matter which, she'd end up making people mad as she went about it. But she got results. And as time went on, she ended up in charge of things more often than not, and got less concerned with whose toes she stepped on."

"Absolute power corrupts absolutely," Jennie said.

"Exactly. I think she was a frustrated Fortune 500 CEO, to be honest." I took a sip of my drink. "So, it wasn't just an accident then?"

"No."

"How can you tell? She went off of Winding Ridge Road in the dark, didn't she? And she told me she couldn't find her new glasses."

"She skidded, but the marks don't make a lot of sense. It wasn't as she was rounding that hairpin turn—it was before—and there was nothing to show why she'd swerve where she did. The car flipped—there's a steep slope right there, and a lot of rocks. She was pretty banged up, but the medical examiner thinks she got a whack on the head after. Hard to tell until he gets a closer look, but there were a lot of loose items in the car, including a bottle of wine."

"You think someone ran her off the road and then made sure they finished the job?"

"It's possible, or it could be from something flying around during the impact, but we need to wait for the autopsy and the forensics on the car. None of this is for public consumption yet," Jennie added. "I'm only telling you because you're in a position to come across information. Not that you should go looking for it."

That last bit sounded pro forma. She wouldn't have told me this much if both she and her boss didn't think I'd be useful. I'd certainly been in the past. I wasn't going to rub it in, though.

"Of course not," I said. "I'm going to be very busy with the book sale this week."

"Right," Jennie said. She pulled out her notebook. "Now, tell me all about your conversation with Anita last night, and anything else you can remember about who was around."

I ran through everything, from the time I pulled into the lot until I left. Jennie stopped me a few times to ask questions. I wasn't completely sure about what order people left in, but I gave it my best guess. When I was done, she sighed again and yawned.

"It looks like any number of people knew she was there and was getting ready to go home," she said.

"Yes, but with the hunt for her glasses, almost everyone was gone by the time she left. Unless they were waiting for her. Did you find them? The glasses, I mean. In her car?"

Jennie shook her head. "Not that I know of. As I said, we're going over the car more thoroughly." She paused. "I did see a bag, though. Bright yellow. Eyes on the prize? Something like that?

"Eyes on You Optical," I said. "I have an appointment with them, actually."

Jennie gave me a look.

"What?" I said. "I think I'm getting nearsighted, or I have an astigmatism or something. I've been noticing it more lately. Then, when I heard about Anita's accident, I got nervous. I called them this morning. I had no idea that's where she'd been. It's just that they're close by and always have really cute frames in their window."

This was all true. It was also true that if Anita needed glasses, she'd shop local and designer. No national chains for her. Eyes on You fit the bill, so that was the first place I'd called. As luck would have it, they were open late on Thursdays and could fit me in.

Jennie didn't look convinced, but she let it go. She must be really tired. At that point Meadow, the co-owner of the Java Joint, came over to see if we needed anything. She had a coffee pot in one hand and a plate of cookies in the other.

"I'm trying a new recipe," she said. "You ladies can be my guinea pigs. More coffee?"

"Sure," Jennie said. Meadow set the plate down and poured. I reached for a cookie.

"Terrible news about Anita," Meadow said. "Heard she was run off the road. Hit and run?"

Jennie sighed and reached for her coffee.

"It's okay—Sam was in talking to Jack earlier. You're not giving anything away."

Jack was Meadow's partner and the other owner of the coffee shop. He and Sam O'Donnell went way back. The aging hippie and career cop made an unlikely pair, but Meadow had told me that the two men had been in a band together when

Jack and she had first come to the area. I'd heard stories of Sam in tie-dye, with a ponytail, but had yet to see pictures.

Jennie opted for middle ground. "We're still investigating, but we believe there may have been someone else involved."

"Well, if she'd been bashed over the head instead, I'd tell you to talk to her daughter. I heard Sloane tell her mother she'd like to kill her, and if she didn't, she was sure someone else would."

Jennie perked up. Opening her notebook, she asked, "When was this?"

Meadow raised an eyebrow, put down the coffee pot, and pulled up a chair.

"Yesterday afternoon, around this time, maybe a little later. They came in separately, Sloane first. She seemed edgy. She ordered decaf iced tea and a salad that she picked at. Anita breezed in as calm and self-assured as always. Once she settled in, the two of them went at it."

"Fight?" Jennie asked.

Meadow shrugged. "I don't know that I'd call it that. It takes two to tango. Sloane was upset, but her mother seemed unperturbed."

"Could you hear what they were arguing about?" I asked.

"Only some. There were a few people in, so there was lot of furious whispering on Sloane's part, and Anita talking as usual. I only heard them because they were sitting near the back, and I was around the corner, doing the bank deposit."

Meadow gestured. I looked to where she was pointing— there was a table for two right near the hall that led to the restrooms. A short wall separated it from the work area. I knew there was a desk right behind it, but it wasn't visible. Meadow would have been out of sight but within earshot.

"Anyway," she went on, "it seemed to have something to do with Sloane's husband getting tenure. Sloane seemed to think Anita was ruining his chances, I'm not sure how. I only caught that much because Sloane was so upset she raised her voice once or twice. All I heard from Anita was "Don't be ridiculous" and "Now you're just being childish." She mostly let her daughter rattle on."

"But you definitely heard Sloane threaten to kill her mother?" Jennie said.

"Oh yes. I'd come out to the register. Sloane stood up and said, 'I could kill you for this. Someday you'll push someone too far, and they'll bash your brains out.' Then she left."

"What did Anita do?" I asked.

"Shook her head, finished her soup, and ordered a cappuccino to go. Chatted with me like nothing had happened. Wanted to know if we needed any more flyers for the book sale, said she'd have someone drop them off. But then, that's Anita."

It was, indeed. Certain that she was in the right in every situation, very little ruffled her feathers. I'd find that hard to live with. My mother often worked on my last nerve, but I'd never threatened to kill her.

"And the daughter—Sloane, you said?" Jennie asked, looking at her notes.

"Sloane Hunzeker Harris," I told her.

"Was Sloane's behavior typical?" Jennie asked.

"She's always been a little high strung," Meadow said. "Some would say that's Anita's fault, but I've always thought it was a matter of temperament. Sloane was always a nervy kid, a worrier. You could see it even when she was hanging out in here with her high school friends. I haven't seen much of her since she got married and moved to Troy, but I doubt she's changed."

"Thank you," Jennie said, closing her notebook.

"Anytime," Meadow said. "Now, how were those cookies?"

"Excellent," I said. "Cardamom?"

"Yep," said Meadow. "I'm going to make little gumdrop shapes with colored sugar for Christmas."

Jennie was giving me a look. "Cardamom?" she said. "You can't even cook."

"But I can eat," I said. "Are you going to have that last one?"

"Yes." Jennie pulled the plate toward her. Meadow laughed and got up to attend to a couple of customers who had just walked in.

"So do you know anything else about Sloane Harris?" Jennie asked between bites of her cookie.

"Not really. I've seen her a couple of times at library events, probably because she was roped into helping by her mother. I know she's an only child, and she has one kid of her own—a little boy, maybe five? I see him with his grandfather in the library pretty regularly."

"Anita's husband?"

"Yes, Richard. I don't know anything about Sloane's husband—Sean, or maybe Steve?—or anything about his family. I'm sure I could find out."

"That's all right. Sam will know something, and he'll be the one to talk to her. He's a familiar face, since she grew up in town."

Jennie's phone beeped. She looked at it and said, "Gotta go. Thanks for your help, and let me know if you think of anything else. And don't go snooping around!"

"I would never," I said.

She rolled her eyes, stood, and walked out the door. I finished my coffee and told Meadow I'd drop off some book sale flyers on my way to work the next morning. Then I was off to finish my errands. Much to my disappointment, I didn't run into anyone I knew on the rest of my stops. The drugstore, the shoe repair—not a single person who'd be inclined to gossip or ask me what I knew. But I could honestly say, if asked, that I hadn't done any snooping once Jennie told me not to. I'd forgotten to mention the Cynthia Baker angle, but I knew Dory would make sure the police heard about it. Besides, I hadn't gotten much out of Cynthia other than some odd questions about a request for a thesis that Anita might or might not have placed. I'd look into that tomorrow and see what else came up. I was sure the library would be full of the curious from the minute we opened. Word would have gotten around by then.

Chapter Four

As I expected, Wednesday morning the library was buzz-ing. The volunteers were in and out, working on the book sale and reassigning the things Anita had been handling. The staff was wound up, with reactions ranging from shock to glee. I was sure I heard Dory humming "Ding Dong, the Witch is Dead." Helene was in an emergency board meeting. She'd told me, when I arrived that morning, to look at the schedule and call in any part-timers I thought we'd need for the rest of the day and the week. If history was any kind of guide, Anita's death would increase library traffic consider-ably. We'd see all our regulars, and anyone who owed us for late or lost books would suddenly remember their fines and come in to pay. Others would decide they needed a library card or wanted to use our Wi-Fi. The place was already a zoo, and it was only ten.

I'd huddled with Jilly over the schedule. There was no story hour this week since the community room was in use for book sale storage, so she was picking up some extra reference shifts and would be available to back up others. She said she was happy to help, but she seemed tense and distracted.

"Are you sure you have time for these shifts?" I asked. "I know you have a lot of activities planned for Saturday."

"It's all right, I have everything under control. The big thing is the kids' costume parade in the morning, but once that's done and we've given all the participants their apple cider donuts, the events are smaller, and the kids are older. It's great that your friends from the city volunteered to help—I don't know what I would have done about the face painting. Now that Brianna has gone off to college, I didn't have anyone to handle that."

Brianna was one of our long-time pages. She'd started working for the library as soon as she turned sixteen, and had always been a big help to Jilly. She'd always done her school community-service hours in the kids' department. She'd started art school in late August, and I knew Jilly was feeling her absence. I'd found her in tears a week ago, and she'd said she was fine, just overwhelmed. I called in the cavalry in the form of two of my oldest friends. I'd worked with Beau for years at a cosmetics company before switching careers. His partner, Ben, was a professional makeup artist. The two had taken me in for a while after my husband, Danny, had been murdered. While they'd understood and supported my need for a change, Beau in particular had had a hard time wrapping his mind around the fact that a lifelong city girl like me could be happy in a small village upstate. He still referred to the place as "Raven's Breath," but had agreed to come up and help.

"They're looking forward to it. Ben's very excited—he spent all last weekend practicing different animals and butterflies and things. They're even bringing costumes."

"That's so nice, Greer. I can't thank you, or them, enough. What's your costume? Decided yet?"

"Um . . . noooo, not really." I'd planned on wearing my usual basic black and having Ben paint a little jack-o'-lantern on my face. I wasn't big on costumes.

"I have some things you could borrow," Jilly said.

Of course she did. Children's librarians put on costumes at the drop of a hat. Jilly tilted her head and studied me for a minute, then said, "Some sort of witch? Nothing ugly or mean," she hastened to add.

I had to head her off. If I wasn't careful, she'd have me tarted up like Glinda the Good. Although, a witch like Juliet Blackwell's Lily Ivory, in some fabulous retro outfit, would be all right, though I suspected that's not what Jilly had in mind.

"Well . . ." I said.

"I have a witch's hat and cape you could borrow. Just wear them with your regular clothes—you already have a lot of black. You'll be a very hip witch—the Samantha Stephens of upstate New York. I've even got a wand—it has a little dragon on the end. And if that doesn't work, I have some other things."

She had me at "dragon wand."

"No, those would be fine. Thank you," I said.

"I'll bring them in tomorrow. And those shifts are fine, really. I'm not worried about Saturday. It's this whole thing with Anita. It's just so awful. Even though she was, well . . ."

"Awful," I said. "You can say it. Everybody else is."

"I know," she said. "That somehow makes it even more—

"Awful," we said in unison.

Jilly gave me a weak smile, then asked, "Do you know what the police are thinking? You're friendly with Officer Webber, aren't you?"

"Yes, but she doesn't share a lot. 'Ongoing investigation.' Like that. I'm sure we'll see her or Lieutenant O'Donnell soon. Probably today."

"Oh, I see." She fiddled with her rings. "Well, hopefully it won't take long." She gave me a little smile. "I'll make a note of these shift changes, and your costume."

"Thanks," I said. I left her at her desk and went to my own. The next time I looked over, she was still twisting her ring around and around and staring down at her desk. Strange. Jilly wasn't the type to brood, but she clearly had something on her mind.

I finished my calls to our part-time staff right before my reference shift started. By the time I got out to the desk, the opening rush had died down, and after placing some requests and giving vague answers to questions about Anita's accident— "No, I'm really not sure what happened," "Yes, we will still be having the book sale"—I went over to circ to help out with a big pile of returns. It also gave me the opportunity to talk to Dory and see if she'd heard anything else through the grapevine.

"Let me give you a hand," I said to Dory. "You check them in, and I'll sort them onto a cart."

"Thanks, Greer. We've been so busy this morning. Of course, we always have a lot of traffic during book sale week, but with the news about Anita . . ." Dory looked up at a picture of the library board that hung behind the circ desk. Anita was front and center. I'd seen Dory glaring at it so often I was surprised I'd never found pins stuck in it.

"I know," I said, "Helene told me to call in all our part-timers. That'll help."

"Yes, it will. It'll be like this all week, I'll bet. And Helene will be tied up. She told me she's expecting Sam O'Donnell and to send him right back to her office."

"I wonder if they've found out anything," I said. "Have you heard any news?"

Dory shook her head. "Only what I told you yesterday. Everyone I talked to says maybe her husband or her daughter finally snapped. But I can't see it. Richard has put up with her for years, and Sloane—well, I hate to say it, but Sloane's always been such a mouse. Nice girl, but not a lot of backbone."

But she still threatened to kill her mother, I thought. Or near enough. At that point business picked up again, and I went back to the reference desk. We had a steady stream of people in for the next couple of hours, and I was glad to see our part-time librarian arrive at lunchtime. I escaped to the staff room and settled in with a brisk cup of tea, a sandwich, and a copy of Edgar Allen Poe's detective stories. I was enjoying the adventures of Auguste Dupin and was engrossed in "The Purloined Letter" when the door opened, and Felicity James peeked in.

"Mind if I interrupt your lunch?" she said. "I've been going over some things with Helene. We're rearranging some book sale responsibilities, and she said to ask you about a few after-hours things someone needs to keep an eye on. There has to be a staff member in the building, and Helene's going to be tied up. Anita's death has thrown the board into a tizzy, and of course, she had a hand in all sorts of things as far as fundraising goes. I don't think I appreciated how much she did. I just got annoyed at the micromanagement."

"I think a lot of people felt that way," I said. "But you're right, she did do quite a bit. How can I help?"

"Well, you know Agnes Jenner has volunteered to take over the bookkeeping?" Felicity gave me what could only be called a "searching glance." Agnes had been known to have a drinking problem for years. She'd been one of my outreach patrons after knee surgery last winter, so Felicity knew that I'd know about Agnes and her fondness for cocktails, even though I was a relative newcomer to Raven Hill. I also knew that Agnes had been attending AA meetings every morning in the basement of the Unitarian church for four or five months. I'd started to see her out walking on my way to work in the morning in the spring, and finally put it together. She often stayed after the meeting for something called "chair yoga," a class she'd recommended to me the last time she was in the library.

"I think that's great," I said. "I always thought she was pretty sharp when she was sober. I'm sure having something to keep her occupied now that she's not drinking will do her a lot of good."

Felicity looked relieved. "That's what Helene said. And she is very sharp—my parents always took their taxes to the Jenners when Agnes's husband was alive. She told Helene she hasn't had a drink in months and really wanted to help. She loves the library. And it's hard to find someone willing to do all that recordkeeping."

"I'm sure she'll do a fine job. What do you need me to do?"

Felicity rattled off a list, which mostly involved me letting Agnes into the Friends of the Library office and staying a little late on Friday and Saturday while she totaled up the cash and receipts. There were a couple of other things, so Felicity said she'd send me an email later in the day once she had everything sorted out.

"Thanks, Greer, I really appreciate it," she said. "I'm sure none of this is in your job description."

"No worries," I said. "I think it falls under 'other duties as assigned.' If Helene is fine with it, so am I."

Felicity left and I went back to my book. I'd just finished my sandwich when the door opened again. It was Millicent.

"Oh, Greer, hello. I hope I'm not disturbing you. The library has been so busy today. I'm sure you could use some quiet."

"I'm just finishing up, actually. I think we could all use some quiet. Anita's death on top of book sale week—it's really an awful lot to cope with."

"Yes, yes, it is." Millicent sat down and sighed. She rubbed her shoulder for a moment. I knew her arthritis had been bothering her lately, but as I looked at her, I thought she looked all of her eighty years, which was rare. She sighed again, and then said, "Well, I can't say I liked the woman, but her absence will be felt. Especially right now. And to have another death associated with the library? It's so unpleasant."

That was one way to put it.

"Anita wasn't an easy woman to like," I said. Understatement. I could think of a couple of staff members who loathed her, Millicent being one. "And yes, this week particularly, she'll be missed."

"Is there any word on what happened? I understand she went off the road, but people are saying it wasn't an accident."

"That's what I've heard," I said, as I stood to rinse my dishes. "It's possible she was run off the road." I didn't mention the potential blow to the head afterward—that hadn't been verified, and the police would release that information when they saw fit.

"Witnesses?" Millicent asked.

"I don't know. It seems unlikely given where she was."

"Hmm. I suppose there will be an autopsy, and a—what do they call it? A toxicology test?" Millicent said.

"I would think so," I said. "Is your shoulder still bothering you?" Millicent was once again massaging the joint.

"Hmm? Oh yes, yes, it is," she said, standing and going to the teapot. "I've tried all sorts of things, but nothing works all that well when it gets colder. My doctor recently recommended CBD oil, of all things. I believe Anita was using it too—ski season is just around the corner."

"I've heard it's good for that," I said. "Well, I'm off. Let's hope we have a quieter afternoon."

I left Millicent to her tea and went back to my office. I was surprised by her comment about Anita. Cannabidiol oil was one of the things I'd given her information about in relation to her knee. I could swear she'd harrumphed at it when I ran through the list of things I'd found. But you never knew. She might have heard the same thing from her doctor that Millicent had.

I'd reached my desk when I realized I'd left my book in the staff room. If I didn't get it now, I'd forget, so back I went. I walked in to find Millicent rummaging through the cabinets. She jumped and gasped when she heard the door.

"I forgot my book," I said. "Are you all right?"

"Yes. You startled me," she said. "I can't seem to find my tea. I picked up a special blend at the new tea shop off Main, and it's not on my shelf."

"A few people have brought things in from there. Maybe someone used it accidentally. I'm sure it's here somewhere." Total Tea was a new addition to Raven Hill. I hadn't tried it yet, but enough of the staff had that I recognized the shop's distinctive tins. I was hoping it was for serious tea drinkers and not too much of a "shoppe." I needed something for my mother for Christmas, and she was a real tea connoisseur.

I turned and picked up my book. From behind me I heard Millicent say, "Ah, here it is," and close the cabinet. She went toward the kettle with a bright red tin in her hand.

"Enjoy your cuppa," I said, taking my leave once again. Back at my desk, I thought about Millicent as I updated the weeding schedule. She wasn't quite herself. Anita's death had stressed us all, but Millicent seemed jumpy, which was very out of character for her. I'd always found Millicent distant and, if I were honest, a little intimidating. But Helene had asked me to help her in the archives over the summer. We needed to shift a large group of bound volumes to make room for a donated collection of records, and Millicent couldn't manage the heavy lifting. It had evolved to me spending a few hours a week with her, doing whatever small tasks needed to be done, leaving her to help researchers. We'd developed an easy camaraderie. She had a wide variety of interests and formidable research skills, and I learned a great deal working with her. I'd eventually shared the story of my husband Danny's murder, and my concerns about the investigation. Millicent had asked thoughtful questions, suggesting a few things worth looking into. I'd thought, a few times, that she seemed a little short of breath and tired easily. It was possible she was just feeling her age. I hoped I looked that good and was that sharp four decades from now, but eighty years took its toll. I'd keep an eye on her.

There were a lot of people that merited keeping an eye on, though for different reasons, I thought as I went through some of the more mundane tasks on my to-do list. When I'd tried to come up with a suspect list the previous night, I'd run out of steam before I'd run out of names. It seemed everyone had some issue with Anita—but enough to kill her? Though you never knew what would flip somebody's switch. And had it been planned or opportunistic? Would that change the list much, if at all? Plenty of people knew her schedule, her car, or where she lived.

But how many knew all of that? Particularly, what time she left here last evening. There had been quite a crowd, but most of the people on the book sale committee left while Anita was still looking for her glasses. Millicent was the most likely suspect among the staff, but I'd seen her leaving as I walked to the reading room. Granted, I hadn't seen her pull out, but neither had I seen her car in the street or the main lot. Jilly had been closing, and she was jumpy about something, but I left before her, and Anita's car had been gone when I walked out. Hadn't it? Pretty sure it had. It seemed like there was something else, though. Something she'd said before she left. Something else to do? I stopped and thought, but the memory was just out of reach. It would come to me. I hoped. I shook my head, sent some reports to the printer, and pulled out a pile of purchase requests.

Anita didn't have many fans among the rest of the staff, but I couldn't see any of them killing her, and certainly not the two that were there Monday night. Same was true of the Friends, as far as I knew. If Jennie asked me to, I'd put together a list of who'd been around when I arrived, but I thought the killer would be found closer to home. From what Meadow had said, Sloane was furious with her mother. If she hadn't actually threatened to kill her, she'd come close. Everyone described her as high strung—I hadn't interacted with her often enough to know—but if that were the case, I couldn't see her planning to off her mother. It would have to be in a fit of rage.

And then there was the husband, usually the prime suspect in cases like this. People always described him as pleasant and mild-mannered. In other words, the nice one. Anita was the mean one. But I'd always thought that if he were so nice, he'd have less tolerance for Anita's manipulative ways. I didn't know a lot about him. I spoke to him when he came in with his grandson or when Anita roped him into doing things

41

for the library. The grandson, Caleb, was about five. Richard had endless patience with the kid and whatever his current interests were. They'd spend hours picking out books, looking things up, and requesting out-of-system items. A lot of them ran toward the mechanical. Right now, they were into circuits and electricity. I couldn't fault him in the grandparent department, though I wondered how well he got along with Sloane.

As far as the library projects went, he served as a general handyman and builder for whatever event or fundraiser was going on. Library maintenance was handled by local tradespeople on contract, but other events were handled by volunteers. Richard had been an electrician by trade, third-generation owner of a family business, since sold. Dory had told me that. "Of course, he went to college," she'd said. "Anita's too much of snob to marry a tradesman. He studied business administration or something. My Bill always said he thought Richard liked the hands-on part of it better. The two of them worked on some new construction together, and he said Richard used any excuse to leave the office and work on-site. But still—he was the owner, and that business was a nice earner. Made a bundle when he sold it. And Anita has expensive tastes."

Had the Hunzeker marriage been a happy one? Hard to get an honest appraisal when one half of the couple was universally disliked. Mary Alice might be my best bet—she'd lived here almost as long as Dory and was more likely to stick to facts. I looked up at the staff schedule pinned to my bulletin board. Mary Alice was in tomorrow. I'd talk to her then. Time to give all my attention to my job. That lasted all of five minutes. I heard a strange, muffled noise coming from the next cubicle. I rolled my chair out to see, and my mouth dropped open.

It was Jilly. She was leaning on her desk, her face blotchy and red, sobbing like a lost soul.

Chapter Five

~

I grabbed my box of tissues and plunked them on her desk as I went by to close the office door. Then I came back and rolled my chair over to her.

"What happened?" I said.

Jilly sniffled. She didn't meet my eyes.

"Or if you'd rather not talk about it . . ."

She waved her hand. "Gimme a sec," she said, and took a big swig of water from the bottle on her desk. She blew her nose and sighed. Then she squared her shoulders and looked at me.

"There's no easy way to say this. I'm a suspect in Anita's murder."

I was dumbfounded. And speechless, which was a rare occurrence. After gaping at her for a moment, I said the first thing that came to mind.

"But she left before you. You had to close. And you're not a killer, Jilly."

I realized, too late, that I should have started with that last bit. Jilly just smiled.

"Thanks for the vote of confidence, Greer," she said. "And for spelling out my alibi. But there's more to it than that." She took another sip of water.

"You don't have to tell me," I said. But I hoped she would. I'd seen Jilly face down toddler tantrums, teenage terminal boredom, and unhinged parents, but I'd never seen her like this.

"No, it's all right. I need to talk to someone. You see, Anita found out something, something about my past. Something—not very nice. She wanted my support for her new building plans, and, well . . ."

"She was blackmailing you?" I was aghast. This was low, even for Anita.

Jilly sighed again. "I guess you could say that. I don't think that she thought of it that way. She didn't come right out and say it, but the implication was there. I really didn't know what to think. I still don't. But I didn't kill her."

"Is there anything I can do to help?" I said.

"I don't know if anyone can help. Helene gave me the rest of the afternoon off. I'm going to talk to a lawyer. But maybe you could help me think it all through. You're good at this kind of thing. I was so shocked when the police talked to me. I pulled myself together enough to say I wanted to talk to an attorney before I answered any more questions. They were very nice about it, but I'm going to have to go make a statement tomorrow. I'm not sure I'll be at work. Would you mind stopping by my place tonight? I can tell you the whole story, and you can pick up the costume. We can order takeout."

"I'd be happy to help, if I can," I said.

"Great. I better get going. I'll see you later."

I went back to my desk while Jilly packed up her things. Once she was out the door, I popped up. I wanted to talk to Helene, and with Jilly likely out the next day, I was going to have to redo the reference desk schedule. Again. Anita was becoming as irritating in death as she had been in life.

Helene was in her office. I knocked, and she gestured to the chair in front of her desk. She looked exhausted.

"I've spoken to Jilly," I said. "She told me what's going on. I find all of this unbelievable."

"I know," said Helene. "I don't know what to think anymore." She rubbed her eyes, then said, "I get the impression from Sam that they don't have a solid case against anyone. They're talking to a lot of people, he said. They're in the archives with Millicent now. He said they'd want to see you too. Everyone who was here on Monday night."

"Well, I'll either be at Reference, checking to see if Cheryl is available tomorrow, or at my desk, making calls. I'm going to presume Jilly either won't be here or won't be in the mood to deal with a busy desk shift."

"I wish I could help," Helene said, "but I'm being pulled all over the place. Maybe Millicent can give you a little more desk time. Although she seems tired lately."

"I think so too. I'll only ask if I'm out of options. I sometimes have to remind myself that she's in her eighties. She's such a force."

"Yes, she is. But I think your plan is a good one. I'll approve any extra hours for the part-time staff. It's not like the board will give me a hard time about it. They don't know if they're coming or going at this point." She threw up her hands. "Well, this is not what they signed up for, is it? Approving budgets, photo ops at library events—that's more their speed. Just keep me posted."

"Thanks, I'll see what I can do with the schedule," I said, and went out to the reference desk. To my relief, our part-time librarian, Cheryl, was happy to pick up the extra hours. She reminded me that she had three kids, and Christmas was less than two months away. "Any day shifts are fine. Evenings, I just have to make sure my husband will be home with the kids," she said.

With one more thing crossed off my to-do list, I went back to my office. I wondered what was going on up in the archives, but I could always drop in on Millicent later. Jennie knew where my office was, so if the police wanted to talk to me she'd come looking. As it turned out, I didn't have long to wait. I'd just started revising the schedule on my computer when she appeared.

"Got a few minutes?" she said.

"Sure, I've been expecting you," I replied, hitting the "Save" button. "Where's Sam?"

"Downstairs, in the book discussion room. He said it would be more private, but I think he wanted to stop in the staff room and get another cup of coffee."

We went down to the manor's lower level, where the enormous original kitchen had been split into a staff break room and a conference room used for book discussions and small meetings. The door to the book discussion room was ajar, and inside sat Lieutenant Sam O'Donnell, a notebook and a cup of steaming coffee in front of him. We exchanged greetings, and Jennie and I sat down. Sam began, with his usual laid-back, informal air.

"We're trying to get a handle on everything that happened Monday night. I understand you were here."

"I was, briefly. I had forgotten something, and since I was off the next day, I came back for it. I got here right after the book sale committee meeting ended."

"Run through it for me, from the time you got here. Who you talked to, who you saw, where everyone was—everything you can remember."

So I did. My chat with Felicity, meeting Anita in the office, talking to Jilly, then checking out my movie and leaving. Sam had me go through it twice, the second time with a lot of questions on who left and when. I made a mental note of what Sam was most interested in. Jennie and I were friendly, and Sam found me useful, but neither would give me any information on a current investigation unless they had to. I'd have to figure it out for myself.

"And you're sure you saw Millicent leaving as you came into the building?" Sam asked.

"Yes. I didn't speak to her, but I saw her walking to the front door, with her coat on, carrying her handbag. She often parks in the old lot, and when she does, she comes and goes that way."

"So you didn't see her car at any time in the main parking lot in the back of the building, or anywhere between here and Main Street?"

I shook my head. "I recognize her car, and it's not usually in the main lot, so I would have noticed, especially since I'd seen her go out the front. No, it wasn't there."

"And when you left, Anita's car was gone?"

"Yes. Well, I think so." I frowned. "Maybe not. I didn't look for it. It wasn't in her usual spot, but there was a minivan partway down the row of spaces near the street. I'm pretty sure that was someone here to pick up the new page. I don't think she has her license yet. I wouldn't have seen any cars behind that."

"Do you remember what other cars were in the lot?"

"Jilly's and David's—they were closing. A few others. There were people in the reading room when I got my DVD, but no one I recognized. I didn't recognize the cars either."

"Hmph," Sam said. He was quiet for a minute. Jennie looked up from her notes.

"Go back to your conversation with Anita. Start at the beginning," Sam said.

I ran through it again. Once again, I felt like I was forgetting something. When I was done, he asked, "Did anything strike you as odd or out of character while you were talking to her?"

"Well, she did seem chattier than usual, more upbeat. Anita was usually all business. And the misplaced glasses—she never did things like that, at least not that I knew of. I'd call her ruthlessly organized, if you know what I mean." I stopped, picturing the file box. Some folders were labeled, some handwritten. More of them handwritten, actually. That was strange.

"You found that file box she had, right? Snap top, with a handle?" I asked.

Sam nodded. Jennie flipped back through her notebook, then nodded as well.

"She always had that at meetings. She worked on a laptop, but she liked to print out documents and take notes by hand. She told me once that she felt staring at a screen 'impeded effective communications,' or something like that, so she never used it in meetings. It was strictly pencil and paper. She would type up her notes later. Then they'd go into a neatly labeled folder. But Monday night there were a bunch of folders with handwritten names on the tabs. More handwritten than not. I don't know what it means, but it seems odd."

"And you got a good look at them?" Sam said.

"I did. I was on the floor looking under things for her glasses. The box was on the floor beneath the table. When she stepped out to take a call, I decided to check the box for the glasses. She'd never admit she tucked them in and forgot, but I thought it was worth a look."

That was not entirely true, but that was my story and I was sticking to it. Sam gave me a long look. I saw Jennie start to smile and look back at her notes. Sam sighed.

"How many folders?" he said.

"Ten? Maybe a dozen. It wasn't full by any means," I said.

"How many were labeled?"

I tried to picture it. "Four, I think. The rest were handwritten."

Jennie tapped her notebook and looked at Sam.

"Are you sure about the number?" he asked.

"Pretty sure."

"Do you remember what the files were called?" she asked. "I know you only had a quick look, but maybe you can remember?"

I sensed a tone but ignored it. If I'd snooped, it was to her advantage.

"I think the labeled ones were 'Book Sale,' 'Historical Society,' 'Grants.' and maybe one more. The handwritten ones were names, mostly. 'J Bean,' 'Ames Family'—those I recognized. 'Sean Harris.' Pretty sure that's Anita's son-in-law. Also 'Ravenscroft Deeds.' Then a couple of names I didn't recognize. One was 'Margaret' something or other, and then 'PJ Waters'? I don't think that's exact, but close."

"Not bad for a quick look," Sam said.

"I have a very good visual memory. All those years in the fashion industry," I said.

That, at least, was true.

"Besides," I said, "the labels were a big font, and the handwritten ones were pretty big too. Maybe her eyesight really was going. But you have the files, right? I'm sure she took them with her."

"We found the file box in the car, yes," Sam said. "I'm just verifying the contents. If those other names, or anything else, comes to you, please let me know."

Not exactly what I'd asked. *They weren't all there,* I thought. That's why they asked how many and that's why they wanted the list. "J Bean" had to be Jilly, and the contents put them onto the potential blackmail. So what else was in those files? I thought he might pursue it, but instead he moved on.

"The phone call. That was from Richard, her husband?"

"It was. She greeted him by name before she stepped out."

"Did you happen to hear anything else?"

"Not much. She went into the little hallway outside Helene's office. It bends, you know, so she wasn't right in the doorway. I only caught a few words. She must have either moved or raised her voice for me to hear those." And I was busy looking through her files, so I hadn't paid close attention.

"You said earlier that she mentioned wine or a gift basket?" Sam said.

"Oh, right, she did. I thought she was planning on hitting up that new liquor store for a donation or that she wanted Richard to do it. But the two weren't necessarily related. And there was something else, I think, maybe another errand? Or she had to do something she hadn't planned on or check something? I'm sorry—I can't remember."

Sam asked a few more questions and then thanked me and sent me on my way with a reminder to call them if anything occurred to me. He added, "We're not sure what we're dealing with, so be careful." It looked like he'd given up on telling me to mind my own business and let the police handle things. Based on experience, he knew I'd keep them informed if I found out anything useful, though perhaps not as promptly as he might like. I also wasn't interested in putting myself in harm's way. I was more of an armchair detective. But I was interested in keeping my coworkers out of trouble, presuming they were not, in fact, murderers, and I didn't think they were.

I went up to the archives to see how Millicent's interview with the police had gone. I was in luck, and she was alone.

"Hi," I said when she looked up. "Mind if I join you? I'm hiding out—I can't face any more questions or any more reasons to redo the schedule."

Millicent gestured to a chair near her desk. "Make yourself at home, Greer. I can't fault you—I don't know what the place is coming to. And I've always hated scheduling," she said with the hint of a smile.

"That, and 'other duties as assigned' has become one hundred percent of my job description. Now I understand why it's in all those position postings. It's one thing to come up here and help out, but dealing with the fallout from a board member's murder is a different story."

"That dreadful woman," Millicent said. "She's been nothing but trouble since the day she joined the board. She developed an absolute mania about this building."

"That's a good way to put it," I said. "From what I've been hearing, she's been stooping to new lows to get her way."

I left it there. I didn't want to share Jilly's story, but I also wanted to see if Millicent had been on the receiving end of some subtle threats. I wasn't sure she'd tell me if she had, but it was worth tossing out the opportunity.

"Really?" she said. She shook her head. "I guess I'm not surprised. I overheard her talking to another staff member, and I didn't like her implication."

We exchanged a long look.

"I never would have pegged her for a blackmailer," I said. "But I don't think there's any other word for it."

Millicent sniffed. "I'm sure she wouldn't have called it that. Anita was the type who could never admit to doing anything wrong, because if it was wrong, of course she wouldn't have done it. With that mindset, nothing is off limits."

"That's true. I guess for her, the ends justified any means. But do you think this centers on the library, or could it be something else? Her family? You would know more about them than I do. Did the police give anything away when they spoke to you?"

Millicent shook her head.

"They were very interested in who was here and when they left. They also asked some questions about the historical society, since I'm a member there too. But they seemed fixated on the manor. Anita had gotten hold of some old rumors about the Ravenscroft legacy to the village. Some letter about a missing will or another heir. Those stories have been around my whole life. What Anita didn't seem to understand was that the Ravenscroft family was its own gothic novel. Each generation was more eccentric than the last. Honestly, the Brontës couldn't have done any better."

I had to laugh. "From the stories you've told me, that's true. But they all seem mostly harmless and shrewd enough to keep their legal affairs in order."

"Try convincing the police of that—or Anita Hunzeker or some other historian on a mission. Though she was off base on this, I have to admit Anita was a good researcher."

It clearly pained Millicent to admit it. Her tone was one of grudging respect. She took a deep breath and said, "Well, I have someone coming shortly to work on a family history.

You will keep me informed, won't you? If you hear anything else about the investigation?"

"Of course," I said. I would too. I was getting the uneasy feeling that if we didn't all hang together, we would certainly all hang separately. So to speak.

Chapter Six

❧

Jilly had an apartment in an older building a few towns away. She'd told me she didn't want to live in Raven Hill because running into the story-hour crowd in the supermarket meant she had to be "on" too often when she wasn't at work. I really couldn't blame her. I liked being able to walk to work, but sometimes it was hard to avoid having to chat when you didn't feel like it.

I called from my car when I arrived and then climbed to the second floor. I'd been to Jilly's place once before. It had a more minimalist style than I'd expected—if she had a stash of finger puppets anywhere, they were not visible. She had told me her costume collection took up all the closet space, but her apartment had a different vibe than her office. The only obvious signs that a librarian lived there were a couple of piles of books on the coffee table, and a framed copy of the American Library Association David Bowie "READ" poster over the couch. When I'd asked Jilly to recommend some professional reading on children's literature, since I hadn't studied it in grad school, she had handed me her own copy of *Dear Genius,*

The Letters of Ursula Nordstrom, she of "good books for bad children" fame. That and the Bowie poster told me everything I needed to know about Jilly's philosophy of librarianship.

Jilly looked composed when she answered the door. No makeup and her eyes were a little red, but otherwise she seemed okay.

"Why don't we order dinner and figure out your costume? Then we can talk while we eat."

"Sounds good," I said.

Jilly ordered Chinese food and then lead me to the spare room. After some rummaging around in the closet, she produced a black cape with tonal embroidery and a matching hat. The cape was a matte wool blend, perfect for a chilly day running in and out of the library. It was embroidered with a repeating pattern of birds in a shiny black thread. They caught the light nicely when I put the cape on and twirled.

"Cool," I said. "These could be ravens, don't you think?"

"That's why I bought it," Jilly said. "I haven't worn it to work in years, though, so none of the current crop of kids will recognize it. Here—try the hat."

It was more of a fascinator. It fit snugly over the top of my head, with a few squiggly pieces coming up on one side, anchored by another small black bird. Jilly adjusted the angle of the fascinator and stood, studying me.

"Perfect," she said. "Couple of bobby pins and it should stay in place. Now the wand."

She produced that out of a small trunk. As promised, it had a dragon at the base. Fire-breathing even. I waved it around. It, too, caught the light nicely.

"I'm ready," I said. "Bring on the sugared-up kids and their crabby parents. I've got a dragon wand, and I'm not afraid to use it!"

Jilly laughed. "Good luck with that," she said. At that point, the doorbell rang. I folded up my costume while she dealt with the food delivery. Once we were settled in the kitchen with our dinner, I tried to figure out the best way to broach the subject of Anita's murder. Saying "So, what did she have on you?" lacked diplomacy, even if it was what I wanted to know. I decided to come at it sideways and give her an out if she decided not to share.

"You seem to be feeling better. Did the meeting with the lawyer go well?"

Jilly nodded. "It was helpful. She put things in perspective, and I've remembered some things that might be important." She paused.

"You don't have to tell me anything if you don't want to," I said, hoping she wouldn't take me up on that.

"No, it's all right. It would help to talk about it. I'm not out of the woods yet, and I'd value your perspective. I feel like I'm too much in the middle of things."

"I know the feeling," I said. Some days, I was convinced I had enough distance from my husband's murder to examine it with detachment. Others, I was in an endless memory loop of finding his body.

"I'm sure you do," Jilly said. "Well, this story goes back years. You know I was married when I was very young, right?"

"Yes," I said. I had met one of Jilly's children shortly after starting my job at the library. She had two kids, both adults. Since she was only ten or twelve years older than I was, I was surprised when she introduced me to her son. He was in the area for a visit, and they were going out to celebrate his twenty-eighth birthday. My surprise had obviously shown on my face, because she'd laughed and said she'd started young. That's the only time she'd mentioned it, until now.

"I got married in college. I was young and stupid. Totally swept off my feet. My parents were against it—they knew I was too young—but I was determined, and Ryan was what everyone considered a nice boy from a nice family. He was two years ahead of me, and he already had a good job lined up. Next thing you know, I'm pregnant. He talked me into leaving school and staying home with the baby. It wasn't hard—I can't say I knew what I wanted to do, so I was a good student, but an indifferent one, if you know what I mean."

I nodded. I'd phoned in a few classes myself, doing enough to get a decent grade, but no more.

"Anyway, once the baby was about two, I started to get restless. I wanted to go back to school part-time. My mom was willing to watch Colin. Ryan wanted me to wait. He persuaded me to hold off until the fall term. By then I was pregnant again, so of course going back made no sense. Or so I was told. He said it made more sense for me to wait until after I'd had the baby."

I raised my eyebrows.

"I know what you're thinking. Yes, I knew how babies were made and how to avoid it. But he'd often try to convince me to skip the birth control, and sometimes he succeeded.

Young and stupid, remember? I thought it was all about how much he loved me."

I didn't say anything. I thought I knew where this story was going.

"By the time Caroline was teething, I didn't have much of a life outside Ryan and the kids. My friends were all starting their careers, and I was younger than the mommy crowd I met at the park. My parents tried to help, but Ryan always had some reason I shouldn't see them or why we should go together. I think they could see what was happening, but I couldn't. Or wouldn't."

Jilly paused, staring down and fiddling with her rings.

"What finally made you see the light?" I asked.

She sighed. "It started getting worse. He got more controlling, watching what I spent, always wanting to know where I was. I'm sure if I'd had a cell phone back then, he'd have been tracking me. One day my mom was watching the kids while I ran errands. I bumped into a girlfriend from my freshman year. We decided to have coffee. Ryan came home early, and my mom left, thinking I'd be there any minute. Well, I didn't get home for another hour. By the time I walked in the door, he was furious. The kids had been acting up, asking for dinner, and he couldn't stand not knowing where I was. He started screaming at me. He got right in my face, then he grabbed me. Something snapped. I shoved at him and tried to get away, and he pinned me against a wall. Then Colin started to cry and ran over. He grabbed his father's leg and wouldn't let go. Ryan yelled at him, then finally let go of me and sent Colin flying. That was it. I hauled off and hit him, right in the nose. He started bleeding. Then he screamed he was going to kill me. So I grabbed a frying pan and hit him over the head. He dropped like a rock. I bundled the kids into the car—Colin wasn't hurt, thank God—and went straight to my parents."

"Good for you," I said. "It's awful, and I'm sorry that you had to go through that, but he had it coming."

"He didn't see it that way. He tracked me down and told me that if I didn't come home and behave, he would charge me with assault and divorce me and get custody of the kids. My dad threw him out and called a lawyer. Then the police showed up."

"That's nerve. He really thought he could get away with it?"

"It gets better. He told them that *I* was the one who threw Colin across the room and then hit him because he tried to stop me. He'd even lined up his parents to help with the kids—it's not like he'd take care of them himself for more than a couple of hours."

"Then what happened?" I asked.

"One of our neighbors had heard us fighting and called the police. When they got there, I had left, but they talked to the neighbor. He'd heard Ryan threaten to kill me. By the time the cops got to me, there were big purple bruises coming up on my arms. I think they believed me and the neighbor, and my parents said they'd be responsible for the kids, so they left. But Ryan insisted on pressing charges. He was so used to me doing what he told me to, and so sure he was always right. But I was done. He was never laying a finger on me or my kids again. It was like a fog lifted. And I was lucky. I had my parents to back me up. I don't know if I could have done it without them."

"I'm glad they were there for you. It would have been almost impossible to do alone, with no job and two kids. But what happened with the assault charges? I can't believe he was successful, was he?"

"Ultimately, no. But he stuck to his story for a while. I ended up filing charges as well, and I got the divorce papers filed first. I had a really good lawyer. In order to get the whole thing settled, we both dropped any charges. I didn't want to give him unsupervised visitation—the settlement was complicated. But in the end, I got what I wanted. The kids saw him regularly for a while, and then he moved on to his next wife and lost interest. It was hard, but they maintained a relationship with Ryan's parents. As they got older and saw the whole thing play out again with his second family, they understood what had happened."

"I'm glad, for them and for you. But you didn't do anything wrong. So what was Anita holding over you?"

"That I was once accused of child abuse but that the charges were dropped as part of a deal. Not a good look for a children's librarian."

"That was nearly thirty years ago, and the charges were false."

"I know that, but as Anita pointed out, a lot of people believe that where there's smoke, there's fire. All it would take is one angry mommy with a lot of social media accounts to fan the flames. I know Helene would back me up, but part of me is still embarrassed at how dumb I was. I don't want people to know any of it."

"You were young and naive, not dumb. How did she even know about all of this?"

"That I'm not really sure about, but I suspect she heard it from my ex-mother-in-law. She mentioned a few months ago that they'd met at an alumni event. They went to the same college. Then more recently she started saying things about how difficult a time I must have had, and how she's not surprised I never spoke about it. It was both subtle and pointed, if that makes sense. She didn't start with the smoke-and-fire analogy until after the last board meeting, when things really didn't go her way on the new building discussion."

"Wow. I don't know that I would ever have pegged her for a blackmailer. She was so direct. No matter what she thought, you knew about it."

"I know. It's not like she ever came right out and said it, but the threat was there. I didn't really believe it at first, but she kept bringing it up."

"But why did she even do it? I mean, it's not like you were against a new building."

"No, but I wasn't strongly for it. She'd gotten obsessive about the new library. I think there's plenty that can be done here, and I wasn't on board with her vision for the children's area in a new one. She was all about the technology. Not enough emphasis on books."

"And if she tried this with you, who else did she try it with? I doubt you were the only one," I said. I thought of all those handwritten names on folders, but it might go beyond that.

"I don't know, but I'm sure you're right. I think she'd reached the point where she'd use whatever leverage she had. I don't think she thought of it as blackmail."

"Then there must be other suspects."

"There are, and I'm pretty sure I handed the police one."

Jilly looked miserable.

"Who?" I asked.

"Millicent."

"But I saw her leave. It was before I talked to you and before Anita left."

"She came back. Not into the building. I'm not sure she left for home. Anita was still in the lot when I walked out. She seemed to be looking for something. I wasn't in the mood to be helpful, so once everyone else was in their car and pulling out, I did too. I left her there."

We all usually left at the same time, with the closing librarian pulling out last, to make sure that everyone's car had started and that they were safely on their way. Anita had closed the building herself plenty of times, though, if she had a meeting that ran late.

"That wasn't too unusual. She's been last out before," I said.

"I know, and I didn't much care. But the thing was, when I drove toward Main, there was a car in Agnes Jenner's driveway. There were no lights on, and I couldn't see inside the car, but I'm sure it was Millicent."

"Did you tell the police?"

"I didn't realize the significance of it until I was going over everything with the lawyer, but yes, they know now."

And Millicent—and the Ames family—had their very own file. And according to Millicent, everything Anita had mentioned was old news, long disproved. Though that was the Ravenscroft family. What about her family? Her father was a doctor, and her mother had worked for Horatio Ravenscroft. But they were long gone. I'd love to know what was in all those files of Anita's. Jennie might tell me about the ones they had if it didn't compromise the investigation. The ones that had disappeared, though, might be even more important.

"Greer," Jilly said, "do you think—I mean, I've joked about it, but—Millicent?"

"I just don't know," I said. "I think—I really believe—that we all have it in us to kill if someone flips the right switch."

"But that's more a heat-of-the-moment thing, don't you think? Looking back, I think that if Ryan had really hurt Colin, or gone after him again, I could have killed him. I'm not sure I would've thought of it as killing him, though. That sounds lame, doesn't it? It's an excuse."

"Defending yourself or your kids is your switch. That's true of most people—defending their families. But there are things people hold dear beyond that, things that they'd kill to protect. I'd agree, though, that it takes a certain temperament to plan it out."

"And Millicent has that temperament," Jilly said. "She's got the brains and steady nerves. What I can't figure out, though, is why now? If she did it, I mean. I hate to think it, but I have to admit the possibility."

"I know. She and Anita have been going at it over the building for years. What changed?"

Jilly shook her head. "If anything, Anita was losing ground. Like I said, the last meeting on the subject didn't go well. The people there were split, and everyone from the historical society to the village attorney were raising issues."

"That doesn't sound like a motive for Millicent—rather the opposite," I said. Although Jennie Webber had told me more than once that motive was overrated. Opportunity and the physical ability to pull it off mattered more.

"Could she have done it? Physically, I mean. Are you sure it was her that you saw?"

"I think so. It was the same color and type of car she drives. Agnes had left her front porch light on, and there's a streetlight near the end of her driveway, so it wasn't completely dark. The car itself was dark. No lights anywhere—the engine had to be off," Jilly said.

"And you're sure there was someone in the car?"

"Yes. I looked over as I went by. I know Agnes doesn't drive, so when I registered that a car was parked there, I was curious. I saw movement in the driver's seat, as though someone were leaning back quickly."

"Hmph," I said. "Then she would have had to follow Anita and somehow run her off the road. Then turn around and get home, all without being seen. It's possible, but not easy. It would take some fast thinking. I don't know, Jilly. She could do it, but it doesn't seem like her style."

"True. And if Anita was trying some subtle blackmail with me, you're probably right that she was trying it with other people." Jilly stopped and threw up her hands. "Listen to us! We're trying to figure out if our elegant elderly colleague could really have murdered our board chair, who was seemingly respectable but had a side hustle as a blackmailer. I should be figuring out next spring's story-hour themes—not this!"

I had to laugh. "I know," I said. "It's awful. But what else can we do? I can't just sit, waiting to see what the police come up with. And you're actually a suspect, though I can't believe you're high on the list, given how many people hated Anita."

"I don't know about that. I don't think that they have many suspects with solid motives."

"I'm told motive is overrated. What the police like is physical evidence. Who had the opportunity? I think that really opens it up. There aren't a lot of houses out near Winding Ridge Road. Probably not a lot of streetlights either. Or traffic cameras," I added. My favorite modern-day detective, Detective Chief Inspector Vera Stanhope, was always demanding CCTV footage, which would sometimes yield a clue. I doubted the police would get that lucky. Though if the murderer had come and gone through a major intersection at the right time, it was possible. I tried to picture the route Anita would have taken. Traffic cameras had become so ubiquitous that I didn't notice them anymore.

"I'll have to look at a map," I said.

"I love the way your mind works, Greer," Jilly said. "And your loyalty. I'm sure you've never run away from a fight."

Oh, but I have, I thought. *And pretty soon, I'm going to have to decide if I'm running toward one.* But Jilly didn't need to know that.

"Thank you, you're very kind. And thanks for dinner and the costume. I should be going, though. We've got some long days ahead. Let me know if there's anything else I can do to help."

"I will," Jilly said. "And if I learn anything else, I'll tell you that too."

When I got outside, there was a wintery chill in the air. I turned the heat on in my ancient car and sat for a few minutes while it warmed up. I'd ask Jennie if they had any camera footage—I wasn't sure if there was more than one route to the accident site. Regardless, it was time to take a look at the terrain. I knew I could get directions and satellite images online, but I wanted to get my hands on some local maps as well. Google Earth did not know all.

Chapter Seven

I was at work bright and early on Thursday, with extra caffeine in a travel mug. I was happy to see that Helene had brought in an assortment of mini muffins from the Java Joint. She'd left a note thanking us for our hard work and encouraging us to carb up and power through book sale weekend. I preferred donuts, but any port in a storm. I took a muffin and went to my office. After a quick email check to make sure there was nothing pressing, I headed to the reading room. I was hoping to talk to Mary Alice before the library opened. I hadn't seen her since the news about Anita had broken, and I wanted to hear her thoughts. She was opening up the circulation desk, so I zipped around, turning on the public computers and catalog kiosks, then joined her. There was no point in beating around the bush.

"So, Anita—thoughts?" I asked.

"Honestly? I'm only surprised no one did it sooner. I'd have liked to strangle her once or twice myself. I should feel bad about saying both those things, but I don't. What happened to her was wrong, but if ever a person worked at being unlikeable, it was Anita Hunzeker." Mary Alice pulled out the cash drawer and started double-checking the total.

"I agree. Though I don't think she ever thought about being unlikeable. What mattered to her was being right." I started straightening a cart of overnight returns and went on. "Have the police interviewed you yet?"

"Yesterday, though I didn't have much to tell them. I was off on Monday, so I haven't seen her for at least a week, probably not since the last board meeting. It's hard to keep track—so many meetings and events this time of year. I will say they asked some rather odd questions."

Mary Alice faced the bills and tucked them into the register, then started checking in books. She gave me a sidelong look.

"I got the impression that Anita had been sticking her nose into things she shouldn't have been—and stirring the pot, shall we say?"

"I have heard that," I said, "though not from the police. I had coffee with Jennie Webber on Tuesday, and she didn't mention it. I think it's a more recent development."

"Shameful. And with all the airs she put on. So principled with her research and her vision for the village. Now I sound like Dory, but Anita always was a snob." Mary Alice sniffed. "You know I don't like to spread gossip, but I was shocked at who Sam was asking me about. Staff members!"

"I know. Jilly and Millicent, right? I don't think I'm on the list this time."

Mary Alice nodded. "Jillian Bean! Ridiculous. She wouldn't hurt a fly. Not that I'm saying Millicent would . . ."

"I agree. Jilly doesn't have it in her, and I can't see Millicent stooping to running someone off the road. And why now? Haven't she and Anita been feuding for years?"

"In a low-key way, yes. It's been worse this last year or so, but murder? No, I don't think so. There has to be another explanation."

"Well, if she was leaning on those two, who's to say she wasn't trying the same thing with someone else?"

"But why? All for a new building? It's not like her name would be over the door."

"I don't know. Maybe if we knew why, we'd know who. Hey, I wanted to ask you about someone. Do you know a Margaret Emerson? I saw the name somewhere, and it rang a bell, but I can't place her."

"Of course. She worked here before you started. She'd retired from one of the bigger libraries, but after a year or so, she got bored and started to fill in here pretty regularly. It was quieter, she said, and only a short drive. She grew up in the village. She went by Peg. You've probably seen her name on things—recommendation cards, old newsletters. She passed away six months or so before you started. That's when they got serious about finding someone full-time."

"Oh, that's why the name was familiar. I've seen 'Peg' signed to a few things, but not many. I'm surprised no one ever mentions her."

"Ah, well. Helene said she'd fill you in about Peg and asked us not to discuss it. Did no one ever tell you the story?" Mary Alice asked.

"No, I didn't know there was a story. Helene must have forgotten."

"It's nothing terrible. Just awkward. Peg didn't retire until she was about seventy, and as I said, about a year later started working here. She did fine for a few years. She was still sharp but a bit frail. The winter before she died, she got pneumonia and never really came all the way back. She filled in for Millicent in the archives for a couple of months—Millicent had slipped on some ice and broken her wrist—and that's when it became clear our elevator was on its last legs. Peg couldn't handle the stairs after the pneumonia, so she went creaking up and down in that old elevator. Then when Millicent came back, Peg stayed down here and only worked Reference. She seemed to be doing fine. She'd started gardening again, and was out and about. Just occasionally short of breath and more easily tired."

"So what happened? Relapse of some sort?"

"No, we think it was her heart. It looked like she'd nodded off," Mary Alice said.

"Did she die in the building?" I asked. Maybe that's why it was so awkward to talk about. It sounded like Mary Alice had been there. "Were you the one who found her?"

"It was a patron, actually."

"What? Where was she—in the parking lot?"

"She was at the reference desk."

"Are you serious?" I said. Talk about dying with your boots on. No wonder no one had wanted to mention it. Any time you took a new job, it was always useful to know why your predecessor had left. That she went out the door feet first after clocking it in the middle of a desk shift wasn't what you wanted to hear.

Mary Alice nodded. "Yes. I was here, on Circ. It was a busy afternoon, lots of people coming and going. Whenever I looked up, she was helping someone at Reference. I didn't think either one of us had gotten a break, but she had a cup of tea at the desk so she must have slipped out for a few minutes. I was about to ask her to keep an eye on Circ while I took a quick break, when the phone rang. There was a patron at the desk when I hung up. She said that the reference librarian wasn't looking too good, and that maybe I should check on her. I apologized for any inconvenience and said she must have nodded off. The woman shook her head and said, 'I don't think so,' or something like that. I went right over. She looked like she was asleep until I got closer, and then I realized she was slumped. I checked for a pulse, but there was nothing. I called an ambulance anyway, but I knew it was too late."

"That's awful. I'm so sorry," I said. "Was it a heart attack or something like that?"

"Probably heart failure, as far as the coroner could tell. There was no autopsy—she died in a room full of people and was known to have health issues. But still, it was upsetting for everyone."

"I'll bet. Well, thanks for filling me in," I said. At that point, it was nearly time to open, so I fired up the computer at Reference and went to unlock the doors. Mary Alice's story made sense, but I still wondered. What did Anita have in that folder labeled "Margaret Emerson"? Other than the fact that she'd died in the library, there was nothing extraordinary about her death. She was older and in a rough patch with her health. But there was something about her that had made Anita decide to look into her, and I wanted to know what it was. Mary Alice wasn't a gossip, but Dory was. I had a feeling if there was anything sketchy about Margaret Emerson's life, or her death, Dory would know. I'd catch her the next time she was in.

Business was steady. The initial excitement about Anita's death had died down, but there were still plenty of people commenting on it. Many expressed shock, but I sensed an underlying "she had it coming to her" sentiment. I kept my ears open but didn't catch anything new. By the time my shift ended, I was looking forward to some quiet time. Unless things got crazy out here, I'd have a few hours at my desk to think while I took care of some run-of-the-mill tasks.

I settled in, ran a few reports—weeding, missing items, inventory exceptions—nothing so exacting or exciting that it required my full attention, and mulled over what I'd learned. I hadn't drawn any conclusions by the time I'd collected the reports from the printer, so I turned to the pile of intersystem loans that had arrived that morning. Interlibrary loan— ILL—for short, was one of my favorite jobs. Searching out books and articles not available in our system had a certain treasure-hunt aspect that appealed to me, and trying to figure out what some of our patrons were actually looking for when they turned in a request that was less than complete required some detective skills. I unpacked today's treasures, checked their condition, made sure all the paperwork was there, and logged into the resource sharing interface.

I'd gotten halfway through the pile when I found a request with a familiar name. It was a thesis, and an older one. Though not typewritten, it looked like it was from the early days of desktop printing, and it wasn't professionally bound. The subject meant nothing to me—it wasn't of local interest as far as I could tell. The author's name, though, got my attention: J. P. Walters. That was one of the names from Anita's files. I'd remembered it as "Waters" when I was talking to Jennie, but I was sure this was the name. And if I wasn't mistaken, this was what Cynthia had been asking about. I fished her card out my bag and checked. Bingo.

I paged through the thesis. I had the time frame right—it was from the early eighties. This was J. P. Walters's master's thesis. He'd been a history student at a small Midwestern college I'd never heard of. I did a quick internet search and found it, or what was left of it. It had merged with another institution nearby. It was now part of the school of liberal arts at a university of moderate size that I had also never heard of. But I wasn't from that area, so unless they had a sports team that was a national contender, that wasn't odd. What was odd, or at least unusual, was that this thesis had not come from the school he attended.

I checked the paperwork again and looked at the return address on the envelope. This copy was from a university library in the western part of New York. That one I'd heard of, but again, it wasn't that big. Theses and dissertations were not widely distributed even now, though there was a database that specialized in them. Forty or more years ago, it was even less likely that you'd find multiple copies. And this topic was pretty obscure. Curiosity piqued, I decided to do a little research.

I went back to the interface and typed in the thesis title. Up popped a record with matching bibliographic information. It showed two holdings—the library at the school Walters had attended, and the library that had sent this copy. I clicked through to the catalogs of each. The lending library showed their copy checked out—that was the one I had in hand. Walters's alma mater showed a status of "missing."

I pulled up the request in the system and scrolled through it. Anita had placed it. She had listed both libraries, with Walters's school first. They'd entered a status of "missing" two days after the request was put in. Anita would have checked the catalog, as I did, so it must have appeared to be there, and she put in the second library as a backup. The first had looked for it, discovered it wasn't there, and moved the request along. All pretty standard. Still, I had questions.

First, why was Anita so interested in this? Was it the topic, or the author? Based on what I'd learned about her files, my guess was the author. I did a quick search on J. P. Walters. Someone named John Patrick Walters came up as the head of the history department at a local private college. It wasn't far—across the Hudson, and a bit north. Though not large, it was well-known for science, and it had a strong nursing program. Not the first place I thought of in terms of history, but they did offer liberal arts courses. There was not a lot of information beyond that. No profile on any networking site, not many mentions anywhere. Unusual for an academic— their work was often cited by others, and they participated in conferences and gave talks. Apparently, J. P. Walters did not get around as much as some of his colleagues.

A little more digging got me an issue of the online student newspaper from a few years ago, in which Walters's appointment as department head had been announced. It was brief, containing the usual types of quotations from college officials and Walters himself, but it did contain a rundown of his previous appointments. His career was a study in mediocrity. Maybe I was missing something, but I didn't see anything that would get him a nice job at a respected private school, even if it wasn't known for his area of expertise. But these things sometimes happened through personal connections, politics, or what have you. It didn't explain Anita's interest, though.

I looked at the time and put the thesis to one side. I could think about this while getting through the rest of my to-do list. I'd do some more digging later. I started to process the rest of the interlibrary loan items. From the looks of them, all were for library patrons. Those requests all went through me—I was system administrator for the library, so I reviewed anything put in by a patron. Helene, Jilly, and Anita all had user credentials, the first two because they were full-time staff members, and Anita as a courtesy to a board member. That meant they could place requests directly without going through me. Helene and Jilly usually did that, only consulting me if they had something tricky. Anita would sometimes do her own and sometimes email me with what she needed if she didn't have all the information—what we called a complete citation. She hadn't sent any requests to me lately; the last batch had to do with grant writing, as far as I could remember, but that was earlier in the fall. She'd sometimes order things related to history, which often had to do with her work with the historical society. Others were personal interest. I thought she had been a history major in college, but I couldn't remember. She was a good researcher, but a thesis was not a typical request. Which led me to wonder what else she might have asked for.

Once finished processing the recently arrived items, I went into the interface and searched for requests from Anita. There were a few recent ones, none of which had gone through me. One was a copy request—those she usually handed off to me because journal articles could be fussy to find. But she'd done all of these herself the previous weekend. The copy request was pending, two items were in transit, and the last was working its way through potential lenders with no luck. If there was a pattern to what she requested I couldn't see it. On the upside, I didn't have to figure out whether to cancel these. Anita wouldn't be needing them, but they were on the way. I could just send them back when they got here. I wasn't sure what the etiquette was in terms of library items for a murder victim. Would the police even be interested? How far did patron privacy extend? Time for a chat with Helene. I doubted we had a policy, but it was her call.

I closed out of the interlibrary loan interface and picked up the stack of books I'd processed, then grabbed the weeding report. With any luck, the page would have time to help me pull old materials. Shelf space was getting tight in some areas. I handed off the ILL books to David at Circ and checked on the status of the page. David let me know that she was shelf reading in the Young Adult area and would be able to help me. I found her, divvied up the weeding list, and got a book cart. I was on my way to Nonfiction when Cheryl called to me. She was standing over the copier with a patron. I sighed, parked my cart, and went to see what was up, hoping it would be a quick.

"This lady would like to scan some documents to a flash drive," Cheryl said. "I must be doing something wrong. I thought all I had to do was switch the function to scanner and plug in the drive. It won't go in, though. Do I have the wrong spot or something?"

I sighed again, this time inwardly, and bent to look at the USB port on the side of the multipurpose machine that was the bane of my existence.

"That's where I tried to plug it in," Cheryl said. "That's right, isn't it?"

"Yes," I said. "I think there's something stuck." I pulled out my phone and clicked on the flashlight. This couldn't end well. Cheryl bent to peer in.

"There is something there," she said. "But what is it? It's not part of a broken flash drive."

I knew what it was, and it wasn't a broken drive. It was the work of Gummy Bear Sinclair.

Gummy Bear, whose real name was Jonathon, was the youngest of the three Sinclair children and the only boy. The Sinclair family were regular library users. We saw them at least once a week. Jonathon was four. He had told me so himself on his last birthday. His sisters were six and eight, or maybe nine. They came in after school with their mom and little brother. Since Jonathon hadn't started kindergarten yet, we still saw him some mornings for story hour. It was on one of those mornings that Jonathon had earned his nickname.

Sarah Sinclair, Jonathon's mom, had always encouraged her kids to ask the reference librarian if they were looking for something in the library and didn't know where it was. Jonathon in particular was a heavy user of reference services. He liked to come over to the desk and stand at my elbow, watching what I typed into the computer after he'd told me what he was interested in that day. On one occasion he suggested that I was spelling something incorrectly. Everyone's a critic. On the morning of the initial gummy bear incident, Jonathon came over to the desk as usual. The rest of the story-hour crowd had checked out their books and left, and his mother was sitting at a table, looking at a cookbook.

"Tissue, please," Jonathon said. I handed him one from the box on the desk. He took it, said thank you, and stood shifting from foot to foot. I waited a minute, watching him.

"Did you want me to look something up for you?" I asked.

He looked down the room at his mother, then at the tissue in his hand, then back at me. His brow furrowed.

"Knights and castles," he said.

I turned to my computer. Out of the corner of my eye, I saw him raise the tissue to his mouth and spit something into it. Always alert to a child about to vomit, I grabbed the trash can beneath my desk and spun to face him.

"Do you feel sick?" I asked him.

He shook his head and held out the tissue. It contained a gelatinous blob in a screaming shade of red so unnatural I knew it was nothing his small body had produced.

"Tastes like rocks," he said. "Yuck."

I had never tasted rocks, so I was willing to take his word for it. At that point his mother looked up from her magazine and then zipped over to the reference desk. She took a look at the tissue and sighed.

"Jonathon! Ugh! What am I going to do with you?"

Her child shrugged. "Rocks," he said again.

"Not rocks, vitamins," his mother said. "I guess you better throw that away."

He crumpled the tissue. I held the garbage can out and he dropped it in. Then he looked up and asked, "Knights?" I found the call number and wrote the numbers on a scrap of paper. He took off toward the children's nonfiction section without making eye contact with his mother.

"He's a fussy eater," she said to me. She went on to explain that the doctor had told her to give him a children's vitamin daily if she was concerned. Jonathon wouldn't swallow a pill, so she'd tried the gummy vitamins, since he loved gummy bears. She had to sneak them in, mixing them with the real thing and changing the time of day he got them. It usually worked, she said, but sometimes he tucked them in his cheek and spit them out when she wasn't looking. She apologized and joined her son in the kid's section.

I told Jilly about it later. She'd found a similar blob the previous week. It was on the floor in the community room after story time. From that day on, we regularly found colorful blobs of goo in all sorts of places in the library, though none higher than the eye level of a four-year-old. Gummy Bear had decided he was better off stashing his unwanted vitamins, since he'd been busted when he tried to throw one away. He'd become as adept as a squirrel at storing them in his cheek until he could dispose of them. Unfortunately, we often found them long after they'd been hidden. We had learned that well-masticated gummy vitamin, exposed to cool, dry air for any length of time, hardened to the consistency of rubber cement and was equally adhesive. I was sure that was what was stuck in this USB port. The uneven, shiny neon green surface gave it away. There was no way I was going to get that out.

"I'm sorry," I told the woman. "I'm afraid we'll need to have this repaired. You can still scan your documents and email them to yourself, then save them to your drive at a public computer or at home." She decided that would be okay, so I left her with Cheryl and went to Circ to ask David to call in the repair.

"Oh, Greer, I'm sorry! Anita asked me to do that Monday night before her meeting, and I completely forgot. I had to referee a fight between the Eldridge twins. You know Maddie likes to put all the board books in alphabetical order, and Macy always wants to arrange them by color. Maddie was singing the alphabet song the entire time she was ordering the shelves, and when her sister started to rearrange them, she let out such a shriek. Went right through me—I had such a headache from the singing! By the time their dad quieted them down and took them home, it had gone right out of my mind. I'll take care of it now. Something stuck in one of the ports, is that right?"

I explained the problem and chose the appropriate sign from our collection of "Temporarily Out of Order" notices. I taped it to the machine while David made the call. Then I retrieved my cart and weeding list and got to work on the overcrowded pet care section. I was starting to get a headache myself, though I couldn't fault David for the forgotten call. Or Maddie, for that matter. I sang the alphabet song when I was shelving too, though I did it in my head rather than out loud. The kid might end up a library page someday. Her sister was probably headed for a career in interior decorating. Arranging books by color, indeed.

I was twenty minutes into my project—did we really need this many books on hamsters?—when I realized I'd missed something important. Anita had been trying to scan something and save it to a drive and couldn't. What had she been trying to scan? Did it have anything to do with those files? And if she couldn't save it to her flash drive, what had she done? She could have emailed it to herself, as I'd instructed the patron to do. Or she could have saved it to her file on the library shared drive. That's what I usually did. It was also the path of least resistance—you had to type in an email, but if you had a folder on the shared drive, you could hit a button, bring up another menu, and choose your folder. For something confidential, email was a better bet, but it was easier to save to a flash drive directly from the shared drive.

That brought me full circle: What had Anita been trying to save? It might be nothing more than updated budgets or meeting minutes from one of her committees. I reviewed what I knew of her Monday schedule. The historical society and the library book sale had been the focus of her day. The Friends kept the minutes for their meetings, though Anita might have had notes for the book sale committee. And David had said she was trying to scan *before* her meeting. So probably not book sale related. That wouldn't be of much interest anyway, but anything from the historical society might be. As would the mysterious missing files. It was worth a look.

I checked the time and saw I had about fifteen minutes before I was due to help Jilly find some props for Saturday's event. After eyeballing what was left of my weeding list, I finished pulling items from the shelf I was working on and shifted things around so that the range made sense by subject. After plucking off one final title that looked like it had been chewed on, I checked in with the page and towed my cart back to my office.

Jilly was on the phone, and the Friends office seemed to be empty. Still, I angled my book cart so that no one could come around the corner and catch sight of my screen. I fished through my tote bag for my own flash drive and plugged it in. Within seconds, I was scrolling through the library's shared drive. I had to go into a few subfolders, but I found Anita's pretty quickly. Nothing in here was password protected because the whole purpose of this was to provide access to anyone who needed to see something. It didn't happen often, and it's not like people were in the habit of rifling through each other's digital files. Yet here I was. I couldn't believe I'd never thought of it before.

As I scrolled through all the files, I realized I hadn't missed much by not snooping sooner. What a snore. Anita had kept copies of every set of meeting minutes, budgets, plans, or what have you, going back years. It was reasonably organized, though there were several folders labeled either "Misc." or with abbreviations I couldn't follow. This would take a while. I could tell that Jilly was wrapping up her call, so I copied the lot onto my flash drive. By the time Jilly popped her head around the corner to see if I was ready, I'd gotten out of the shared drive and pocketed my flash drive. I'd study it later, at home. Finding something useful was a long shot, but worth a try.

Jilly seemed much calmer now than she had been all week. Neither one of us brought up the murder, instead talking over different elements of the book sale. She had already asked Millicent if there were any old picture frames she could use for a photo booth, and had been directed to a rarely used section of the top floor.

"She said that if there are any—and there probably are—they'll be against the wall in the north corner, near the tower," Jilly said. "We'll have to look under all the dust sheets, and she doesn't know what kind of shape they'll be in, but we can take whatever we need. The two of us should be able to manage, but we might need to shift some things around to get to them."

"I'm surprised she's not supervising," Jilly had added as we came up the final set of stairs. "She's usually so protective of everything up here."

"True, but she seems to be letting go a bit. She's let me have input in the new arrangement of the archive. I think she's getting tired."

"Yes, I've thought that as well, and so has Helene. You don't think she'll retire, do you? It's hard to imagine the place without her."

"It is," I said. We picked our way through the attic, peeking under sheets at likely looking piles, making our way to the corner. So here we were. Millicent had said she'd check in with us after we'd had time to hunt around.

Jilly and I viewed the tarp-covered heap with some trepidation. We were in the far back corner of the attic, having wound our way through an assortment of old furniture, stacked crates, and unknown objects draped in sheets. There was a layer of dust, visible to the naked eye even in the dim light, over everything around us. This was the part of the attic never used by staff or volunteers. Even Millicent had given up on creating order here.

"This must be the pile she meant," Jilly said. "I guess we better pull this tarp off."

"Right," I said. "But let's open the shades on these windows. If anything scurries out from under that stuff, I want to know what I'm dealing with."

"Good idea." Jilly sidled around the pile to the window on her side. I had to walk a few feet to the one closest to me, but at least the path was clear. I could hear Jilly coughing as she struggled with the window shade. Mine went up easily, with only a squeak of protest. I squinted in the sunlight and waved away some dust. I had a view of the back parking lot and the woods beyond.

"Ready?" Jilly said.

"Ready," I said. We each took a side of the tarp and lifted it gently, trying not to stir up more dust. We draped it over an old bureau behind us and took a look at our find.

"Wow," I said.

It was the motherlode of overwrought Victorian portrait frames. Some painted, some varnished, all solid wood, carved, and ornamented to a fare-thee-well.

"Is that one in the back full length?" I said, trying to get a closer look.

"I think so," Jilly said. "If it is, it's perfect for the event. We're going to have to move everything to get to it, though. Help me pile the small ones over here."

It was like an oversized game of Jenga. We shifted things around, gently untangling and spreading them out. The frames were in great shape considering how old some of them must be. Jilly found a couple in different sizes that would suit her purpose, but we still wanted to get to the big one.

"Look out," Jilly said as the light reflected off something in the pile. "I think one of those has glass in it."

I eased a couple of frames to one side. A face stared at me from behind streaks of dust.

"There's still a picture in it too," I said. I lifted it carefully and held it up so Jilly could see. "Looks like an old black-and-white photograph."

"I'd have expected to find a daguerreotype in this heap," Jilly said. "Hold it steady." She used a corner of the tarp to wipe the glass. "Still grimy, but you can see it's a woman. Must be a Ravenscroft."

"Probably. I guess she's not downstairs with the rest of them because this isn't a formal portrait," I said. "Millicent might know."

I laid the picture on a chair behind me. We continued to move things until we could slide the full-length frame out and get a better look at it. We were happy to see that it had an attached stand that folded out from the back. We set it up in the aisle between all the piles and stood back.

"Well, compared to a lot of this stuff, it's positively tasteful," I said.

"True," Jilly said. "But it's still interesting, and it will photograph nicely."

We heard a cough, and Millicent appeared, visible through the frame and waving her hand in front of her face.

"Have you found any treasures under all this dust?" she asked.

"A few," Jilly said. She pointed out the frames she'd chosen, ending with the full-length one that Millicent had just stepped through.

"That standing frame is awfully heavy," Millicent said. "Will you be able to get it downstairs?"

"I have some volunteers coming tomorrow," Jilly replied. "We can do it."

"Look what else we found," I said, picking up the photograph and turning it so she could see it. "Do you know who it is?"

Millicent stepped closer and tilted the picture.

"I believe that's Harriet Ravenscroft. In fact, I'm sure it is. Horatio's older sister. Older by quite a bit, actually. She raised him and his brother, Hieronymus, after their parents died. Ran the whole place, actually. Managed the household and staff and kept the farm going until she decided it was wiser to sell off the land and invest the money. It was Harriet who set up the Ravenscroft Trust. She hired my mother when her eyesight got too poor to be able to manage all the financial paperwork."

"Why isn't there a portrait of her anywhere?" Jilly asked. "It sounds like she did quite a bit for the family fortunes."

"She was considered eccentric at best, and the local lunatic by the less charitable. Never married, spent her days studying the stock market and innovations in farming and building. Smoked a pipe. Not very social, though my mother attributed that to her being very intelligent and very impatient with those who weren't."

"So because she was shrewd with money, an accomplished businesswoman, forward thinking, and didn't tolerate fools gladly, the village decided she was crazy?" I said.

"Yes," Millicent said. "In such an uncertain world, isn't it nice to know that some things never change?" She smiled and added, "Leave me a list of what you're taking. You know how everything has to be accounted for. It's long past time some of the things buried in this house saw the light of day." And then she glided off.

Jilly and I looked at each other, saying nothing until we heard the attic door close in the distance.

"Well, that was something," Jilly said. "Maybe she is retiring. I've never heard her talk like that about the family."

"Neither have I," I said. "And 'Hieronymus'? Who does that to a kid?"

"Seriously. Let's get the stuff we're taking closer to the stairs and then shift the rest back."

We discussed the eccentricity of the Ravenscrofts and how best to get everything downstairs. I kept the picture of Harriet aside, though, and took it back to my office. I'd clean it up and display it there. Raven Hill might not have appreciated Harriet, but I certainly did.

Chapter Eight

When I got back to my office, I tucked Harriet's picture under my desk and braced it with a cardboard box of donations so it wouldn't fall and break. I'd clean it up and find a spot for it later in the week. I'd just finished dusting myself off and was signing into my computer when Sloane Harris appeared.

"Sorry to bother you," she said, peeking into my cubicle, "but I can't find Helene, and the librarian out front told me to check with you."

"No problem," I said. "I'm sorry about your mother. I'm sure this is a difficult time. Whatever I can do to help." And hopefully do a little subtle probing and decide whether Sloane merited a closer look as a suspect. I'd been hoping I'd get a chance to talk to her, but was afraid it wouldn't be until the funeral.

"Thank you," Sloane said. "It was a shock. I still can't quite believe it."

By the look of things, the shock had not yet worn off. Sloane was pale and had dark circles under her eyes. Whenever I'd seen her before, she'd been carefully made up. Today it looked like she'd made a half-hearted effort to put herself together. The makeup consisted of mascara and lipstick; her hair was in a messy bun; and her jeans, loafers, and sweater, though of good quality, were well worn. Combined with her slender build and current wide-eyed stare, she looked like a sorority girl after a rough weekend.

"None of us can," I said. "Anita was a real force to be reckoned with."

Sloane gave a lukewarm smile. "Yes, she was. Though many people would say she was a bull-in-a-china-shop type of force."

"I can see that, but she did get a lot done." I smiled in return. Sloane looked lost. "Now how can I help you?"

Sloane hesitated, then took a deep breath. "Well, I'm trying to tie up some loose ends," she said. "You know, take care of some things. Personal things that my mother was working on. Home repairs, banking, a couple of things for Caleb—my son—that have to do with summer camp. And I can't find the paperwork. I was wondering if she left anything here."

It came out in a rush. Then Sloane stood, biting her lip. That was quite a list and didn't make a lot of sense. Summer camp? January maybe, but October? No. Even I knew that. What was she after?

"Not that I know of. Wouldn't a lot of that be on her computer?"

"Oh, you know my mother. She liked to make notes by hand. She was old school—still printed a lot of things out. She always carried a file box. Plastic, with a handle. Maybe you've seen it?"

"Yes, of course. I know just what you mean. She had it Monday night. I saw it in Helene's office when I stopped by. I thought she left with it, though." I knew she had, but did Sloane?

"She did. The police have the box and her computer, but not the things I'm looking for. I thought she might have missed a couple of the files or left them here for some reason."

"I'm pretty sure she didn't." Though I really wished she had. Going through all those digital files wasn't going to be easy. But it might be worthwhile to keep Sloane talking. "You know what, though? I have a little time before I leave, and I'm tired of staring at a screen. Let's take a quick look in the most likely spots."

"Well, um . . ." Sloane looked uncertain. I bounced up before she could say no.

"We'll check the Friends office and then Helene's. Let me get the key."

"Okay, thanks," she said.

I opened up the Friends of the Library office, and Sloane followed me in.

"If somebody found it, they'd probably leave it right here on the desk," I said, pointing to the empty surface. "But we can take a peek in the file cabinet—there's nothing confidential in there. You know what you're looking for, right?"

"Sort of. But anything with my mother's handwriting is worth a look."

We did a quick search of the cabinet and found nothing, as I expected. Helene's office yielded the same result, though the board did have a couple of file drawers for their own use if needed. We rifled through and came up empty. Anything of Anita's had her neatly printed labels on it. There was nothing handwritten. By the time we were done, Sloane was biting her lip again.

"And you're sure the police don't have them? I hate to raise a painful subject, but in car accidents things do fly around inside the vehicle. Maybe they were knocked loose from the box?" I asked. "Did you tell the officer specifically what you were looking for?"

"Yes, um . . . no—well, not exactly. I wasn't really thinking straight."

"Understandable," I said. "This must be very hard. I think it's worthwhile asking them again, and I'll certainly keep my eyes open. Things turn up in the oddest places sometimes. Am I just looking for anything with your name on it? Or Caleb's?"

I wondered what she'd say. The only file I'd seen related to her family had her husband's name on it.

"Oh, anything with 'Harris' on it, I guess. I'm not really sure. She had her own system, you know. But if you find anything, anything at all, just give me a call. Please." Sloane pulled out a notebook, scribbled her contact info, and handed the page to me.

"Will do," I said. "And tell the little guy I said hello. It's so nice to see him come in with his grandfather. They have such a good time."

Sloane got a funny look on her face. "Yes, like peas in a pod, those two. My dad would be lost without Caleb. Thanks again, Greer."

With that, she left, the set of her shoulders just as tense as when she'd arrived. Shock and grief affect people differently, but Sloane seemed a lot more upset about some missing files than she was about her mother's death. I doubted she'd follow up with the cops—whatever she was looking for, I got the feeling she didn't want anyone else to see it. I'd have to check with Jennie.

As I got ready to leave for the eye doctor, I pondered the bigger question: If the police didn't have the missing files, and Sloane didn't have them, where were they? I knew they existed—I hadn't imagined them. Was it possible they'd been returned to Richard? Unlikely—Sloane would know, and I didn't think the police had handed anything over to the family yet. Another thing to check with Jennie. Maybe I'd get lucky and find something in Anita's digital files. If so, I'd suggest to the police that they take a look at the shared drive. They might have already done that, but I doubted it. They'd have to do it from inside the building—we weren't set up for remote work. And they'd probably need a warrant. Those missing files might have nothing to do with Anita's death, but still—they had disappeared. Who had taken them, and why?

I was still puzzling over that when I arrived at the doctor's office. I was a little early. Medical staff were discreet, but Anita's death was a big enough story that I hoped it would loosen tongues. I didn't expect to get anything from the doctor, but with any luck I'd find a chatty receptionist. After I'd handed over my insurance card, I sat and filled out forms while the woman who'd checked me in fielded calls and helped another patient pick out sunglasses. I returned my paperwork to the desk, then drifted around, looking at frames, hoping there'd be a lull and I could do some snooping.

Once the sunglass buyer had left, I moved a little closer to the desk. The receptionist—Courtney, according to her name tag—smiled at me and told me it would just be a few more minutes. "You're the last patient," she said.

"I'm so glad you could fit me in," I said, "and on such short notice too. A woman I work with recommended you. She said she'd gotten some lovely glasses here for driving at night. I feel like I'm not seeing as well at night either. I'd decided to make an appointment, and that very night she was killed in a car accident, so I got nervous and called right away."

Courtney's eyes widened. "You must mean Ms. Hunzeker. I heard about that. My mother worked with her on a committee. Village Green beautification? Something like that. Anyway, it's awful. We live out that way. My mom always said she thought Ms. Hunzeker was indestructible."

"She did seem that way," I said. "I work at the library, so that's how I know her. She's on the board. Incredible energy, nothing seemed to faze her. I was surprised when she mentioned the vision problem. She was going to show me her new glasses—I think she'd just picked them up—but couldn't find them. It's scary to think she'd go off the road without them."

I was stretching the truth a bit, but it was a good cause, and Anita wasn't around to contradict me. Courtney looked dubious.

"I wouldn't think that would do it. Not having the glasses, I mean. I don't think her vision would get that bad that fast. Of course, I'm only part-time. Dr. Lewis's wife does the eyeglass fittings. You could ask either one of them if you're worried."

"Thanks, I will. Now maybe you could help me pick out some frames? I'm sure the doctor will tell me I need glasses."

"You just have to think of them as an accessory," said Courtney. My kind of girl, even if she hadn't been able to give me as much information as I'd have liked about Anita's vision issues. By the time the doctor was ready for me, I'd chosen a few librarianesque cat's-eye frames that Courtney assured me looked great with my face shape and would work with most prescriptions.

Once seated in the exam room, I ran through my list of concerns, emphasizing what had happened to Anita and mentioning her by name. This received no more than a "hmm" as Dr. Lewis took a look at my eyes. He ran me through various tests, put some drops in my eyes, and while we waited for my pupils to dilate, I returned in a roundabout way to the subject that interested me most.

"Issues with night vision usually affect people much older than you are," he said. "They often have to do with cataracts. And it's unlikely that had anything to do with your colleague's accident, so I don't think you need to worry on that count. You don't appear to be dealing with anything worse than some presbyopia and a slight astigmatism, both common in middle age."

I gave him a look. He smiled. "Early middle age," he said.

That was better, but not much. He decided my eyes were suitably dilated and finished up the exam. After writing up a prescription for reading glasses, he said, "You're not driving tonight, are you? No? Good. Those drops should wear off by bedtime. Pop back in if you have anything else come up with your vision." Then he ushered me out to Courtney and said goodnight.

I arranged to come back and see Mrs. Lewis about getting my reading glasses made. Courtney wrote the appointment on a card and handed it to me along with a sample bottle of drops for dry eyes "since you said you spend a lot of time on a computer" and a coupon for some vitamins to support eye health. Then I was out the door. I could hear Courtney locking up behind me as I headed up the small side street toward Main. My vision was still distorted. I could see well enough to find my way home, though I found myself weaving a bit.

I hadn't learned much, but it seemed clear that even the lack of her new glasses shouldn't have been a big contributor to Anita's accident. No, something else had happened. But what? Jennie said there were skid marks in an odd place, and someone else had mentioned Anita being run off the road and asked about witnesses. That was Millicent, who had also asked about toxicology. Hmm. Maybe someone had doctored her eye drops. Hadn't Agatha Christie poisoned a character that way? Was there a method of poisoning Agatha Christie *hadn't* used to kill off a character? I thought not, but I also decided this was a real reach as far as Anita was concerned.

I turned on to Main Street. There was that new wine shop on the corner. Anita had said something about wine when she was on the phone, hadn't she? And a gift basket? This was a new business in town, so she'd probably hit them up for something to use as a door prize at some event or another.

They were still open, but I decided it wasn't a good idea to go in already staggering. Or maybe it was. If I couldn't see, I'd have to ask for the type of wine my coworker had suggested. And I had friends coming to town—a good reason to get a couple bottles of wine.

The bell on the door of Adventure Wine and Spirits gave a cheerful jingle as I walked in. The man behind the counter—Eric, the proprietor—introduced himself and gave me an equally cheerful greeting. I explained my mission: friends coming to town, would like to try something new, coworker had recommended something, but I couldn't remember, and my vision was blurry.

"And to make matters worse," I went on, "she was in a terrible accident, so I don't want to ask her husband, though he may have been the one picking it up. But the way she described it, I'm sure my friends would enjoy it."

"Hmm, when was this?" he asked.

"Probably Monday," I said. "And they might have hit you up for a donation too. Anita was involved in every fundraiser in town."

"Everyone wants a donation," he said. "But if you're talking about the lady from the library, she was looking for a gift. That's what her husband said when he came in, anyway."

"That could be it," I said.

He led the way toward a tidy display with a map of Italy above it. "I heard that someone died in a car accident earlier this week. That wasn't your friend, was it?"

"Actually, that was Anita. Not a friend—she was on the library board. I happened to be helping her with something that evening, and she mentioned the wine. With everything that's happened, I'd forgotten about it until I was walking by."

Eric tsked and shook his head. "That's terrible. I'm sorry. But as far as the wine goes, you're in luck. It's from a boutique vineyard, and I didn't get a big shipment. The gentleman took three on Monday. Said they'd bought it before, and his wife loved it. There's one left. I've ordered some more. If you decide you like it, give me a call. I'll put some aside." He handed me a bottle. I was glad to see the price was well within my budget.

"This is great, thanks. And I'd like something for my landlord. He's French, and a little bit of a wine snob."

"I think he's been in a few times. Does he have a small dog?"

"That's Henri. And the dog is Pierre."

"I've got just the thing. Very elegant but won't break the bank."

Perfect. Eric gave me a brief rundown of the kind of stock he carried while he packaged up my wine in a neat little carryall with a handle. I'd definitely be back, and I'd send Beau and Ben in if they had time.

I walked home with my purchases, wondering how to ask Jennie about the wine in Anita's car without revealing that I'd been snooping. By the time I got back to my apartment, I was so tired I decided to cross that bridge when I came to it. It had been a long day.

Chapter Nine

The following morning, I was working my way through the items I'd pulled for weeding, when Dory walked in.

"Morning, Greer. Beautiful day, isn't it? I hope the weather holds for the sale. I've got an hour before my desk shift starts, and thought I'd get through some of these repairs. The smell of the glue won't bother you, will it?"

She settled in at our processing desk. This was a mixed blessing—I had a lot to do before my afternoon reference shift, and Dory would want to chat. On the other hand, she had an encyclopedic memory for local gossip, so if there was something to be known about Margaret Emerson in general, and her death in particular, she would know it. She might also have new information on Anita's death. Much of it would be speculation, but there was often a kernel of truth in the wild theories that came out of the village hive mind. And I could always get through these carts on Friday night.

"No, it won't bother me. I hope the weather holds too. I think we'll be in luck. So, what's new?"

"Well, not a lot," Dory said, and then launched into a recap of everyone she'd seen in the village since we last spoke, and what their thoughts were on Anita's death.

"Of course, they always say look close to home," Dory said, "but no one can see Richard or Sloane having the guts to do her in. I think you have a point about what a cornered animal will do, so I can see one of them suddenly snapping. But if she was run off the road—wouldn't that take planning?"

"I would think so, unless they just happened to be on the road at that time, which is a stretch."

"Well, I know Richard was out and about that night, running errands for Anita. Last-minute book sale things. Bill ran into him. Sloane's another story—she lives farther away. Do you happen to know if she has an alibi?"

"I don't," I said.

Dory looked disappointed. "I thought maybe Jennie Webber might have said something, since you girls are friendly."

"I haven't seen her. I think this case is taking up a lot of time. And you know, she's pretty tight-lipped about work stuff." Unless she wanted to know something, at which point she might offer up a crumb. All of which I could respect.

"Hmm," Dory said. "I did run into Cynthia Baker—did I tell you? No? Well, I asked how she was doing, given how shocking this whole thing is. Then I mentioned how dangerous Winding Ridge Road is—so dark and twisty. And then she said she was used to it, having lived there so long, and she only worried about it when it was icy. She said she was out that night, but not anywhere near there, and when she went home, the road wasn't even wet, so she can't imagine how Anita went down the bank."

"She volunteered all that?" I said.

"Yes, she did. I thought it was odd too. She was really rattling on, not at all like her. And then all of a sudden she seemed eager to get away."

That last part wasn't that odd—many people were eager to get away from Dory. But the first part sounded like the lady was protesting too much. It's possible the thought of a murder in her neighborhood, especially of someone she knew, made her nervous. But taken in combination with the conversation I'd had with her, it sounded suspicious. Cynthia really was a terrible liar. So was Sloane Harris, for that matter. I marveled that they'd gotten this far in life so completely lacking in the ability to dissemble, though I was grateful that they gave so much away without knowing it. It made a girl detective's job much easier.

"I suppose someone has told the police about the fight your cousin overheard?" I asked Dory.

"Oh yes, they've spoken to Angela. She said they took everything down, but she couldn't tell if they thought it was important."

"Well, at least they know," I said, and then before Dory could launch into another murder theory, I added, "I wanted to ask you—well, I probably shouldn't discuss it, but . . ."

Now I had her full attention. "Oh, Greer, you know you can ask me anything. I know how to keep quiet if I need to."

I let that one go.

"Thanks, Dory. It's just that I came across something with the name Margaret Emerson on it. I asked Mary Alice, and she told me the story of how she died here in the building. I couldn't quite believe it, but I didn't want to press her for details. She still finds it distressing, I think. But then she was right there at the time, from what she said."

"She was at Circulation. I remember that day well. I was here too—I'd gotten in early and was having a quick bite in the staff room." Dory then told me the same thing Mary Alice had, with one notable exception. "It was so busy that day, no one could get a break. When I was walking in, Millicent was in here fixing two cups of tea. I commented on it, and she said one was for Peg—Margaret went by Peg—because she hadn't been able to get away from the desk. I wasn't surprised—the parking lot was jammed, and the two of them were friends."

"Oh, that's sad. Millicent isn't close with many people, is she?"

"No, and I think it's more that she and Peg knew each other as little girls. You know Millicent's mother worked here, first for Harriet and then Horatio; and Peg's mother—she was also Margaret—was close with Harriet. Peg was a late baby and an only child, and I don't think her mother really knew what to do with her. Very bright, the whole family—father was a professor. So sometimes she'd bring Peg to visit when Millicent was going to be here with her mother."

"Playdate, before that became a thing?"

"Exactly," said Dory. "There's a picture of the two of them out there on the lawn. They must have both been in grammar school. It's in the library centennial collection, in the archives."

"That's really too bad then. It must have been quite a shock."

"Well, Peg had had pneumonia, and she never really came all the way back, you know? It's harder when you're older. But it was still unexpected. Though I saw her a few days before, and she seemed a little under the weather. Distracted, and a little low. So maybe she wasn't feeling well and didn't like to say. I know she enjoyed coming to work here. Said it kept her sharp."

"Didn't she live in the village? I thought that was what Mary Alice said."

"At the edge of town, actually, near the orchard. The house she grew up in. She went away to school and came back to Albany to work. She told me once she had a little apartment downtown for a while, but when her parents got older, she moved home. She had a good job, though, and she enjoyed it, so she kept working. Her parents had someone come in to help them, so Peg didn't have to give up her career."

"That was enlightened of them," I said. "Unusual decision for the time."

"Very forward thinking, the Emersons. My mother once told me that in her time the family was considered a little eccentric. Not as odd as the Ravenscrofts, but who was? Anyway, Peg started cleaning out that house when she retired, and was still at it when she died. It had a big attic, she said, that ran the full length of the house. I know she found some things that went into the archives—her family had lived here for quite a while. She told me she enjoyed reading the old letters and journals, but she had no one to pass them on to, so anything related to local history she was giving to the library. I'm not sure Millicent has gotten through it all yet."

"How interesting. I'm sorry I never met her," I said.

"It's too bad, what happened. I thought maybe she *would* retire soon. I know Helene and the board had been thinking we needed someone full-time again. They'd been making do for a while because of the budget. Helene never told you the story? Well, maybe she didn't want to scare you off. And things got awfully hectic right about when you started—that's when Anita really started agitating for the new library."

"I'm sure it slipped her mind," I said.

"I guess so," Dory replied. "These should be ready to go back on the shelf in a couple of days." She piled bricks wrapped in craft paper on top of the repaired books and put away her supplies. "Well, I'm heading out to the circulation desk. Need me to take any of that?"

"No thanks, I'm still going through it. I'll see you later."

Once Dory had gone, the office was quiet, and I made a good dent in my cart of potential discards. Once I'd made a pile of books that could go back on the shelf, and another of those that needed to be reordered or updated, I could give some thought to what Dory had told me. There was not much I'd consider suspicious, I thought as I stamped and scanned the withdrawn books. The bit about Millicent bringing Peg her tea was news but didn't necessarily mean anything. It was a busy day, and the two women were long-time colleagues. Their relationship was friendly. It was interesting that Peg's mother was also Margaret. Which woman was the subject of

Anita's file? My money was on the younger Margaret, Peg, since she had not only worked at the library but had also died here. But Margaret the elder, having been friends with Harriet Ravenscroft, could tie into the "Ravenscroft Deeds" file. According to Millicent, there had always been rumors of a missing will or missing heir or some such. If there were any question about ownership of the manor, the discussion of a new building wouldn't have gotten as far as it did. Would it? I'd have to ask Helene.

My phone buzzed. Jennie. I picked up and said hello.

"Do you have a couple minutes?" she asked.

"Sure," I said. "I'm in my office."

"Is anyone else around?"

"No, not at the moment. Why?"

"This is confidential. I need some information."

"Hang on," I said. I walked over to the door, looked around, and shut it. There was no one in the hall, but if someone walked into the office, they might hear me before I realized they were there. The Friends office was locked and empty. I went back to my desk and sat.

"Go ahead," I said. "There's no one else here right now."

"Can you remember the names you saw on Anita's paper files, the handwritten ones?"

I rattled off what I could remember and then added, "and I gave you the name Waters, but that wasn't right. I'm sure it was Walters, J. P. Walters."

"You're positive?"

"Yes. Well, as sure as I can be without seeing the file again. Anita requested a copy of his thesis. It arrived late yesterday.

I only put it together with Anita's file because Cynthia Baker asked me about it."

"Cynthia Baker? Really? Hang on," Jennie said. I heard some muffled conversation. Then she was back.

"What did she want to know?"

"She wanted to know if Anita had left any research materials, something like that. They were working on something for the historical society. To be honest, I didn't quite believe her, but not for any solid reason. It was the way she asked. I think she even wrote it down for me."

"Has she contacted you since?"

"No."

"Good. Don't tell her anything if she does. And see if you can find whatever she wrote."

"Okay, I'll look. What's this all about?"

There was a brief silence. I could picture Jennie debating how much to tell me. I heard a man's voice—Sam's, probably—and then Jennie spoke.

"J. P. Walters was found dead this morning."

"What? Did someone kill him?"

"We're not sure. It could be an accident. Or suicide. Hard to tell from the scene. We'll know more later. If Cynthia Baker shows up or gets in touch, don't say anything, and let me know. And hang on to that thesis."

"I will. Call me if you have any more info?"

"If there's anything I can tell you. Will you be home tonight?"

"No, actually." I told her about the sale preview and that I had friends arriving late.

"Okay, if you don't hear from me, I'll stop by the sale tomorrow."

We hung up. I found the thesis and locked it in a desk drawer. I'd find the card Cynthia wrote on later. It was in my bag somewhere. I grabbed the pile of books to shelve and went to the reading room. I was putting the last book from my stack back in its spot when I heard a piping voice from the end of the aisle.

"Hi! Hi! Hi!"

I looked to see a little boy bouncing on his toes and smiling at me. There was no one else in sight.

"Hiya, Caleb," I said. "Where's your grown-up?"

"Grampa," he said, and waved his arm in the direction of Circ. "Got my book?"

Caleb bounced some more. He was a good-natured kid, generally happy, who didn't seem to have inherited his mother's nerves. He was smart too. He'd figured out a while ago that when he and his grandfather ordered what they called a "special book," I was the one who would eventually produce it.

"Not yet," I said. "Maybe when the mail comes, but no guarantees. You know we always call as soon as it gets here."

He looked disappointed. Time to redirect to something I knew would get a positive response.

"Are you coming to the costume parade tomorrow?" I asked.

Caleb nodded and smiled again.

"What's your costume?"

"Circuit board," he said carefully and clearly. "I light up!"

"Wow! That's really cool, Caleb! Did your grandpa help you make it?"

"Yes, and pumpkins too. Scary ones."

"Nice," I said. "I can't wait to see."

At this point we were joined by Caleb's grandfather. Richard Hunzeker was a pleasant-looking but otherwise nondescript man. Whereas Anita always sported a colorful accessory, usually a scarf, her husband dressed as though trying to blend in. Not much of a talker, he was easy to overlook.

"Caleb just told me about his costume, and the scary pumpkins, and that it all lights up," I said.

Richard smiled. "That's true. Caleb and I have been studying circuits, haven't we, buddy? We figured out how to make everything blink."

Caleb nodded. "But no book yet, Grampa."

"It'll get here. It always does," Richard told him.

"I think there's some new puzzles out," I said. Caleb looked at his grandfather, and when Richard nodded, zipped off to the kid's area. Once he was out of earshot I turned to Richard.

"I'm sorry about Anita. I've always appreciated that she and Helene were willing to take a chance on someone with so little library experience." This was the most personal thing I could think of to say. Praising her work ethic and efficiency didn't seem appropriate.

"Thank you, Greer."

There was a brief silence. The arrangements were probably on hold because of the police investigation, so I didn't want to go there. I could satisfy my curiosity on a couple of points, though.

"We had a nice chat on Monday night, Anita and I. She needed a hand finding her glasses. She'd just gotten some new ones, she said, and misplaced them. She recommended the eye doctor, though. I was glad to hear her say she was happy with him—I'd made an appointment there."

"Yes, she had just been to the doctor. She was having a hard time accepting the vision problem, but she broke down and went. I think it was worse than she let on, but she's always been so healthy."

"She did seem indestructible. We weren't able to find the glasses, though. I feel a little bad about that."

"I wouldn't worry, Greer. I'm sure they were in the car somewhere. We were both running so many errands that day—they probably slipped out of the bag and went under the seat. I know I had a carful of things when I got home, and I'm sure she did too. I barely made it to the pumpkin patch before they closed."

"Well, in any case, I'm glad we had time to talk about something other than business. She was in a good mood. She even recommended the new wine shop and some particular brand, but I can't remember exactly. Maybe you know—she said you were picking some up for a gift basket or something like that."

Richard tilted his head and thought for a minute. "I'm not sure . . ." He frowned.

"Oh, that's all right. I'll stop in and ask." He didn't need to know I already had. "It's a small business—I'm sure someone will remember."

"Yes—oh, wait a minute! Now I remember. Monday was so busy—it's all a blur."

"Understandable," I said. "Maybe I shouldn't have asked. It's just such a nice memory of Anita to have." Even if I'd made it up.

"No, no, it's all right. I was confused when you said 'gift basket.' I was picking up a few things for us, but she sent me specifically for a gift for someone. She was working with a professor from one of the local colleges on something for the historical society and wanted to get him a thank-you gift. It's someone who works with Sloane's husband, Sean, so I wasn't sure how all that would look. There's grant money involved, you see. But she insisted. I don't remember the name, but I'm sure I have it written down somewhere."

"Oh, that's all right. I can ask at the shop or just see what they suggest. I have friends coming to town for the weekend." Richard looked distressed, so I moved on to a happier subject.

"Your little buddy seems pretty excited about all the Halloween events. Will you be entering something in the pumpkin carving contest? Caleb is just about old enough, isn't he?"

"Not quite. Next year. It's nice how Jilly has all the little kids make designs, and the adult volunteers carve. I picked up all the pumpkins Monday night. Caleb's are for his house. His mother worries about any kind of flame, so we found battery-operated candles and doctored them up. Bright orange lights that flicker."

"That sounds great. It's so nice that you're able to do that kind of thing with him and that he's so interested."

Richard smiled. "Yes, his mother jokes that Caleb is my 'mini-me.' I had fun with Sloane when she was small, but she was never interested in electronics and engines like Caleb is.

By the time he could crawl, I'd decided to sell the business and spend more time with him. The kids got free childcare, and I got all the fun! It's true that being a grandparent is the better deal. I don't know what I'd do without him."

Though I'd never for a moment wanted children, I could see his point. At least if they weren't yours, you could hand them back when you got tired of them. But I doubted Richard did a lot of that. Anita, probably yes.

"Sounds that way," I said. "Well, I'd better get back to work. I'm sure I'll see you tomorrow. Bye."

Richard nodded and headed toward Caleb. I went back to my office. It didn't sound like Richard had a firm alibi for the night of this wife's death. The police would be checking that—if he could produce time-stamped receipts, he'd be okay even if he did something as retro as pay cash, and every place had cameras. Well, a lot of them anyway, even in Raven Hill. And who knew where Sloane had been. I'd ask Jennie. Sloane was nervous about something, but from what I'd heard she was always nervous about something. The fact that she was after the files but couldn't say quite what for, and Cynthia Baker was after something related to one of those files as well made me wonder.

Once again, I searched for J. P. Walters to make sure I hadn't missed anything. I took a look at the department directory, and it hit me. Sloane's husband worked for Walters—he taught in the history department. Dr. Sean Harris had gone from adjunct to full-time a few years ago, according to his biography. He specialized in early twentieth-century history, with an emphasis on labor movements. He lived in the Capital

District with his family and enjoyed hiking, gardening, and the local minor league sports teams.

Nothing there said he had a reason to kill his mother-in-law. I wondered how the two had gotten along. They had a shared interest in history, though different time periods. And though Richard spent a lot of time with his grandson, and so had more interaction with the Harris family, I'd never gotten the sense that Anita was very involved.

I wasn't having a lot of luck putting all these pieces together, so I went back to my actual job and let my subconscious work on it. I had a list of things to get through, including touching base with Helene.

Chapter Ten

Book sale preview night was something I didn't mind working because it also gave me a bake sale preview. Though many of the goodies would arrive early on Saturday, plenty of volunteers dropped things off on Friday afternoon. While Saturday's spread would be outside the entrance, Friday night there was a table, outside the community room, with a nice assortment of things for those shoppers who were going to be late for dinner and got a little peckish. I nipped upstairs while the line was still forming for the sale. There was a big platter of Felicity's famous artichoke squares, surrounded by assorted baked goods. On the theory that they were vegetable based and therefore counted as a healthy dinner, I took two of the artichoke squares and then loaded up a plate with cookies and brownies. Agnes would be staying late with me and might want a snack, and if she didn't—well, oatmeal and peanut butter made nice breakfast cookies.

I paid one of the volunteers and went back to my desk. The Friends and a couple of the board members would handle the preview crowd, which was usually made up of used booksellers, homeschoolers, and regulars who couldn't make it to the event on Saturday. Admission required an annual membership to the Friends of the Library, which could be purchased on the spot. The fire doors at either end of the main hall were closed and locked, so as long as the Friends on duty kept anyone from wandering down the front stairs, no one could get into the reading room. The moth-eaten velvet ropes pulled out of storage for such occasions weren't much of a deterrent. All I had to do was make an occasional tour of the place and round up any stragglers, but for now I could do some work.

Forty-five minutes later I heard someone coming into the office. I leaned out of my cubicle and saw Agnes.

"Hi Greer," she said. "The volunteer on the door told me to come right in. I know I'm a little early, but I wanted to get settled and take a look at how the Friends are doing their bookkeeping. Felicity went over it quickly, but I'd like to make sure I'm clear on everything before all the cash comes in."

"Sure," I said, getting up and getting the key to the FOL office. "Make yourself at home. I'm here catching up on my ordering until you're done tonight, so I can drop you home. I need to make a couple rounds of the building, but otherwise I'll be at my desk."

Agnes knew where all the necessary files were kept, so I left her to it and took a quick tour of the manor. Every door that should be locked was locked, and every room that should be empty was empty. A good sign. I stopped outside the community room to chat with Darla Van Alstyne, one of our longtime volunteers.

"How's business?" I asked.

"Pretty good," she said. "A lot of the usual suspects—you know: dealers and resellers. A couple of serious cookbook collectors. And a few looking for reference books. I'm just glad no one is asking for old encyclopedia sets anymore. That went on for years after the library got rid of them. People couldn't get over it. No matter how often we said it was all in a—what do you call it? A database?—they were upset. One man said 'Well, a database doesn't look too nice on a bookshelf, does it?' and then stomped off. Haven't seen him at one of these since."

I laughed. People had been putting attractive volumes that they never read on their shelves for centuries, and the invention of e-books and databases hadn't changed that. Darla made change for someone buying some brownies, and then continued.

"I'll tell you what, though: I'll be glad when that elevator project is done. Getting all these books up here using that old elevator is a lot of work. We even used the dumbwaiter for some things, but that's just as ancient and wheezy as the elevator. Any idea when the work on that will start?"

"I know the library got the grant funding and some matching funds, so the money is there. Helene said at the last meeting that the board was getting bids, but that takes time. And they have to make sure the electrical system can handle it. Probably by next year's sale."

"That'll be good. I didn't agree with Anita on the need for a new building, but she was right that this one needs work," Darla said. "And the electrical system—I've lost count of how many times we've lost power during a storm, and the lights flicker an awful lot for no good reason."

I had to agree. The power did go out a lot. The electrical system had never been meant to handle all the technology needs of a modern library. The place met code, but accessibility was an issue. The original elevator had been cutting edge for its time, but its time was a previous century. You could fit a wheelchair and one other adult in it, but it was tight. The dumbwaiter next to it was sturdy enough, but it was designed for domestic use, not hauling books or archival material. The plan was to use the space both took up for one larger elevator, but that required careful engineering. Not to mention the need to keep the original look of the hall intact to the extent possible. The elevator and the dumbwaiter had been disguised behind the same woodwork that ran throughout the main floor. Someone had to point them out to me when I'd first started. The manor wasn't a historic landmark—it was a large home that had been expanded over generations, resulting in a hodgepodge of styles. But it had a quirky charm, and most of the residents of Raven Hill loved it.

Darla went to attend to her customers while I checked to make sure the archives were locked, and then went back downstairs. The crowd coming in had thinned, and the volunteers had everything under control, so I returned to the office. Agnes peeked out as I walked in.

"Oh, Greer, you're back," she said. "I thought I heard you come in a few minutes ago, but when I looked, no one was there. This building does make some odd noises, doesn't it?"

"It does, though it could have been one of the volunteers," I said. "How's it going?"

"Pretty well. I'm ready to go when the sale ends. Are they still busy upstairs?"

"Slowing down, but we have another hour until they close up. I'm going to make some tea, so if you want, I can show you where everything is in the kitchen. I snagged some cookies earlier too—would you like some?"

"That would be nice, Greer." Agnes stood and came out of the office. "I have a terrible sweet tooth since I stopped drinking. If I weren't walking more and going to yoga, I'm sure all my pants would be too tight."

"You seem to be doing well," I said, as I locked the office. Agnes had probably just heard old house noises, but better safe than sorry.

"Thank you. It's been nearly six months since I've had a drink," Agnes said. "It's been hard, but I'm changing my routines, trying to do some new things. And some old things, like the accounting. I needed to brush up, but I can still do it."

"I'm sure you can. How long has it been since you retired?"

"A little over five years. My husband and I were going to travel after we sold the business, and then a month after the sale went through, he had a heart attack. It's no excuse—I was always fond of a cocktail, and so was he—but I was lost without him, and with nothing to do."

"That's hard. After my husband was killed, I felt lost too, or maybe 'confused' is a better word. Once the shock wore off, anyway. And I still had a job, so there was some sort of routine, at least."

"I'm sorry for what you went through, Greer. I hope I haven't brought up a painful subject. I'd heard the story, but I forgot."

"It's all right, I really don't—hang on," I said. We'd reached the lower level, where the staff room and book discussion room were. There were two doors at the end of the hall. One was a closet, and the other led to the basement. I rarely had a reason to use them and never remembered which was which. One of them was open.

I walked down the hallway. This end was dimly lit, and I wished I had my flashlight. There was one somewhere in the staff room if I had to check the basement and the bulb was out. When I got to the door, I was relieved to see it was the closet. I looked in—nothing but some extra mops and brooms and a couple of traffic cones. I pushed the door shut. As I turned, it swung open again with a creak. I closed it again, this time turning the knob and waiting to hear it click. It stayed closed.

"Is everything all right?" Agnes asked as I walked back to the staff room.

"I think so. That door doesn't stay shut. I'm sure one of the Friends needed something and didn't notice." But I was starting to get uneasy—odd noises and open doors. Tonight's volunteer group were all regulars, as far as I knew. I left the staff room door ajar so I could keep an eye on the hallway, and decided I'd do another patrol after we had our break.

I showed Agnes where everything was. While the electric kettle heated, we talked about what we were reading. Like me, Agnes was a mystery fan. She said she'd been to a signing in

Albany that Monday. It was a Vermont writer we both liked whose new book had come out the previous week.

"I went with a friend from my yoga class. She drove—I'm just not sure about getting my license again. It's been so long." She told me about the signing and how nice the author was.

"I've heard that, though I've never met him," I said. The kettle popped, signaling it was done.

"I really should get one of those," Agnes said. "It heats up so quickly." She rummaged around in the cupboard. "Now where is my—oh, here it is. Felicity told me to leave whatever I wanted on the Friends' shelf. It looks like everyone is trying that new tea shop. Nice to see more small businesses in the village. Have you been there yet?"

"On my list," I said. "What do you have there?" It looked like the same red tin that Millicent had.

"A rooibos blend. I'm trying not to have caffeine after lunch. It keeps me up. This is a red tea, so no caffeine. I wasn't too sure, but it has a nice flavor. I'll try some others too. I don't know much about tea, but the owner said she puts all the red teas in red tins, so I'll work my way through them. Makes it easier when I don't have my glasses," Agnes said with a laugh.

Odd, I thought, getting my mug. Millicent was a lifelong Earl Grey woman, as devoted to her blend as I was to Irish breakfast. So what had she been doing with a red tin, which likely held a red tea? Maybe she was having trouble sleeping too.

"Anyway," Agnes said, "we had dinner after the book signing, so we were coming back late. And there was something strange. That was the night Anita died, Monday night." She hesitated.

"Yes," I said. "Go on. What was strange?"

"Well, we were near Winding Ridge Road—not at the intersection, but close. It's so deserted at night—we only passed one other car from the time we turned off the main road in Albany. I remember because it was a funny color, sort of metallic. Anyway, all those roads are twisty, and we were on a stretch that's pretty straight, but coming up on a curve. It was very dark—there's no lights out there—and I was thinking how different everything looked in the car headlights. The bare trees and the rocks and the way the ground falls away in places—it's eerie, going in and out of the light. And then something came at us on the road. It was like a big, speeding shadow. Then the headlights hit it, and it was a truck, I think, with no lights on, and it just flew by."

"No lights? That's dangerous on any road."

"Yes, but that's not the strangest thing. We swerved because Debbie was startled, and I turned around to look, and the truck was gone. There was nothing I could see on the road behind us. It was only a few seconds since it had passed us."

"What time was this, do you remember?" I asked.

"Close to ten. I thought about it when I heard about Anita, but she was on her way home from a meeting here, so her accident would have been earlier. And there was something else, something that struck me, and I woke up in the middle of the night, but in the morning I couldn't remember what it was. But I think it was important."

"Have you spoken to the police?"

"Oh, Greer, what would I tell them? That we saw a dark truck that disappeared into thin air, and then I thought of something important in the night that now I can't remember? They'll think I'm hitting the bottle again." She gave me a weak smile.

I smiled back. "I'm not sure about that, and I don't know that they have a firm time of death. I think Lieutenant O'Donnell or Officer Webber would take you seriously. Jennie will be stopping by the sale tomorrow. You could mention it to her then. Or I'll mention it, if you'd rather."

"Yes, that's a good idea. I don't want to waste anyone's time, but I can't shake the feeling that it's important."

"I'll tell her."

"Thank you," Agnes said. We moved on to other subjects, finished our snack, and went back to the office. I checked the closet and basement doors before I left. Both were firmly shut. I decided to take my flashlight with me on my next round of the building, just in case. In case of what, I wasn't sure, but having the hefty light in hand made me feel better.

I left Agnes loading paper into her old adding machine. "I use all those computer programs, but for adding up cash I'm old school," she said. "You go ahead. I'm fine here."

I closed the office door behind me and stood in the empty hall. From my right, I could hear voices coming from the direction of the service stairs. That would be the volunteers and book sale shoppers. I turned left and walked to the reading room. I stepped in, leaving the lights off. The library was closed, after all. I could see well enough with the light from the hall and the windows. I stopped and breathed in the scent of books and furniture polish and the cold autumn air that found its way in despite all the weather stripping devoted to keeping it out. This kind of peace and quiet was rare, so I enjoyed it for a moment and then started a circuit of the room.

The windows at the back gave a partial view of the parking lot. It looked like there was still a decent crowd. Plenty of cars, and a few shadowy figures moving around. I turned and walked the length of the room. The floors, which so often shrieked in protest when walked upon, remained silent. I reentered the main hall near the front door. Tonight I was not in the mood for the Ravenscroft ancestors whose portraits lined the hall, interspersed with rippling antique mirrors that reflected their disapproving stares. I stopped at the bottom of the staircase and listened. I couldn't hear anything going on at the book sale preview—the community room was toward the back of the manor. Things must be winding down. Time to visit my favorite place in the manor—Horatio Ravenscroft's study.

The small octagonal room was wood paneled, with floor-to-ceiling bookshelves on most walls. There were two windows—one looked out onto the side yard, and the other to the front of the manor. There was a small fireplace, a desk, and two overstuffed leather chairs. The desk held all the things you'd find in a home office in the forties or fifties—fountain pens, letter opener, and a wooden tray for mail, complete with a couple of addressed envelopes, ready to be mailed. A carved wooden box weighted down some papers. A blotter, a notebook, a small globe, and an ashtray completed the scene. Everything a pipe-smoking scholarly gentleman would need.

Perched on its own special shelf on one wall was a large raven. As an example of early taxidermy, it was marvelous. Its feathers were glossy and black, its beak gleamed, and its eyes seemed to follow you. Positioned with a view into the hall, the raven had been guardian of Horatio's study for decades. His beady-eyed stare had done more to keep the curious of any age out of the room than a physical barrier ever could. He hadn't stopped me, though. I loved this room and visited whenever I could, chatting him up each time. Admittedly, it was a one-sided conversation, but it was a way of ordering my thoughts. After my first few visits, I'd started to feel welcome, and now reported in regularly. A couple of times, I'd thought I smelled pipe smoke—a hint of woodsy cherry atop the usual scents of leather, wood polish, and musty volumes. It would linger for a moment, and then it was gone.

I stopped a few feet into the room and looked around. Here, too, everything was in order. I leaned against the nearest armchair and looked up at the raven.

"Someone finally got rid of her. I'm shocked, but not surprised. The police think it might be one our own, you know. I'm not so sure."

There was no response. The only sound was the wind in the trees outside. A branch tapped against the window. "'Suddenly there came a tapping,'" I said, quoting Poe's famous poem, and walked over to look out. No sign of the manor ravens, or any other living thing, in the side yard or on the path. The branch tapped again, near the top of the frame. *That'll need to be cut back,* I thought. I'd let Helene know. I turned back to my feathered friend.

"Agnes saw something that night, out near Winding Ridge Road. Something strange, she said. She didn't want to tell the police, but I think it could be important. I'm going to tell them. She's a recovering alcoholic, but she's never been stupid. They'll take her seriously. I'll keep you posted. Got to finish my rounds."

I was at the door when I heard a muffled clang from the corner of the study. I whipped around. Lifting my flashlight, I turned it on, aiming it at the corner of the room. There was nothing there. I found the switch for the overhead light and turned that on, then spun in a circle, checking every corner of the room. I was alone.

I walked back to the corner where I'd heard the noise. Nothing had fallen, but at the edge of the carpet I spotted a metal grate in the floor. It was part of the antiquated heating system. Grates were all over the building, but I'd never noticed this one. The only time I had to pay attention to them was when the boiler signaled distress by clanging and gurgling. It echoed all over the manor as the sound traveled through the vents. The last time it happened, we'd had a chilly few days and a big repair bill. But one clang did not a broken boiler make. I'd give it another couple of minutes, though. If I heard anything else, I'd have to go check.

I flipped off the overhead light and waited. I'd decided we were in the clear, when I heard another metallic clang, followed by a cough. That wasn't a mechanical noise. Someone was in the boiler room. *Or possibly the basement,* I thought as I calculated where I was in relation to the rooms on the lower floors.

Probably a perfectly good explanation, I said to myself, patting my back pocket to make sure I had my phone, and then speeding down the main hall. *Perhaps a confused volunteer.* The Friends were always conscripting spouses, children, and unwary neighbors to help with big events, and they did sometimes wander off. Or flee. Either way, I decided to snag one of the volunteers on door duty on my way to the basement. Hopefully someone who could manage the basement stairs quickly if need be.

I was in luck. A regular library user and retired Marine named Mike was sitting on the stairs, looking bored. His wife, a volunteer, was talking to someone holding two loaded shopping bags. I caught Mike's eye and gestured. He jumped up and came over.

"Borrowing him for a few," I said to his wife with a wave and a smile.

Once out of earshot, I said to him, "I've been hearing some odd noises in the basement. I think either someone's lost, or the boiler's acting up. Not sure which, but I wanted backup."

He nodded, straightened his shoulders, and looked at my flashlight.

"Nice and heavy," he said. "Got another one of those?"

"There's one in the boiler room. We'll check there first."

"Lead the way," he said. "I've never been down here. Boy, this place is a maze once you leave the main floor."

"It's all the old servant's stairs and utility rooms," I said. We went down another half flight next to the staff room. The boiler had been added long after this part of the house was built, fit in by expanding and cementing an old root cellar. I opened the door, turned on the light, and handed Mike the flashlight on the shelf above the switch. The beast of a heating system was humming along. No lights on the control panel were flashing, and there wasn't a clang or a gurgle to be heard. Mike made a quick circuit of the room.

"All clear," he said. "But this thing is ancient. I can see why you'd worry."

We closed up the room and went back up to the staff room. I looked in as we went by—empty.

"This way," I said. We got to the end of the hall.

"I found this closet open earlier," I said. It was closed now, but I checked inside anyway, shining my light around. No vents or grates, so whatever I'd heard had to have come from the basement. I shut the closet door and turned to the basement. Mike turned his flashlight on. As I reached for the knob, the door swung open.

I gasped and stepped back. There was a man standing inside in the door frame. Mike swung his light up, temporarily blinding the stranger, who threw up an arm and staggered back toward the stairs behind him. Mike grabbed him by the arm and hauled him out. Something went flying and landed with a clatter. Without releasing his hold, Mike steadied the man and then turned off his flashlight. I took a closer look. Though dusty and dressed for dirty work, he was recognizable.

Richard Hunzeker.

"Richard? What are you doing here?" I asked.

I looked at Mike and nodded. He let go of Richard's arm. Richard sighed. "Checking the fuses," he said.

"After hours on a Friday?" I said.

He looked abashed.

"Anita had asked me to look at them before the book sale. One year the sound system wouldn't work because a fuse blew. It knocked out some other things too. It was chaos, with all the little kids in their costumes and the sale going on. Since then, every year she'd have me come in the week before and check them all. There's also been a lot of issues with the wiring lately. I wanted to give it a good going over. But—well, with everything going on, I forgot until this afternoon, when Sloane called to double-check what time to bring Caleb to the costume parade." He shrugged. "It didn't occur to me to check in with anybody. I'm sorry."

"I'm sorry for your loss," Mike said. It sounded perfunctory, but Richard took him at his word.

"Thank you," he said. "I still can't quite believe it."

"Neither can I," I said. "I don't think any of us can. Here, I'll help you gather these tools. Mike, they probably need you back on door duty. I'll see him out. You are finished, aren't you?" I said to Richard.

Mike gave a wave and said he'd put the flashlight back on his way upstairs. I knelt down to help Richard with his toolbox.

"I've got it," he said. "No need for you to get dusty and dirty too."

"It's fine," I said, handing him some things that had rolled away from the box. It seemed an odd assortment of items, but then I wasn't handy, and I knew nothing about electrical systems.

Richard piled everything into the box. "I'll tidy it up later," he said, snapping it shut.

"Okay, I'll walk you out. I need to check a few things." I had no reason to think he wouldn't leave, but I'd had no reason to think he'd be roaming around the building tonight either. I decided I'd see him to the door.

"Are the fuses all in order?" I asked as we walked.

Richard shrugged. "They're all recently replaced, but the wiring in the whole building needs an upgrade. I know it's inspected regularly, but it worries me. Anita didn't go about it the right way, but she made a good point about the maintenance on the manor."

Once Richard had walked out to the parking lot, I went back downstairs and made sure all the doors were closed and that nothing was on in the staff room. I turned off the lights to discourage anyone from going down, and then stopped to check the alarm panel. No blinking lights signifying that people were moving around where they shouldn't be, but the system didn't cover the whole building. That was something else that needed upgrading. More than once I'd thought that there was someone else in the building when I was alone or closing with one other person, but I'd never been able to prove it. I hadn't done a careful search for secret passages, but I'd tried to get my hands on a copy of the building plans. Apparently, there were none, which struck me as odd. There'd been plenty of work done on the manor, and the original building was of interest to local historians, but no one could find anything related. I knew Helene had tried years ago, because I'd asked her. And I'd heard Anita say she'd like to find some as well. That was recent.

Had she? Helene hadn't mentioned it. I would have seen anything Anita had requested from another system. But she did have connections through the historical society and whatever other organizations she was involved in, so she might have found something. Who would know? Richard or Sloane, maybe. Possibly even Cynthia Baker. Worth checking. I'd add it to my list.

The rest of the evening passed without incident. The Friends wrapped up their sale, secured the remaining baked goods, and handed off the cash to Agnes. Mike and his wife stayed—she was in the office organizing table signs for the next day, so Mike accompanied me on my final tour of the building.

"You know," he said as I checked doors and windows on the second floor, "I always liked this place. I wouldn't want the library to move. But it's not too secure, is it? In the last year I've started to think that maybe that Hunzeker woman had a couple of good points. But still. It's going to sound fanciful, but the manor has always reminded me of a book I read as a kid. *The Secret of Terror Castle*. Ever heard of it?"

"My dad had it. Alfred Hitchcock and the Three Investigators," I said. "I read it too."

"I read them all," he said. "And I'm fond of the manor, but I'll bet it's got plenty of secrets. Sometimes I really wonder about the place."

"So do I, Mike. So do I."

Chapter Eleven

❦

Book sale day dawned bright, clear, and crisp. I got in early and managed to catch Helene for a few minutes. I explained the dilemma with Anita's interlibrary loan requests and the interest from other parties, including the police.

"We had something like this happen once before, years ago. Check it out to the reference card and give it to me. I'll lock it up until I talk to Sam. That way it's out of your hands."

"I'll get it for you," I said. And if anyone else asked, I'd say I had nothing and encourage them to place a request for any items they might need. It would be interesting to see if they did.

"Thank you, Greer, and thank you for letting me know," said Helene. "If anyone is looking for me, I'll be in my office until the costume parade."

Helene looked exhausted. My guess was that the board was having a collective meltdown, and a lot was landing on her. Anita's murder left a leadership void and required a delicate balancing act in terms of public relations. She'd been closely associated with the library, and there had been a great deal of heated debate around the subject of a new one. The person who would normally handle that kind of problem was Anita, so the remaining board members had to be scrambling. There was not a lot I could do to help with that, so I decided to offer the best support I could think of. It was something that always worked for me.

"I think the donuts just arrived," I said. "Would you like me to bring you one, along with the thesis?"

"That would be nice, Greer—thank you."

I snagged a donut for each of us and went to my desk. I pulled out the thesis and processed it, then decided to take one more look through it. I couldn't imagine what could be so important about this. I flipped pages, stopping here and there to read a paragraph. My eyes started to glaze over. I liked academic mysteries but didn't want to live one if it involved slogging through this kind of reading.

I was putting the thesis in an interoffice envelope when something niggled. Academic mysteries. Missing documents. Research. It seemed like there was something I should be thinking of. A book I'd read? Nothing came to me, but still, I hesitated. I pulled the thesis out and found something to prop it open with. Then I got my phone out and took pictures of the title page, table of contents, and bibliography, making sure I got all the details on each page.

"Why are you doing this, Greer?" I muttered, hoping my subconscious would burp up a reasonable reply. It remained silent. Well, I could always go home and stare at my bookshelves and see if something jumped out at me. It's not like I'd have time to do any research at work today. Besides, the library didn't arrange fiction by genre. Satisfied that I'd gotten the best shots I could, I packaged the thesis, marked it "Confidential," and brought it to Helene, along with her donut. Then I put on my cape and fascinator, armed myself with my wand, and went to wake up the computers in the reading room. Ben and Beau would be arriving any minute, and I wanted a chance to say hello.

I was still zipping around when Beau strolled in, sporting a frock coat and looking like he could have stepped out of one of the Ravenscroft portraits in the hall.

"Great fascinator," he said. "Are you the Wicked Witch of Raven's Breath? Where's your broom?"

"Watch it," I said. "I've got a dragon wand, and I'm not afraid to use it. And that's Raven *Hill* if you please. You shouldn't mock it—take a look at the pictures out there, and you'll see you fit right in. Nice of you to come as an early Ravenscroft."

"I'm the Marquis de Lafayette."

I raised my eyebrows. "Not a common Halloween choice."

"I got it for a watch party when *Hamilton* started streaming. It's my go-to costume now."

"It does show your legs to advantage," I said. "And what's Ben's costume?"

"Aladdin. He was in a summer stock production ages ago that folded suddenly. He never got paid, but he kept the costume. It still fits, so he pulls it out once in a while. He figured the kids would like it. He even brought a ratty old carpet to set up the face-painting station on. Though you seem to have plenty here," he added, lifting the corner of the rug with the toe of one shiny, buckled shoe.

"Don't be a snob," I said. "These are all the real thing, just too stained and moth-eaten to be worth preserving. There's more stashed in the attic and basement."

"The place is a museum. Speaking of the basement, Jilly sent me in to get a frame. She said it was downstairs and to get a dolly from the boiler room, and to yell if I needed help."

"I think you can manage it on your own—you're tall enough." I gave him directions and sent him on his way, promising to be out when I got a chance. That turned out to be a few hours later. We were mobbed from the minute we opened, and the phone rang off the hook all morning. I was glad Helene always had the whole staff scheduled on book sale day. Everyone did some time in the reading room, but there were enough of us that we got a few breaks. The volunteers directed traffic at each door and the halls, so things went pretty smoothly. Everything would quiet down after lunch, when all the activities except for the book sale were over.

It was a little after eleven when I made it outside. I'd already admired the finery of the costume parade participants who had come into the library after the big event. Caleb's costume did both light up and blink. He was so happy I figured he wouldn't take it off until his batteries ran out. Richard was beaming at his grandson, obviously thrilled with Caleb's reaction. Sloane trailed behind them, occasionally taking a picture with her phone. She looked anxious and exhausted. She didn't even greet me when I walked by—just stood there biting her lip, laser-focused on her father and son while seeming impervious to their joy.

When I got to the lawn, it was mostly bigger kids and adults, here for the pumpkin carving and the sale. Beau was manning the selfie station—the frames we'd found in the attic were set up in front of a blank screen, with a big box of props nearby. He was trying to convince Millicent, of all people, to get her picture taken. Ben was hard at work painting sugar skulls on the cheek of a tween dressed as a character from *Coco*. His Aladdin costume, complete with carpet, was a hit. I saw two people stop to take his picture—one from the local paper. Both Ben and the kid in the chair hammed it up for the photos.

When the photographers left, the boy getting his face painted called out to me, "Are you going to do a selfie, Ms. Hogan? I am when my face is done. You're a witch, right? I mean, your costume." The last bit was a hasty add-on. Beau smirked.

"I will if Ms. Ames will," I said. "Or how about the two of us together? It would be great for the website."

"Oh, I don't think so," Millicent protested. "I really don't photograph well."

"Nonsense," Ben said. "You have wonderful bone structure. Absolutely classic. How about you and Greer in that horizontal frame? Beau?"

"Got it," Beau said. "Ladies?"

"Go ahead, Ms. Ames. Wait—you need a costume too." The boy jumped down from his chair and rummaged around in the trunk. "Here," he said, holding up a mortarboard, complete with tassels. "You can be a professor. Is that okay?"

"It's fine, thank you," Millicent said. She took the cap and we both stood in front of the backdrop. Beau propped the frame on something Jilly had rigged up to hold it, and then took my phone and snapped a couple of pictures. Then he did the same with the library's digital camera.

"If you don't have your phone, I'll send you these," I said to Millicent.

"I should carry it, but I don't. It's upstairs. I would like them, thank you."

"Now just you." Ben appeared, holding a different frame. Millicent protested, shaking her head and sending her mortar board tumbling. Ben retrieved it and whispered something to her that made her laugh. I took a few pictures of them and some of Millicent once Ben had coaxed her back into the hat and the frame. She seemed to be enjoying herself. Maybe she really was winding down—she was usually so reserved and formal. Possibly she'd tried the CBD oil her doctor had recommended. Would it have this effect? I didn't think so. In retrospect, she had let her hair down a bit when I was working with her the past few months. We'd had a few laughs. But Jilly was right when she said she couldn't imagine the library without Millicent. I'd only been there a year, and neither could I.

When Millicent had had enough, Beau took a few shots of me in the big standing frame. Then I made him pose. "I'm going to blow it up and add it to the gallery in the main hall and see if anyone can tell you're not a Ravenscroft." When I was done, I turned to find Jennie Webber watching from a few feet away.

"Hi. Can I interest you in a selfie? Or perhaps some face painting?" I asked.

"No, thank you. I'm working," she said.

I introduced her to Beau and Ben, and then the two of us walked toward the manor. I gave her a quick rundown of what Agnes had told me, and her fear of not being taken seriously or of wasting police time. As I expected, Jennie wanted to talk to her.

"Even when she called in last spring and said someone had tried to run you over, she was clear and consistent on a few points. She'd obviously been drinking—quite a bit—but she never wavered. What she was saying made sense to her, even though it didn't to me. I want to hear what she has to say. Is she at home?"

"She's here, actually. She's taken on the bookkeeping for the Friends. She'll be in their office. You can talk privately there if you want to. But first, tell me about the Walters guy. What happened?"

Jennie looked around to make sure we couldn't be overheard. We'd stopped at a small terrace outside the back entrance, one with a bench where I often ate lunch. You could see anyone coming before they got close enough to hear you. Since I often chatted with the manor ravens while giving them crumbs, I liked that. It wouldn't do to be thought too eccentric so soon in my tenure. No danger of eavesdroppers today, though—there was a group of children bouncing around on the lawn nearby, chanting a counting rhyme about birds at high volume. "One for sorrow, two for joy . . ." It was an old rhyme, but it had made a comeback as a rock ballad.

Satisfied that there was no one else around, Jennie said, "He was found yesterday. He has a cabin up on the escarpment, near the lake. He was due at a meeting Thursday afternoon and never showed. He's got a faculty apartment on campus, but he wasn't there. His assistant tried to reach him at the cabin, but cell service is spotty up there. No landline. He had emailed to say he wasn't feeling well and wouldn't be back in the office until the end of the week, so she didn't worry until he missed the meeting. Even then she thought it was possible he'd forgotten. By Friday morning, though, the dean was looking for him, so she decided to go check. Very out of character, she said, so she got nervous. When she got there, the back door was open and she found him dead on the kitchen floor."

"Do you know how he died yet?"

"Still waiting for some information from forensics. We're not even sure exactly when. Remember, the door was open at least some of the time, and it's been cold at night."

"What's your best guess?" I asked. "You said it could be an accident, murder, or even suicide. That's not sounding like a violent scene. No blunt instruments lying around? Bloody knives? Smoking guns? Nothing?"

Jennie made a face. She hated when I played detective. Unless I unearthed something useful.

"If I had to guess, I'd say he ingested something that acted on his central nervous system."

"Poisoned? Hmm," I said.

"You could put it like that. That's what the assistant thought. She was screaming, 'He's been poisoned!' on the 911

139

call. Since she had to phone from the convenience store at the base of the road he lived on, it's probably common knowledge by now."

"I haven't heard anything, but there's been plenty of excitement here. Nothing will eclipse the news about Anita unless it's about someone else from the village. But you still think it could be an accident? Or suicide?"

"He could have ingested something accidentally. From what we've learned about him, he doesn't seem the type to commit suicide. 'Very fond of himself,' according to a colleague, and he'd just inherited the cabin and some money. But you never know. And until we know what it was that killed him, we won't know much. The crime scene people are still working, and pathologists only toss out brilliant suggestions on television."

"It's got to be tied to Anita somehow. It would be too much of a coincidence otherwise."

"I think you're right, and Sam agrees, but right now we don't have anything to prove that." Jennie yawned, then said, "Sorry. Not getting much sleep. I better talk to Agnes—we have a meeting at the station later. It would be nice to have some new information."

"I'll take you in. Why don't you come to dinner tonight? Henri is cooking—he invited Beau and Ben as soon as he heard they were coming. He told me to bring along anyone else too tired to cook after the sale." Henri was my octogenarian landlord. He was smart, kind, and a fabulous cook. He was a widower whose grown children didn't live in the area, so I helped him out with some things from time to time. We'd become friends.

Jennie looked tempted. She had sampled Henri's cooking once or twice before. "I'm not sure how long my meeting will run," she said.

"Come whenever you're done. He won't mind. He loves feeding people. And Beau and Ben won't quiz you about the case."

"Okay. If I'm going to be too late, I'll text. Thanks."

We went inside and I left her with Agnes, then went back to the reading room. I was busy until right after lunch, when everything but the book sale was done. Ben and Beau helped Jilly pack everything up, and then left, saying they were going to do a little sightseeing and meet me at Henri's for dinner. Cheryl and the circulation staff had everything under control, and Jilly had volunteers to help her, so I was able to retreat to my office. I took off my costume—the fascinator was giving me headache, and most of the kids had come and gone. Still a little wound up, I decided to pop up to the book sale and see how things were going.

There was still a good-sized crowd. I hoped that meant there wouldn't be a lot of leftover items. I greeted a couple of people I knew in the hall and was heading into the community room when I saw another familiar face. Cynthia Baker was standing in the line right outside the door. She had an armload of books and was waiting to pay. Mindful of Jennie's warnings, I decided to broach the subject of Anita's research while there were plenty of people around. I waved and walked over to where she was standing.

"Did you find some good ones?" I asked, nodding at the stack.

"Oh yes. I got here later than I usually do, but there were quite a few things of interest left." She shifted and looked around. Everyone in earshot was involved in their own conversations. She lowered her voice and said, "I suppose you haven't found the item we discussed? Or anything that seems related?"

"I'm sorry, no, I haven't got a thing," I said. "But I'd be happy to place a request for you if you'd like to send me the information. You were working on a grant, you said? I'd hate for the historical society to miss out."

She hadn't mentioned a grant, but Richard had. It was a shot in the dark, but I wanted to see what she said.

"Um, not exactly," she said. I stood there, letting the silence stretch, trying to look both innocent and inquisitive.

"I mean, it was more for background, I guess you could say. I don't actually need it, but it would be helpful to see, if you know what I mean."

"I see," I said.

"Unfortunately, I don't know exactly what I'm after. Anita was handling that aspect of the research. So that's why I'd like to see anything that she had."

"Oh, that *is* unfortunate," I said. I wouldn't have been able to tell her even if Anita hadn't been murdered. That's why I'd let Helene decide how to deal with the police. "Well, you can always cast a wide net and see what you come up with. You can stop by the reference desk anytime, and I can do it, or I can show you how to do it at home."

"Thank you, I'll keep that in mind," Cynthia said. She turned to pay for her purchases, so I said goodbye. As I went down the stairs, I wondered what she had meant by "anything related." I'd have to take a close look at the other items Anita had requested.

*   *   *

The next couple of hours passed peacefully. Jilly was in and out, and I could hear the muffled noise of Agnes's old adding machine and some occasional muttering as she totaled up the bake sale receipts and the midday take from the book sale. The balance of that would come down a little after four, and she'd assured me it wouldn't take her long to finish up. By the time the cash arrived, I had finished my not very ambitious to-do list. Cheryl wouldn't need my help until closer to five, when it was time to round up any strays and close the library. I was looking in the various boxes around and under my desk, for something to bag my costume, when I remembered the picture of Harriet I'd found in the attic. I slid it out and turned it to face the light.

Harriet Ravenscroft, from what I could see of her, was what you'd call a handsome woman. Unfortunately, the glass was so grimy that I couldn't make out much detail. I made some room on my desk and laid the picture down. I knew we had glass cleaner somewhere, and a brief search yielded both that and a fresh roll of paper towels. I got to work.

The years of accumulated dust took some elbow grease to remove, but I managed to get rid of most of it. The area close to the edge of the frame, and the frame itself, would need a little more effort. The engraved wood would take more than a duster to clean, but I thought it would stand up to the compressed air I used on my keyboard. I'd have to take the glass out to clean that thoroughly. I flipped the picture and examined the back. There was a label in one corner, indicating the picture had been professionally framed. It looked it: the wire was in good shape, though bent in the middle. This had hung somewhere for a time. There were turn buttons holding the backing in place, rather than the bent nails I'd been afraid I'd find. They were digging into the back. It looked like some-one had stuffed something between photo and frame to hold everything in place. Probably old newspaper, but that would be fun to see too.

I pushed at one of the buttons. It wouldn't budge. I took an old letter opener from my desk drawer and wedged the point under the small piece of hardware. I pushed down on the backing and with a little maneuvering, managed to push the turn button back to the frame. One down, seven to go. It took me a while, but I got the rest off without damaging the backing or the frame.

I lifted the back carefully and set it aside. As I expected, there was newsprint folded around a lumpy bundle. It was from the now-defunct village newspaper, and it was decades old. The paper was crumbling at the edges and tearing where it was creased. Whoever had done this hadn't done a very neat job. My desk would be a mess if I wasn't careful. I got up and grabbed a flat cart from the processing area and rolled it over to my desk, then covered the top with a layer of interoffice envelopes. I moved everything onto it, then gently lifted the newsprint bundle out and laid it next to the frame. Using the broad end of the letter opener, I flipped the newspaper open.

It sent up a puff of dust, and one violent sneeze later, I found myself staring at something completely unexpected.

It was a library newsletter, old, but not as old as the newspaper. Toward the bottom was a small piece of cardstock. I recognized it as one of our old recommendation cards. Once handwritten, they'd since been updated to a modern-looking PDF that could be filled out and then printed. This one had "Recommended Reading" across the top. Underneath, where the blurb would go, there was nothing but the name Peg Emerson and a date just under two years prior. The "recommended by" line at the bottom held Peg's initials, in script. All were in blue ink, unfaded.

Had Peg decided to bring Harriet's picture out? If so, how had it ended up back in the attic? I lifted the old newsletter and card, expecting to find more of the same. Instead, I found a pile of letters, postcards, and handwritten pages that had been torn from some kind of journal. Some of the writing was a faded copperplate hand that I associated with vintage library catalogs, drawers full of neatly lettered cards carefully ordered. The pages and postcards were in a more sprawling cursive. At a quick glance, most seemed to predate the yellowing newspaper. And yet, Peg Emerson had added something only two years ago. What was going on here?

"Greer?"

I jumped and slid around the cart, placing myself between it and anyone coming toward my cubicle.

"Yes?"

Cheryl poked her head around the corner. "I'm sorry to bother you, but would you mind coming out a little bit early? We've had a last-minute rush, and the page went home sick."

"Give me two minutes," I said. "Just got to finish something."

"Great, thanks." Cheryl disappeared back into the hall.

I turned and eyed the pile on the cart. The newspapers were too big and fragile to carry, but I tipped the rest of the papers into an envelope and put it into my tote bag. I put the rest of the picture back together—with only the newsprint sheets, it was easy to reattach the backing. Then I tucked it out of site under my desk.

I looked in on Agnes before I went out. She was counting change.

"How's it going?" I asked.

"Almost done, just double-checking a few things. Looks like they had a good day. Felicity said she'd stop by right before five to pick up the deposit, so if it's all right I'll wait here and then leave with you. I'd like to do a little tidying up."

She looked bright-eyed and happy. I smiled and said, "Of course. I can give you a lift home if you'd like."

She waved a hand. "That's all right. I'll walk. I missed my class this morning, so I'd like the exercise."

I left her to it and went to help Cheryl. Things were under control at both desks, so I volunteered to go upstairs and do the closing check. The second floor was quiet—the Friends had broken down the tables and packed up any leftover books from the sale. They'd get all their stuff out Monday some-time. I checked the community room windows and closed the doors. Still mindful of Friday night's adventures, I opened every door, checked in every closet, and looked in the stair-wells before turning off the lights. The Friends had created an intricate barricade of boxes at the base of the attic stairs, and it appeared undisturbed, so I didn't go up.

I stopped at the door to the archives last. It was locked. Millicent worked by appointment on Saturdays and took care of closing the room. I stood with my hand on the warm wood, watching dust motes drift through the shaft of late daylight from the leaded glass window. Normally, I would have taken what I'd found behind Harriet's picture to Millicent. Even if she couldn't identify it, she'd store it properly until it could be researched. But the thought of handing it over made me uneasy. It was such a strange assortment of things, and the card that Peg had signed and dated so recently—that made me wonder. If there had been no Margaret Emerson file in Anita's stash, maybe. But there had been, and now that file was missing. No, I'd look through everything first and then decide what to do with it.

Chapter Twelve

The library closure had been uneventful, but it still took a little while to make sure everything was buttoned down and the staff was safely on their way home. Then I went back to my apartment and changed. By the time I got to Henri's for dinner, Beau and Ben were already there, and the three gentlemen had emptied their first bottle of wine. Henri's French bulldog, Pierre, ran to greet me. I handed the bottle of wine to Henri and bent to give the dog some attention. I was glad I'd picked up the French red to bring along. Henri was delighted with my offering and told me a little about the region it was from while he opened it and poured me a glass. He was equally delighted when I told him I'd invited Jennie and that she'd promised to come if she could get away.

"She is looking very tired. I think she is working too much," Henri said.

"I know she's been busy with this case, but she's also said she doesn't sleep much. And I think she doesn't sleep well when she does rest, though she hasn't said."

"The war. She was in Afghanistan, was she not?" Henri shook his head. "Ah well, we will give her a good meal and good company."

We moved into the living room and spent some time talking about the events of the day. Ben had enjoyed his gig at the book sale and had a wonderful time exploring the village and the surrounding area afterward.

"You've got that great coffee shop and so many nice old houses. Lots of open space—I'm sorry we're too late for the foliage. We'll definitely be back," he said. Even Beau had to admit that the area was quite scenic, and he was having a good time. Maybe now the two of them would stop calling the place Raven's Breath and singing the *Green Acres* theme every time I phoned.

"And—we've been invited to tea at Millicent's tomorrow afternoon," Ben said. "She told me you're welcome to come. She wasn't sure she'd see you before she left the library."

"Wow," I said. "You must have made quite an impression. I'd known her for nearly a year before I was invited. The house is lovely. So is the garden—you should see it in the warm weather."

"That's what Millicent said too. But she's got lots of plants that provide year-round color. I told her how pretty the area around the manor was, and that I had a little plot in the community garden on the roof our co-op building but didn't know what to do with it in the winter. The conversation took off from there, and the next thing you know we had an invitation."

"She said we reminded her of close friends from college, and she rarely had the chance to show the place off to people who'd never seen it," Beau added.

"I never knew she liked to show it off," I said. "Though it is lovely."

"Millicent used to participate in the garden club open house, back when they still did that sort of thing," Henri said, as he topped off my wine and his own. "It has been many years. My wife and I used to go. A lot of those families are gone now, or the younger generation doesn't have time. And of course, the developers." Henri gave a classic Gallic shrug. "But still, there are some who keep lovely gardens. The master gardeners are quite active also, with the vegetable gardens at the cooperative extension, and most have beautiful landscaping at home."

"Millicent did tell me once both her parents gardened, though her father was more interested in medicinal plants. There's even a little greenhouse attached to what was his office," I said. "She still works in there, though I believe she hires someone to help with the grounds."

"That is true," Henri said. "She uses the same young man who trims my trees each fall. His family used to own the pear orchard. He still has the house and some of the land, but the rest has been sold off."

"I just love this small-town feeling," Ben said. "It's so much more interesting than suburban New Jersey."

"That's only because you didn't grow up in a small town," Beau said. "Trust me—it's pretty stifling when you're young."

"That's because you were in the middle of nowhere. You didn't even have a mall," Ben said. "It's very pretty there, even if it was a little humid when we visited." Beau was from the Carolina low country. "Besides, there's a lot more happening in your hometown now. And here—well, Albany is just a short drive away. There are theaters and restaurants and things, right?"

"True," I said. "It's not a big city, but there are things to do in the area."

"And the roads are much better than when I came here, so the snow is less of an issue," Henri added. "Ah, I believe Mademoiselle Weber has arrived."

Introductions were made as Jennie took off her coat. Since she was not technically on duty, "though I'm waiting to hear what forensics found," she accepted a glass of wine and we all started in on the hors d'oeuvres. Pierre moved from his bed to a more central location, hoping for crumbs, or better still, a dropped serving of baked brie.

"What's new with the case?" I asked. She gave me a look. "That you can discuss, I mean," I added. We all looked at her expectantly. She sighed, but I saw her lips twitch as she hid a smile. She took a sip of her wine and settled back in her chair.

"All right, there are a few things I can tell you. And Sam asked me to follow up on a couple of things with you. Most of this is already out there, but we'd still like you to keep quiet about anything we discuss."

We all nodded.

"First, Anita definitely did not go off the road without help. Without boring you with the details, the skid marks are wrong, and there are some dents and bits of paint on her rear bumper that couldn't have been caused by the accident. Second, she got more than one whack on the head after impact."

"Someone finishing the job," I said.

"Or maybe insurance," Jennie added. "She would have died from her internal injuries, but not right away. And the extent of those injuries wouldn't have been obvious. The accident scene wasn't pretty, but I've seen people walk away from worse."

"And she was in a newish SUV," I said. "There must have been a lot of safety features."

"Did she have that thing that automatically calls 911?" Ben asked. "You can put an app on your phone, but some cars have it built in, don't they?"

"She wouldn't have had her phone on," I said. "Anita was vehement about not using a cell phone while she was driving. She always had it off and tucked into a specific pocket in her handbag. She didn't want to be distracted. It came up when Dory got her new car—she's got all the bells and whistles. The car itself will call in if it senses a crash. Part of—what do you call it? The onboard diagnostics?"

"She didn't have either," Jennie said. "No app on the phone, and it was off, though we found it on the floor of the car, under her bag." Jennie frowned, then shook her head and continued. "Her vehicle had all the standard equipment. No advanced safety features. It was a couple of years old, but well maintained. If she hadn't gone off the road where she did, the car wouldn't have flipped and rolled."

"Sounds like someone knew what they were doing," I said.

"Or they got lucky," Jennie said.

"What did she get whacked with?" asked Ben. "Do you know?"

Jennie nodded. "Heavy-duty flashlight. Similar to what I carry. You can buy them easily enough online. A lot of people have them. It's likely she had it in the car. There were a lot of loose items."

"I've got one in my car, but I keep it tucked into the pocket on the back of the passenger seat. I can reach it, but it's not going anywhere. Although if the car flipped . . ." I stopped. I wasn't sure. Maybe everything had gone flying, her handbag upended, things all over the floor.

"My theory is that she had it secured but within reach, like you do, and that the killer used it because it was at hand. That part seems impulsive, not as well thought out. The flashlight was tossed away, but it didn't go far. There's a stream that feeds into the Ravens Kill not far from the accident site. I'd have dumped it in there."

"Better yet," I said, "use a rock or a tree limb, then dump that in the water. Less likely to be found, let alone with trace evidence."

Beau looked at me. "I've always loved the way your mind works, Greer."

Henri chuckled. "I do as well. But now, my friends, give me a moment. I will serve the cassoulet. The kitchen is small, and we are comfortable here, so I will bring it in. If someone would lend me a hand?"

"I will," said Ben.

"And I'll get more wine," Beau added, and followed the other two men into the kitchen.

"This is sounding like someone who knows their way around that area," I said to Jennie. "Though then they'd also know about the stream. But as you said, that might not have been part of the plan."

"I think you're right about them knowing their way around. And I don't think the crime was opportunistic—I think it was well planned. If not, it had to be someone with local knowledge who was able to think fast."

"Does that eliminate anyone? All the likely candidates are local. Although," I added, "the Walters guy isn't, and I don't think Sloane's husband is from around here. I think she met him in college."

"Why do you put Walters on the suspect list?" Jennie asked.

"He was in Anita's files." I shrugged. "Other than that, I've got nothing. Just a feeling that there's a connection. Cynthia Baker is still sniffing around—she was at the book sale and asked me again about any research Anita was doing. The only thing I've found so far relates to Walters. Oh, and Sloane stopped by."

I told her about the conversation and added, "She was lying about something. I'm just not sure what. Whether it was what she was looking for or why she wanted it, she's on edge because she doesn't have it and doesn't know where it is. To be honest, I'm not sure she even knows exactly what she's looking for, only that there's something. My guess is it relates to the file labeled 'Harris' in Anita's collection." I raised an eyebrow. "Or was that one of the ones that was missing?"

"You're fishing," Jennie said, and then took a healthy swallow of her wine.

"Only kind of," I said. "It was pretty obvious when I rattled off that list to you and Sam that I'd seen things that you hadn't. Come on—spill. You never know what I might come across." Especially since I'd downloaded Anita's digital files to a flash drive for further study. But she didn't need to know that yet.

"And where might you 'come across' them?" she asked.

"I have some ideas, but it would help to know what I'm looking for. All kinds of odd things turn up in the manor."

Jennie thought for a few seconds, then said, "Harris, Walters, and Ravenscroft deeds, but you didn't hear it from me."

"So that might explain what Sloane's after. But I still don't get the sense she's entirely sure *what* she's after. And if not, would she do in her mother?"

"Hmm," Jennie said. "Sloane and her husband alibi each other, but Sam talked to them and he thinks there's something hinky there. That's where you come in. Do you know anyone at St. Catherine's? Librarian, professor—anyone at all?"

I perked up. "Sam's looking for gossip? Nothing interesting in the background check?"

Jennie gave me a look. "Any information that you feel would be helpful. Right now, that's any information at all. Sam says academic communities are always 'a hot bed of scandal and innuendo.'" She put air quotes around the last bit.

"Most small communities are. Witness the Village of Raven Hill." Jennie made a face but didn't disagree.

"I don't think any of our local professors that use the library work there, or used to. Most of them are retired anyway. Wait—Sister Mary Josephine!"

Jennie looked skeptical.

"She works in the St. Catherine's library. The diocesan archives are housed there—she's in charge of that. She also handles some of the nursing school collection. She told me once that that's what her degree is in. I've spoken to her a few times."

"You think you're going to get a nun to spill the tea?"

"Do tell," said Beau, as he walked back in with dinner. "I thought those couple of years in Catholic school had put you off nuns." He handed me a plate while Ben did the same for Jennie. Henri followed with his own meal and the rest of the wine. Once we were all settled, I continued.

"It's a small college. I'm sure she knows where all the bodies are buried. So to speak. She's been there forever. I've always found her willing to chat. She has some pretty firm opinions. And I've got nothing against nuns in general, only the ones that made my life miserable in grade school."

"If you think it's worth a try," Jennie said.

"I think Greer is correct," Henri said. "This Sister, she still wears the habit, but also the most colorful running shoes. She was always very active in the community. I remember her from my teaching days. Several of my students went to St. Catherine's. She has never been the most traditional of religious."

"When do you think you can talk to her?" Jennie asked.

"Monday, earliest. If she's in the library or archives. I'm not sure what her schedule is."

"I'll let Sam know. Thanks."

"I'm happy to help. I don't want to see Millicent or Jilly under suspicion. Though I guess Jilly is in the clear, right?"

"No one is in the clear except maybe Richard Hunzeker. No, neither one can account for her whereabouts that night once the library closed. Millicent insists she left about fifteen minutes before closing, which is when you saw her. But no one saw her after that."

"But I thought Jilly did, parked in Agnes Jenner's driveway."

"So Jilly says, but no one else noticed that. The rest of the staff left before Jilly, but none can say for sure whether or not there was a car in that driveway, let alone what it looked like. Then Jilly took what she calls 'the back way' home because it was a nice night and she wanted to clear her head. From eight o'clock on, there's no one to vouch for either of them."

"And Richard? He told me he was running errands for Anita all evening," I said.

"He was, but he was home before Anita left the library. One of his neighbors places him at home a little before eight. The neighbor was watching television, and apparently when a car turns into the Hunzeker driveway at night, the lights flash across the windows of his den. He always looks out. He's retired, and I think he's bored. He saw Richard pull in, get out of his car, and go into the house."

"Oh, I guess that lets him out then," I said.

"But," Jennie said, holding up her hand. For someone who was usually so close-mouthed, she seemed to be enjoying herself. Maybe it was the wine.

"But what? He left again?" I asked.

"No, but someone else came by. Cynthia Baker. The neighbor described her car—you know, she has that metallic paint job. Said he saw a woman get out and ring the bell. When no one came to the door, she walked around to the back of the house. Then after a few minutes, she came back and left."

"What was she doing there?" This from Henri, who was frowning. "The two ladies, they did not get along. Everyone knows this."

"That's what we asked her. According to Cynthia, she and Anita had had a disagreement about their approach to getting some grant money for the historical society. She said she thought about it and decided Anita was right and should go ahead, so she stopped on her way home to discuss it. No one answered, but she knew Richard was home because of the car, so she walked around to the back, thinking she'd talk to him. She said they've all known each other since high school. I got the feeling she always got along better with him."

"Most people do," said Henri.

"Dory said something like that too. And Richard confirmed her story?" I asked.

"In a way, yes. He was in his workshop, which is at the back of the property. He said he was finishing up his grandson's Halloween costume and working on a couple of other projects. He noticed headlights and thought it was Anita coming home, but he wanted to finish what he was doing, so he didn't check. Cynthia Baker says she saw lights in the workshop and heard some machinery, but when she stepped onto the lawn, she decided it was too wet and muddy to make the walk. It had rained all day, remember. She decided to call Anita when she got home, and she left. Their stories match, and the neighbor confirms the times."

"But did she go straight home? She could still have taken Anita out, either before or after," I said. There was something else, something Jennie had just said. "Wait—Cynthia's car has metallic paint? Didn't Agnes see a car with that same finish when she was on her way home?" I asked.

"She didn't mention the color when I talked to her, but I'll check. As for going straight home, she says yes, but her husband was out at a meeting. He got home at ten, and she was there."

"Does no one in this town have a security system? And what about cameras? No traffic cameras? Anywhere?" Ben was indignant. "You can't make a move in Manhattan these days without someone watching."

"I was wondering that myself," Beau said. "I've only seen a couple of cameras at intersections, and only on busier roads. I understand they wouldn't be on the all the local roads, the ones farther out into the woods, but I thought you'd have more on the main roads."

"Very good questions," Jennie said. She looked genuinely impressed.

"Thank you," said Ben. "We've been watching a lot of crime shows ever since . . . um . . ."

There was a brief silence.

"Ever since Dan was murdered. It's okay, I appreciate the reason," I said.

"We only want to help, Greer," Beau said.

"I know. We'll talk about it later. But I was wondering the same things," I said to Jennie.

"There are only cameras at the major intersections in that area. Those roads that go up into the escarpment don't see a lot of traffic, even during the summer. There's one where

Raven Hill Avenue meets Winding Ridge Road, and one where Winding Ridge ends and the three roads that go into the hills start."

"Can you get onto Winding Ridge any other way?" I asked. "I can't remember, but it seems like I went that way once when there was an accident on Raven Hill Avenue."

"One road. It runs between Albany and Winding Ridge. Sam said it was used a lot before the county route was extended and widened. Now it's only used by people that live out there or need an alternate route. It's not on every GPS though. And no camera."

"So, someone could get onto Winding Ridge without a camera catching them, but neither Cynthia nor Richard could leave home, run Anita off the road, and then get back without it being clocked by the traffic camera? Is that right?"

"Yes, that's right. And there's no sign of them doing so. But we don't have an exact time of death, so Cynthia could have killed Anita before stopping by the house," Jennie said.

"She'd have to be a cool one, to do that," Beau said. "I don't think I could pull it off."

"Good to know," I said. "I'm not convinced Cynthia could either."

"You never know," said Jennie.

"What about home security systems that time-stamp when they come and go? Or something with a camera?" Ben asked.

"Some do, but not anyone we're interested in. The Hunzekers have an alarm system, but Richard said he rarely sets it. Anita used to, but he was in and out so much he didn't bother. He said she armed it when she left, but when he came back midday, he turned it off and left it off."

"Convenient," Ben said. I thought so too. Jennie went on.

"The Bakers have a system with a camera, but wildlife kept triggering it, so they stopped using it. They went back to a basic alarm but are also inconsistent about using it. To be fair, the only calls about break-ins I've ever gotten up that way are bears looking for a snack getting into sheds and trash cans."

"Well, everyone just go right ahead and leave a key under the flowerpot," Ben said, throwing up his hands. "Though I have to admit, that kind of crime rate sounds appealing."

"One of my neighbors actually does have a key under a flowerpot," Jennie said. "No matter how often I tell them not to do it."

"Mine is safely with Henri," I said when Beau raised his eyebrows at me.

"And vice versa," said Henri. "And now perhaps dessert? I have made a lovely chocolate torte. Coffee?"

We all stood and gathered our dishes and glasses. Jennie's cell phone rang.

"Sam," she said. I took her plate and left her to take the call, hoping it was an update she'd be able to share. As I handed over the dishes, I tried to hear her side of the conversation but caught nothing more than some murmured "mmhm's." Then suddenly a *"What?"* that carried into the kitchen. We all stopped for a second, looked at each other, and then continued with our tasks in silence. Henri handed me a tray with the coffee cups and creamer and gestured me into the living room. I was in time to hear, "Yes, I'll ask her." I set the tray on the coffee table and took a seat. After a "Yes, I'll be there," she hung up.

"Any news?" I asked. "That you can share, I mean."

Jennie pursed her lips and shook her head. "This is confidential. Sam okayed this because we've asked for your help. The report came back on Walters—he died by poison, as everyone in town probably knows by now, thanks to his assistant. Something plant based. They're still trying to narrow it down."

"Are you ruling out suicide? Or accident?"

"There's no sign of the substance anywhere else in his home, so yes. It was in his wine. There was an open bottle in the kitchen—there are traces of the poison in what's left and on the cork. Nowhere else. One wineglass. Only his prints on the glass."

"What about the bottle?" I asked.

"His prints, and one other person's. That's where it gets strange."

"Do you know whose?"

Jennie nodded and blew out her breath.

"Anita's," she said.

Chapter Thirteen

❧

There was a collective silence in the small apartment. I looked into the kitchen and saw that Beau, Ben, and Henri had all stopped what they were doing and were staring into the living room. Jennie sighed and muttered, "Forgot they were there," then plopped back into her chair. I made a face at the group in the kitchen as I took my own seat and they went back into action, appearing moments later with plates of dessert and coffee. Henri poured while Beau handed us our torte. No one said anything—which took some effort—until we were all seated. Jennie was frowning into her coffee cup. The rest of us exchanged looks, and I decided to wade in.

"So where does that leave us? I mean, does Sam think Anita killed Walters? Could she even have gone up there that night? Would someone have seen her?"

"We're putting together a time line. And we're going to have to go back over some things. This is—unexpected." Jennie pulled out her notebook. "Sam wanted me to ask you—you mentioned wine, a gift basket, something like that. Something you overheard when Anita was talking to Richard."

"Yes, she did say something about wine. That new shop that opened on Main."

"That makes sense. From what Sam said, this bottle didn't come from a strip mall liquor store. We'll check it out."

"Um, I think I can save you some time," I said. She looked up. "I stopped in there the other night to pick up a few bottles since Ben and Beau were coming. That's where the red I brought for Henri came from."

"The one we drank tonight?" she asked.

"Yes," I replied.

"Ewww," Ben said.

Henri clucked. "It was fine. It did not taste even the tiniest bit off."

Jennie added, "Don't worry, if it were going to kill us, we'd already be dead, based on what the pathologist said. Besides, we know it wasn't red. White, Sam said. The same as the broken bottle in Anita's SUV. We're not sure how the poison was introduced—Walters would have noticed if the bottle had been opened and recorked. Sam plans to get a bottle that hasn't been opened and see if we can figure it out."

"I may be able to help you there too," I said. I told her about my conversation with Eric, the store proprietor. "I was being nosy, I admit it. I wanted to know if she'd hit him up for a donation. She really was shameless that way. Anyway, he told me Richard was in buying a gift. He said he'd recommended this white and sold me the last bottle he had. It's upstairs. He said he'd be getting more in, but I'm not sure when. Do you want me to get it so you can see if it's the same?"

"Please," she said, pulling out her phone and starting to text.

I zipped up to my apartment and took the bottle of wine from the fridge. After turning on the bright light over the stove, I set the bottle down and took a closer look. There was no foil over the cork—Eric had explained that was getting less common, since nowadays it was for aesthetics rather than to protect the cork from insect damage, which was its original purpose. I ran my finger around the lip of the bottle. The cork was fitted tightly. There was a stamp on top—it looked like the vineyard logo burned into it. This would be tough to tamper with. I placed it right under the light and took a couple of pictures with my phone, then got a few of the label. Maybe one of the others would have some ideas. I put it in a bag and went back downstairs.

Jennie was waiting outside. I noticed Henri had packed up her dessert for her and given her coffee in a travel mug.

"Do you have to go to the station?" I asked.

"Not tonight, but we're meeting early, and I want to go over my notes."

"I'll carry this to your car. I see Henri is not letting you leave empty-handed."

"When I said I had to go, he insisted. Told me that I was working so hard, I was in danger of getting too thin."

"He tells me that too. It's one of the things I love about him." I handed her the bag after she'd put her other packages in her car. She slid it out of the bag, looked at the label and the cork, and shrugged.

"This is the same brand, but I'm not sure how it was tampered with. I've never been able to pull out a cork and then get it to go back in. But then, I don't drink a lot of wine," she said.

"Don't feel bad, I've never been good at it either. I'm sure Eric could give you some insight."

"We'll be talking to him. He may know if anyone else associated with the case has bought any of this."

"Actually, he said something like that. That several people from the library had been in since he opened."

"Do you know who he meant?" Jennie asked.

"No, it was just a passing comment. I'm not even sure when—he's been open for a few weeks now. Everyone's been talking about that and the new tea shop, including Anita. And it could have been anyone associated with the library— staff or volunteer or the board members."

"We'll see if he can narrow it down. Thanks."

I turned to go, and Jennie stopped me.

"Wait—I have something for you. I almost forgot."

She reached into the car and pulled out a big envelope. She handed it to me.

"It's the police file on Dan's murder. I asked for copies last spring when I was checking up on you after Joanna Goodhue died. I thought you might want to see it, and I figured that while your friends were here . . ." She paused. "It's up to you. I can hang onto it for now."

"No," I said, hugging it to my chest. "It's time. I'd like to look through it. And Beau and Ben will help. We all lived in the same building. They came to my apartment and took me home with them that night. They saw, well, you know."

Jennie nodded. "If you have any questions, I'll give you whatever help I can," she said.

"Thank you. And I'll let you know what I find out from Sister Mary Josephine."

She reminded me not to take any chances, that I probably knew the killer, and that I wasn't a detective. It was her usual speech, and I nodded in all the usual places. She thanked me, got in her car, and drove off. I stared at the envelope in my hands for a minute and then went back inside.

The gentlemen were in the living room, discussing Anita's murder between bites of torte. I took my seat and started in on my dessert, listening as they discussed various theories.

"Do you think the woman is capable of murder?" Ben asked me.

"I don't know. I wouldn't have thought she was the type to blackmail people, but it seems pretty clear she was. Still, I have a hard time seeing it. Unless she'd really gone off the deep end and it wasn't obvious," I said.

"I would agree," Henri said. "The blackmail—it is extreme, but she was one who liked to feel in control. She enjoyed power. Still, I cannot see her stooping to murder. It seems out of character. And there is one other possibility."

"That the poison was meant for her?" I asked.

Henri nodded.

"I wondered about that, but I can't think how the killer could be sure she'd be the one to drink it," I said. "We don't even know if both bottles were poisoned, though I'm sure the police are checking the one in the car. Ugh, my head is spinning. It's been a long day. A long week."

I was feeling confused and defeated and a little sad. Not because I would miss Anita, but because I had a feeling nobody would. And the more I learned, the less I was able to make sense of it all. Maybe it was the wine making me feel maudlin and uncertain. Tomorrow morning, before I went to Millicent's, I'd put together what I had and see what I could figure out. I'd been going full tilt ever since I'd found out about Anita's death—a good night's sleep and some quiet could be just the thing. I shifted, and the paper envelope crackled. I sighed. At some point soon, I'd have to deal with that too.

"Whatcha got there, ducky?" Beau asked, nodding toward the envelope.

"It's the police file on Danny's murder. A copy, anyway. Jennie got it for me."

There was a brief silence. I saw Ben and Beau exchange a quick glance. Ben opened his mouth and shut it again. Henri came to the rescue.

"Have you never seen it before?" he asked.

"I've seen pictures of the scene and read some statements, but the not whole file, no."

"And you are certain, Greer, that the man in jail did not kill your husband?"

"Certain? No. But too much doesn't add up. I want to know for sure. I have to know."

"I thought maybe you'd changed your mind," Beau said. "You hadn't mentioned it the last few times we talked. And you haven't been back to visit since last Christmas."

"I only get so much vacation time, you know. I'm sure Helene would be sympathetic, but I can't just say, 'Hey, I need to go back to the city and try to figure out who killed

my husband—not sure how long I'll be gone,'
town. I need to have a plan, to know where I'm

I sounded cranky. I was cranky. They only w.
I took a deep breath, trying for a calmer tone. ...ing the
envelope, I said, "Maybe this will help. There was so much
that doesn't make sense."

"We've been talking about it, and we think you're right.
About things not making sense," Ben said. "When we
helped you list things for the insurance company and then
helped you pack. The Ginsburgs think something's off too.
You should talk to them. Whenever you can come to the
city."

The Ginsburgs had been my next-door neighbors. They
were nearly as old as Henri, and Herb didn't hear very well.
Goldie was still sharp as a tack.

"December," I said. "I've got to work Thanksgiving weekend." I yawned, a wave of fatigue washing over me. "I'd like
to talk to them. I got some information at Sarah Whitaker's
wedding too. You remember my friend Sarah? I went to her
wedding in Lake Placid last month. Anyway, I need to tell
you, but not tonight. Tomorrow, after Millicent's?"

They agreed. It was time to call it a night. Beau began
gathering plates and waved Henri back into his chair when
he rose to help.

"We'll take care of the cleanup," he said as Ben gathered
the tray of coffee cups. Pierre followed, still hoping for a handout. Henri reached out and touched my arm.

"If you would not mind, Greer, I would like to look at
the file. Perhaps I can help. A fresh set of eyes. And I think

you will be busy with your friends, and with Mrs. Hunzeker's death, for a few days more."

I was surprised, and then not. Henri had seen a great deal in his lifetime. He had a keen mind. Though he had never pressed for details about Dan's death, he had always listened well when I did mention it. He understood that I'd kept it buried for too long, and how the inconsistencies disturbed me. I handed him the envelope.

"Thank you," I said.

"I appreciate your trust," he said. "I will take good care of it and do my best to help. I would like to see you resolve this, for your own sake. And if that man is not responsible, for his as well."

I wasn't worried about leaving the file with Henri. I knew he would be careful, and I suspected Jennie had another copy. She was like that. I was touched by the number of people willing to help me, whether or not they thought I was making any sense. Some days, I wasn't convinced I was.

Once the kitchen was clean, I leashed up Pierre for his last outing of the night and walked Beau and Ben to their car. We made plans for the next day and said goodnight. After a short walk, I returned Pierre to Henri and climbed the stairs to my own apartment. *Tomorrow,* I thought as I climbed into bed, *I will get a handle on this.* It was as I was drifting off that a question I should have asked earlier flitted through my mind: *Why were there only two sets of prints on the wine bottle?*

Chapter Fourteen

After a decent night's sleep, I made myself a breakfast of bacon, eggs, and toast, with a leftover peanut butter cookie from the bake sale for dessert. A girl detective could not live on coffee alone, though I had plenty of that. I spread out the tools of my trade on my coffee table—laptop, notebook and pencils, the flash drive containing the files I'd downloaded from Anita's folder on the library shared drive, and the papers I'd found behind the picture of Harriet Ravenscroft. Before I did anything else, I looked up addresses for the chief suspects and then mapped and printed directions from their last known location to the Hunzeker house. I didn't have an exact address for the accident, but it wasn't hard to determine when I looked at the map.

"It's important to be familiar with your crime scene, Greer," I said as I spread the printouts across the table. I paused. "Crime *scenes*, actually. Hmm." I did a quick search for J. P. Walters's address, but all I found was his faculty apartment. The inherited lake house didn't come up. Not surprising, since he hadn't been there long and there was no landline. I went to the county home page and searched the online records. The deed would have had to be transferred, I thought, in order to settle the estate, unless Walters was already on it. Either way, there'd be a record with an address. I found it easily enough, and because I'm nosy like that, also checked the property value. Not bad. He must have been his aunt's favorite nephew. I considered what I knew about him. More likely her only nephew.

I mapped directions from St. Catherine's to the lake house, and from there to the Hunzekers' for the sake of consistency. After that, I used a red pen to mark the accident scene and the location of the traffic cameras. I studied my work. Once I felt I had the lay of the land, I moved on to Anita's files. I had no idea what I'd find, and I wanted to do it while I was fresh. I pulled my notebook toward me and made a quick list of the handwritten files I could remember from Anita's box: *J Bean, Millicent/Ames Family, Margaret Emerson, J. P. Walters, Ravenscroft Deeds*, and *Sean Harris*. Based on the questions Sam had asked, not all of them had been there when the police went over Anita's car. They obviously had the files on Jilly and Millicent. According to Jennie, the ones on Walters, Harris, and the Ravenscroft deeds were missing by the time the police searched the car. I tapped my pencil against the list. I had a feeling those missing files were important. But why just those three? What did they have in common? Maybe I'd be able to tell once I'd gone through Anita's digital files.

I took a look at the list of folders on the drive before I dug in. I was hoping that whatever Anita had scanned would show up as a random PDF file with Monday's date on it, and I was in luck. She hadn't had time to move or copy anything once she'd sent it to her folder. There were several files with the right date—she must have divided things by topic to make it easier to sort out later. I clicked on the first. Handwritten notes about some historical society project. At least her penmanship was good. I skimmed them, but nothing seemed relevant, so I moved on.

The next couple files were more of the same—meeting notes, a couple of estimates for work on the current library and an annotated list of grant sources for making buildings wheelchair accessible, created by Helene and added to by Anita. The next item was more interesting. Anita had a copy of the original documents for the Ravenscroft family trust, including the addendum that gave the building and grounds to the village for use as a library. There was a lot of legalese referring to things the village was required to do and keep, as well as references to the ability of any heir to change the terms of the bequest and what acceptable reasons for said heir doing so would be. There was also a copy of the Last Will and Testament of Horatio Ravenscroft, and that of Harriet Ravenscroft. All of these were copies of the original typed or handwritten documents. Anita would have had to go downtown, request the documents, and make or pay for copies. None of this was online.

Why had she done that? The trust documents had to be in possession of the library or its attorneys. She must have wanted to read them herself. Maybe she was trying to see if there was a loophole. She wanted a new building in a new location, but there were issues with the wording of the trust. I remembered hearing that last spring. She'd seemed willing to settle for a new building in the current location, but I wouldn't put it past her to try to find a way to sell the manor and use the proceeds to fund her dream library and local history center. I scrolled through the documents again. On the last page, I could see a square outline with some writing. She'd stuck a Post-it Note onto the copy. There were a few words: *missing codicil—rumor? Harriet check records*, and *H. Heir?*

I couldn't make any sense out of it. I'd heard rumors about a missing codicil. Millicent had even mentioned it. I didn't know what the rest meant, unless Anita was trying to prove that either Harriet or Horatio weren't the actual heirs. Or Hieronymus, the poor guy. Millicent had said the family was its own gothic novel, so who knew? This would take more digging. I printed out the documents so that I could study them myself later, and moved on.

The next item was pretty mundane—a copy of her son-in-law's CV. An academic résumé made for dry reading, though Sean Harris had published several interesting articles, if the titles were any indication. He'd even authored a chapter in an upcoming book on twentieth-century labor laws, *The Girl on the Sidewalk: Frances Perkins, the Triangle Shirtwaist Factory Fire, and the Reinvention of the Sweatshop*. I wasn't sure what he meant by the last phrase, but maybe he was staking out new ground in a well-known story. As far as I could tell, Harris wasn't setting the world on fire but had solid credentials for his age. He might be able to land a tenure track position at a school with a more prestigious history department than

St. Catherine's, but maybe not. I read the whole document and was reminded why I had decided against an academic library—too many committee meetings. There were no notes on this, but I printed it out anyway. If Anita had a file on Sean, it might be important.

The next file I opened contained three obituaries: Jonathon Ames, Elizabeth Ames, and Margaret Emerson. They were standard newspaper obits—nothing out of the ordinary about them. They weren't from the village paper, which usually included more detail. If anyone wanted to read those, they could check the archives. Maybe she was just doing a thorough background search. Curious.

The only other item of interest was a copy of a title page, table of contents, and bibliography of another academic thesis. It was from the same time period as the Walters thesis, but I didn't recognize the author's name. I did recognize the school—a well-known liberal arts college in Vermont. It had been written a couple of years before Walters had written his. I printed all the pages. This would definitely require more research. I only hoped I wouldn't have to read either thesis. I yawned thinking about it.

I got up and went to the printer on the desk in my bedroom. I gathered the pages and put them in a folder. I'd read through everything again later. I'd probably need a lawyer to interpret the things in the will. Maybe Felicity could help. She'd put her law career on hold when she'd had kids, but she'd always done most of the grunt work in her late husband's practice. Since his death, she'd brought in a new attorney and taken over other clients herself. I thought she specialized in trusts and estates, but I wasn't sure. Worth asking. I scribbled her name on a sticky note and put it on the copy of the will.

Back on the couch, I put the folder and my laptop to one side and spread out the sheets of directions. Each one gave me part of the picture, and there was plenty of overlap, but what I really needed was one map to rule them all. I should have copied the page that covered the crash site from the local atlas we had at work. I shifted my printouts around. I'd actually need a couple of pages from the atlas, or I'd have to enlarge parts of a local map. Either way, I'd be taping things together. And I didn't know for sure what time everyone was on what road—there were two to three hours where no one could account for their whereabouts, and there were no witnesses to place them anywhere in particular. This part of my investigation would have to wait. I slid those pages into the folder with the others.

I got a fresh cup of coffee and started to sort through the papers I'd found behind Harriet's picture. There were letters, pages that looked like they had been torn from a diary, a couple of postcards, and scribbled notes. I had already noticed that the handwriting was not the same on all of them. I sorted the papers into piles—one for the neat, old-fashioned script that reminded me of vintage card catalogs. "Library hand" they had called it. These were nearly all letters signed by Harriet Ravenscroft. All the letters but one bore the salutation "Dear Margaret." The one that didn't was more formal and was addressed to Dr. Jonathon Ames. This one was signed by Harriet, with a note at the bottom that I thought said "file copy."

I went to my desk and got my magnifying glass. I put the lamp on and examined the letter in better light. It did say "file copy." Apparently, Harriet kept copies of her business correspondence. At least, she had until her eyesight went. Or maybe until carbon paper was invented? I set the letter aside and went through the rest of the stack. The journal pages were tricky—not all had dates, and some pages started in the middle of a sentence. These were all in a more modern cursive, as were a couple of postcards with notes on the back. Those hadn't been mailed. Maybe they had been kept as souvenirs.

That left only the recommendation card that Peg had initialed and dated, a clipping from the village paper, and a sheet torn from one of the message pads we used at the library. The clipping was a brief article about Hieronymus Ravenscroft. He had done a bit of traveling and after several months away had returned with some wonderful photographs, interesting artifacts, and plant specimens. It was standard human interest for a small-town paper. The last couple of lines were torn off, and there was no date on the part that was left. I couldn't see how it was important, but these were the Ravenscrofts. It was possible the artifacts were cursed, and the plants an invasive species, poisonous, or both. I started to put it aside, then paused. Walters had been poisoned. Jennie had said it was something plant based. I shook my head. I was reaching.

I set the clipping down and picked up the last item. The library notepads hadn't changed in decades. They had an etching of the manor on top and the library's logo, address, and contact information on the bottom. They were used for everything from phone messages to short reading lists for patrons. Helene had told me that the one time she had suggested updating them, or just using scrap paper, the outcry had been incredible. And so the message pads remained as they had always been.

This was Peg's handwriting again, though not as tidy. No date, but the blue ink looked similar. Same ballpoint pen, or same brand. Probably written around the time of the recommendation card, but there was no way to know for sure. She'd written a series of questions:

> Hieronymus trip abroad—dates?
> What did Harriet mean?
> Hieronymus died away—death certificate?
> Why not Dr. Ames?

All interesting, but it was the last one that got my attention. It had been underlined three times.

<u>Where is the missing will?</u>

Chapter Fifteen

"Where is the missing will? You mean there really *is* a missing will?" I was talking to myself, something I only did when it was something I shouldn't be saying out loud at all. At least there was no one to hear me this time.

"And how would Peg know about it?" I asked. I looked at the time and eyed the pile of papers in front of me. The answer could be in there. I had an hour before I had to shower and change to go to Millicent's. No time like the present.

I'd ordered things by date to the degree that I could when dividing up the piles, so I started with the earliest document I had. This was a letter from Harriet to Margaret, the latter having recently left for the family summer home in the Adirondacks. After the usual greeting, and Harriet's expression of hope that the drive had not been too arduous and that the cottage roof had held up to the winter snows, she moved into something more interesting.

I appreciate your concerns about Hieronymus. His health has never been good. When he was a child, I feared we would lose him to the rheumatic fever, and then to the mumps when he was thirteen. Though he never completely recovered from the rheumatic fever—the family has always suffered from ailments of the heart—I do feel he is strong enough to make this trip abroad. He is a cheerful and curious young man, and the most easygoing of us all. His brother is content with his research, and I with the management of the manor and the family trust, but Hieronymus needs the company of others. A few months of adventure with his school friend will do him good, and since they will be traveling with Christopher's family, I know he will be well looked after. He deserves to enjoy himself while he is able.

Then she moved on to other things, none of which seemed to have anything to do with Peg's cryptic notes. I made a note of the date of the letter, since Harriet had not mentioned exactly when her younger brother would be taking his trip abroad. It was fair to say it would have been within the next few months. I put the letter aside and sorted through the journal pages to see if there were any dated close to the same time. There was something from about a month later. It was only one page and began with a lament about mice in the pantry and a suspected leak in the roof. It was the last line that interested me: *H. seems unconcerned, but I cannot help but think that this trip abroad has been hastily conceived and not thought through.*

That was it. I placed the page with the letter, hoping that if I got everything in one pile in chronological order a more cohesive narrative would emerge. Then I went back to the letters. The next one was dated years later, and the handwriting, though still very precise, was larger.

My dear Margaret—I am happy to hear that both you and little Peggy are doing well! I look forward to the day when you will have found a suitable nanny and can once again join me for an afternoon of tea and conversation.

In other words, you're welcome to visit, but leave the baby at home. Not that I blamed Harriet on that front, and as women of means, that kind of help would be typical. Margaret, being an older mother at a time when that was unusual, might be happy to ditch the kid for an afternoon. I read on.

My eyesight continues to fail, but now that I have Elizabeth Ames to help me with the day-to-day office work, I am able to manage my personal correspondence without too much difficulty. My eyeglasses are sufficient for that, and I have acquired a powerful magnifying glass that I use to read the newspaper. Elizabeth is a treasure—highly intelligent and competent at any task I've asked her to undertake. She has quickly become a great favorite of the entire family. When not assisting me, she has lent a hand to Horatio, who is still researching Poe. Hieronymus conscripted her the other day, as well—I found her helping him to identify and mount a variety of insects. I was concerned that this would put her off, but the two of them were laughing and seemed quite at ease.

Elizabeth was a better woman than I. Mounting insects?

I am so pleased that Jonathon Ames recommended I speak to her. He was here to see Hieronymus and realized I was having trouble with my eyes. Elizabeth was growing bored, and he needs someone with nursing skills to manage his office, so there was little for her to do there. I believe they are hoping for a child, but they married later in life, so that may not be in the cards. Although—as you can attest, one may always be surprised! There appears to be real affection between them, so it may yet happen. Meanwhile, we have a good arrangement for all concerned.

Hieronymus continues to have periodic episodes of dizziness and difficulty breathing. Dr. Ames feels it is time he see a specialist, but Hieronymus is resistant. He does not like to think that he is truly ill. It is the way of the young to believe they are immortal, is it not?

Harriet then moved on to village news. I looked through the journal pages, but those that were dated were from later and those without dates at all didn't seem to jibe with what I was reading. I went back to the letters, the next of which was written about a year later. It looked like Harriet had unbent sufficiently to allow Peg to visit along with her mother before the Emerson family was once again off to summer in the Adirondacks. Dory had said Peg's father was some kind of academic, hadn't she? That would explain the free time. After agreeing with Margaret that the baby was clearly intelligent as well as pretty, Harriet moved on to her own family.

Speaking of babies—my right hand, Elizabeth, is expecting her own later this year. I had thought she seemed unwell for a stretch, but then better. She told me this morning. She hadn't wanted to say anything until she was further along, as both she and Jonathon had concerns in the early months. But all seems well now, and she insists that she is happy to continue her employment as long as possible, if I find that acceptable. As you know,

I am not one who believes a woman's place is in the home caring for offspring! She may continue with me as long as she wishes, and may return if she would like and can make suitable arrangements for the child. Elizabeth seemed most gratified, so we shall leave that door open and see what comes of it. She has a lively mind—devoting herself to homemaking would be good for neither her nor the child. Nor Jonathon Ames, for that matter.

She went on to discuss her eyesight and recently prescribed drops that seemed to be helping. She had enjoyed the novel her friend Margaret had recommended, though it had taken her some time to finish it, and she looked forward to the next from that author. The last paragraphs were of greater interest.

We have finally reached an agreement with Hieronymus. He will see a specialist for his heart but will do so in Boston! He wishes to visit his friend Christopher, who has invited him for the summer. The family will spend the month of August at the shore—a small town on Cape Cod—I have never heard of it—but they will be in the city prior to that, and so he will see a doctor there. We have a recommendation, and Dr. Ames is satisfied.

Horatio has recovered from the cold he had just before you left. Spring colds are the worst, don't you think? While convalescing, he made quite a pet of one of the manor ravens. He feeds it scraps and has taught it a few words. I was not aware of what progress he had made until last Tuesday. He has taught it to say "God Save the Queen" when a certain member of the garden club arrives for a meeting! At first, I thought I was mistaken, but I have now heard it twice, and the second time found my brother snickering at the window of his study. I won't name names, but

I'm sure you'll know who I mean when I say I can hardly fault him!

I had to give Horatio credit. I'd heard ravens could learn words, but hadn't ever tried to teach any of my usual lunchtime companions. I'd have enjoyed hearing one of them croak out "God Save the Queen" whenever Anita walked into the building. I felt briefly ashamed of that thought, then realized she would only have taken it as her due, and so with a clear conscious I read on.

Elizabeth's pregnancy had obviously resulted in a healthy baby, I thought, looking at the date again. Peg Emerson was a year or two older than Millicent. I'd thought she was a couple of years younger. Hieronymus still had the energy to travel, regardless of dizzy spells. His health was getting worse, but according to Millicent, he had died when she was a little girl, so he still had time left. And Elizabeth had remained employed after Millicent's birth. I wondered how old she was before Harriet had allowed her to visit.

I found a journal page dated a few months later. Margaret was back in Raven Hill and had just hosted Harriet for the afternoon.

I knew it! Harriet has just confirmed something I suspected all along. There is a story behind Hieronymus insisting he would only see a heart specialist in Boston. There is a woman involved! His friend Christopher has a younger cousin, Aileen, and Hieronymus has become quite fond of her. She is a widow with a young child. Apparently, she eloped right out of school and went off to Europe with her husband, who was an opera singer! Of all things! They had quite the Bohemian lifestyle, and then before the baby was even born, he was killed in a car crash somewhere in Italy. Christopher's family took her in, and she has been with them ever since, having never gotten on with her own family. Hieronymus met her when he traveled abroad with Christopher, and they renewed their friendship this past summer in Boston.

Of course, the way that Harriet presented it, the story seems quite aboveboard, but I do wonder . . .

So did I. I reached for the pile of journal pages and found the sentence continued on one of the undated ones.

. . . about the timing. I mean the trip, the age of the child, the convenient death of the girl's husband—it does seem rather suggestive. When I broached this to Harriet— diplomatically, of course—she rolled her eyes and accused me of reading too many gothic novels! She may have brushed me off, but I can tell she is concerned. Harriet has never been a maternal person, but she has taken care of her half brothers ever since her father and stepmother died when the boys were quite young, and she has all the concerns of a parent. She and Horatio are very much alike, both brilliant like their father, though considered a bit odd. Hieronymus, the baby, has always been such a nice boy. Exceedingly kind and trusting, and never entirely well. I worry about him being taken advantage of. Harriet indulges him, but she did say before she left that I wasn't to worry—that I'd got the wrong end of the stick, she would sort things out, and it would come right in the end. And that . . .

And that was all, as far as Margaret's commentary went. There were no pages that followed up on the story. Read in the context of Peg's list of questions, the story was suggestive. But you would need firm dates to make it hang together, and Margaret didn't give them, hence Peg's question about the dates of Hieronymus's trip abroad. It could also amount to no more than a sociable young man whose options were limited by location and bouts of bad health finding a ready-made family and enjoying life in a city and at the seashore. Aileen was a nice young woman with a tragic story, attached to a good friend's family. But still. I could see where imaginations would run wild, particularly in a small town with a family as eccentric as the Ravenscrofts.

Harriet's next letter once again jumped ahead in time. Young Millicent was now a regular visitor at the manor.

I admit she is a winsome little thing—very bright, with a mischievous sense of humor. Both of my brothers encourage her to call them "uncle." Horatio performs magic tricks, and she is learning to do some on her own. Hieronymus teaches her about the local butterflies and insects. She is not, thankfully, a squeamish child. Elizabeth tells me that Millicent also has a keen interest in the garden and all the things that can be made with the plants in the greenhouse. She is very much like her father in that regard. This is all well and good, but as you know, I believe that what a woman really needs is a solid financial education so that she may maintain whatever independence she chooses. Perhaps in a year or two, I will teach her about the stock market.

Hieronymus will be off to Massachusetts in a week and will spend the month with Christopher's family on the Cape. This annual trip is something he looks forward to all year. He will see the specialist in Boston, but from what Dr. Ames tells me, there is little that can be done. His heart grows weaker, and the doctor would like him to have regular appointments with someone in Albany. Dr. Ames has said that, all things considered, he thinks it best that Hieronymus be under the care of someone other than himself.

Hmph. Not sure what that last bit meant, but perhaps I was reading in. Someone with a serious heart ailment probably did need regular appointments with a specialist. And Millicent had certainly had an interesting education outside of what she'd learned in school. There was no further mention of Aileen or her child.

There was one more letter, dated late the following year, but a few journal pages written before. I skimmed them, but only stray phrases caught my eye.

Jonathon Ames came to pick Millicent up from Peggy's birthday party. His daughter is clearly the apple of his eye, and the apple does not fall far from the tree. I heard her saying that she was anxious to get home so he could teach her how to "decoct the potion." Honestly!

And then,

Harriet tells me that H. wishes to leave money in trust for Aileen's young son, for his future education, with Christopher as trustee. I still wonder.

Later,

My poor friend Harriet! Her vision is really fading fast. Thank goodness for Elizabeth Ames—the whole family has come to rely on her. Good research skills and a head for figures are invaluable, as my husband will attest. The professor is lucky to have me!

There was nothing else before the next letter. This one wasn't written during the Emerson's usual summer trip, and a couple of sentences in I could see why.

My dear friend Margaret, it began, *thank you for your kind letter. Please, do not chastise yourself for being unable to attend the funeral. Influenza is not to be trifled with, and I am glad to hear that you are feeling better. We knew that Hieronymus did not have much time left, and I am glad that he was enjoying himself with friends at the end. Christopher's family has done everything one could wish. Still, we grieve. Even Elizabeth burst into tears when I told her. Young Millicent will not let her "uncle" Horatio out of her sight when she is here. In the way of children, she is convinced that Hieronymus would still be alive if he hadn't gone away in the wintertime. And to answer your question—yes, the child has been taken care of. Both children. A sum in trust for Aileen's son, and a smaller sum, along with his books and the butterflies she helped to catch and mount, for Millicent.*

She went on to give the details of the funeral and the reaction of mutual acquaintances who had visited and who had written. It seemed her younger brother had been well liked in the village. She closed with,

I am afraid this is the last handwritten letter you will get from me, Margaret. I now have to dictate all of my correspondence to Elizabeth. Even with the special drops, my vision grows darker. I look forward to a visit when you have fully recovered.

The only thing left was the copy of her letter to Dr. Ames. It was brief and straightforward. She thanked him for his care of her brother and the good advice he had given them. She also expressed her appreciation for his efforts to delay the total loss of her vision, including his "old country herbal remedies, which gave her comfort, and the modern medicine he prescribed, which had helped tremendously." She closed with a request for an updated account so that she could pay him, and wished him joy in the coming year.

There was much to think about in this pile of documents. Peg thought they meant something, though they could just as easily be exactly what they appeared to be. She had spent time with the Ravenscroft family, and with Millicent's family, as a child, and her mother was Harriet's closest friend. If she thought something was up, something probably was. But what, exactly? I could see a few possibilities. I'd have to review everything later. It was time to get ready to go. I folded everything up and tucked it all out of sight on my bookshelf.

Chapter Sixteen

I was a little early, so Beau and Ben had not yet arrived when I pulled into Millicent's driveway. She lived in a lovely Dutch colonial close to town in one of the older residential neighborhoods. Her home was within walking distance of what you'd call downtown Raven Hill, though situated in a wooded area that provided privacy. She'd told me that the land backed up to an old orchard, but the grove was no longer farmed, which added to the quiet. When her father had an active practice, people arrived by foot, on bicycles, and in cars, depending on where they were coming from. Dr. Ames had enjoyed having his office attached to his home and had never been tempted to move or take on a partner. When he had retired, a local physician group in the next town had taken on his patients, but Dr. Ames had left his office as it was, retreating there to keep up with professional reading and his gardening journals. Millicent said he'd gone in there for a couple of hours every day until he died, and she'd never bothered to change it. She had let me peek in. Like Horatio's study, it was a time capsule.

When Millicent answered the door, I was glad I had dressed up for the occasion. She looked elegant in a country gentry sort of way. Her tweed skirt, silk blouse, and cardigan were all in soft colors that flattered her pale skin and silver hair. I had gone the skirt and twinset route, and like Millicent, chosen low-heeled shoes that would hold up to a walk around the grounds.

After a warm greeting, Millicent asked if I would mind helping her in the kitchen. "I decided to give my mother's china one last hurrah—I don't entertain often anymore, and handwashing is an awful lot of work. But I thought it would be nice to use today. We'll have tea in the sunroom. It's more comfortable and has a lovely view."

This was true. The sunroom, which had once been her mother's study, was where Millicent spent much of her time. It had the advantage of being close to the kitchen, which I appreciated as I carried plates, cups, and silver to the antique sideboard just inside the door, praying all the while that I wouldn't trip on the wide-plank floors. Once everything was safely deposited, I went back to the kitchen and arranged tiny sandwiches on a tray. I was happy to see some were cucumber—I loved cucumber sandwiches.

Millicent and I chatted about nothing in particular as we worked in the kitchen. After a pause while she ran hot water to warm the teapot, she turned to me and said, "Greer, would you mind staying for a few minutes after Beau and Ben have left this afternoon? I have a favor to ask, and I'd like to explain a little about why I'm asking. Feel free to say no to either request."

"Of course I'll stay," I said. "Whatever it is, I'm sure I'll be happy to help."

"Thank you, Greer. I'm glad we've had the chance to get to know each other over the past few months. And I appreciate all the help you've already given me."

"I'm glad too. And I've enjoyed working in the archives more than I thought I would, especially going through all the ephemera in the old vertical files."

She gave me a thoughtful look. "I'm glad to hear that. I had something in mind—oh, that must be them. I'll get it. If you'd keep an eye on the kettle?"

I heard Millicent greeting the guys as I finished placing slices of cake on a plate. All three appeared in the doorway. Millicent had a lovely bouquet of cut flowers.

"—not at all necessary, but so lovely! Let me find a vase. Greer's been helping me with the last-minute things, so we're about ready. Come through to the sunroom," Millicent was saying.

I greeted my friends and agreed that the flowers were beautiful. "The water's boiling—would you like me to make the tea?" I asked.

"Please," said Millicent. "There's an open tin in the pantry. I'll just be a minute."

I went into the old-fashioned butler's pantry off the kitchen. It was as orderly as you'd expect, complete with an alphabetized spice rack. I could admire it without feeling inadequate—since I didn't cook, I didn't have a spice rack, and my pantry consisted of a couple of cabinets of what most people would consider emergency rations. I found the open tin of Earl Grey. It was the only one from Total Tea and was nearly full. There were other boxes of loose tea of various types, all black teas of good quality. One unopened box of decaf tea bags, probably for guests. There was no bright red container of rooibos. Perhaps that was something new Millicent was trying at work. It wouldn't hurt me to cut down on the caffeine later in the day either.

The only other item of note in the pantry was a shiny new metal box, partly open to reveal electrical switches. Next to it was a blinking panel with the logo of a well-known security system on it. Ben would approve. I doubted Millicent left a key under a flowerpot. I went back to the kitchen and made the tea, putting the teapot and cream and sugar on the tray Millicent had left out. I carried it into the sunroom and placed it on the coffee table. Ben was exclaiming over the china as Millicent arranged her flowers. Beau was studying a collection of framed photographs on the bookshelf. I didn't recall seeing them on my last visit, so I went over to look.

"Millicent, is this you as a little girl?" I asked, pointing to a picture of a child and a middle-aged man I believed was Horatio Ravenscroft.

"Ah, yes," she replied, setting the vase on the sideboard and coming over to where we stood. "My mother used to bring me to work with her sometimes when school was out. The Ravenscroft family was very kind to me—to all of us. Harriet had no real interest in children, but she was amused by the fact that I liked to come and play office. Once I was old enough, she taught me to read a stock ticker. Useful way to learn fractions, really. And Horatio gave me the title of research assistant, since I was an avid reader. The Ravenscrofts had quite a library of their own. He also taught me magic tricks—Horatio loved puzzles and tricks of all sorts. I had the run of the library and the grounds. It wasn't a typical childhood, but it was an interesting one."

"There was another brother, wasn't there? You once mentioned him—Hieronymus?"

"Yes, he died when I was quite young, though. He'd had rheumatic fever as a child, and it damaged his heart. He was never really well, from what I understand. It was too bad—I think he was most inclined to have a family."

"And this must be your mother and father," Beau said, pointing to pictures of an attractive young woman seated at a typewriter and an older man working in the greenhouse. Both were smiling, though the woman looked somewhat wistful. When Millicent nodded, Beau went on. "Now who are these lucky fellows with the young and glamorous Millicent?"

He held up a black-and-white photo of Millicent with two young men. They all looked about twenty, and the tallest of the boys was wearing a letter sweater. Millicent was in the middle, and they all had their arms around each other and were laughing. It was a good-looking trio. Beau was right—Millicent looked rather glamorous in a fifties film star way.

"Oh, that's a long story," Millicent said. "Ancient history." But she smiled, more at the photo than at Beau.

"We're all ears," Ben said. "If you're willing to share, I'd love to hear. You're absolutely channeling Grace Kelly in that shot—I'd been trying to figure out what movie star you remind me of."

"Well . . ." Millicent said. She was quiet for a second, and then held out her hand for the picture. She took another look, and then said, "Oh, why not? Perhaps I'm getting old and nostalgic, but it would be nice to talk about them, my beautiful boys. I warn you, though, it's not a happily ever after."

"Sympathetic cry? I'm your guy," Ben said, settling into the chair in front of the teapot. "And may I pour? I'd like to think all those hours watching Downton Abbey weren't wasted."

Beau snorted and rolled his eyes, but Millicent laughed and agreed. We all took a seat. Ben started to hand around cups, and Millicent set the framed picture on the table. Once everyone had their tea and finger sandwiches, Millicent started to speak.

"This may come as a surprise, especially to Greer, but I was once engaged to be married. To Alexander," she said, pointing to the boy in the letter sweater. "It was when I was at Bryn Mawr. Alexander and Charlie were a year ahead of me at Haverford."

She went on to tell us about how she'd met Alexander at a dance. They'd gone out a few times, and she'd met his friends, including Charlie, who had been his roommate freshman year. Alexander was more of an athlete—he captained the crew team—and Charlie was a talented clarinetist. But all three enjoyed music and the theater, and soon were inseparable. School activities, trips into Philadelphia to dinner and the symphony, and the occasional off-Broadway play.

"We had a wonderful time," Millicent said. "Of course, we were all fortunate—our families had the means to give us that life. Alexander's family was very well-off, Main Line Philadelphia going way back. Charlie and I were both the children of doctors, and so comfortable enough. And then one day, out of the blue, Alexander asked me to marry him. I guess I shouldn't have been surprised—it was the beginning of his senior year, and a lot of the girls I'd started with were already engaged or even married. It was a different time."

Millicent paused and sipped her tea.

"And what did everyone's parents think?" Beau asked.

"That's what was so surprising, at least at the time," Millicent said. "I'd thought Alexander's family would want him to marry someone from their social circle, but they were delighted. They were very welcoming. My parents thought him suitable, and my mother had always encouraged me to spread my wings and make a life for myself outside of Raven Hill, though she did ask if I was sure I wanted to be married. It had never really been a goal—I'd thought I'd get some kind of academic job—but at that point I couldn't imagine life without either Alex or Charlie. They were the best friends I'd ever had. I guess you could say that I loved them both. That we all loved each other."

"Was there going to be a big society wedding?" Ben asked as he passed the sandwiches around again. I beat Beau to the last smoked salmon and got a dirty look, but we kept quiet, not wanting to interrupt Millicent's story.

"Oh no. We both wanted something much more modest. And we were planning a long engagement—my parents wanted me to finish my degree first, and Alexander was applying to law schools. He wanted to get away from Philly and try someplace new. He'd spent his whole life there. Charlie had big plans for a career as a professional musician. He certainly had the talent. We were going to get married after I graduated, and all of us were going to live in New York and be very cultured and sophisticated."

"That was my plan too," Beau said.

"So glad you joined us there," Ben said.

"What's this 'us,' Mr. 'What Exit'?" I said to Ben, mocking the standard New Jersey turnpike question used by state residents to place each other.

"Didn't you grow up in the Bronx, missy? Spare me," Ben replied.

"Kids," Beau said. "I will stop this car . . ."

We all laughed.

"Now," he continued, "I'd like to hear the rest of the story."

Millicent gave a gracious nod. "Thank you. Well, that year was a lot of fun, with all the planning for our new and exciting lives. Then spring rolled around. The weather was uniformly bad, unusually so. Late snow and endless rain. As I said, Alexander rowed—that's what he lettered in—and it was a wonder none of them caught pneumonia. Most years, a day at a regatta was lovely, but not that year."

I nodded. I'd often walk along Boathouse Row in Philadelphia when I was in grad school there, or my friends and I would find a nice, grassy spot and study between races. It wasn't something you wanted to do in a cold rain, though.

Millicent continued. "Then we had one really nice weekend. The weather had been bad all week, but it was sunny and breezy by Saturday. The race was in Delaware, but Charlie and I and some other friends made the trip, to watch. When we got there, I remember thinking that maybe no one should be out on a boat. It was windy, and you could see that the water was rough. But the first few races went off without a hitch. Then the wind started picking up, and there was discussion of holding off on the last one—Alexander's race. They decided to go ahead, though. It all went smoothly at first, but then there several strong gusts in succession. Something happened—the rowers in a couple of sculls got off pace, someone caught a crab and lost their oar—and the wind kept pummeling them. It was so furious it took my breath away. One boat was swamped and another capsized."

Millicent stopped, staring into her teacup. I had a bad feeling about what was coming.

"Did they stay with the boat?" I asked. "That's what you're supposed to do, isn't it?"

"Yes, it is," Millicent said. "And most of them did, including Alexander. But one boy panicked and started to swim for the bank. They were all shouting at him, and another scull tried to get to him, but it was a melee. Alexander was a strong swimmer. He hung on to the boat with one hand and grabbed a loose oar with the other. He maneuvered himself closer and tried to get the other boy to grab the oar. I guess he thought he could pull him in. I talked to the coxswain later and he said that's what it looked like. But the boy was flailing. He grabbed at the oar and pulled it as he went under. It ended up hitting Alexander in the head. Then he went under. No one could get to either one, though people tried. Neither one came up. They both drowned. Alex must have been knocked out. He would have been all right, otherwise."

"I'm so sorry," I said. "That's horrible."

"A real tragedy," Beau added, and Ben murmured agreement.

"And what did you do then? And Charlie?" Ben asked. "That was a horrible experience, and it wasn't the age of grief support groups and mental health checks, was it?"

"No, indeed it was not," Millicent said. "We all grieved, of course. But for the most part, we went on with our studies and our plans. It was what you did. Charlie finished his senior year that May, and he went to New York. He played in various orchestras—theater, clubs. A year later, when I graduated, I moved to the city too. I'd gotten a job in a private library through an alum. We'd get together sometimes, Charlie and I, but it was never the same. I thought he was drinking too much, but at the time I attributed it to his career. Being a musician was such a bohemian lifestyle, from my perspective. Anyway, I worked there for a couple of years, and then my mother became ill, so I came back here. I only saw Charlie once or twice after that. He was drinking too much, and he died in his forties. I don't think he ever recovered from the loss."

"And you?" Beau asked. "Is that why you never married?"

Millicent smiled. "Not exactly. I grieved for a time, for the loss of both of them really. But I found I liked my independence. Looking back, I think Alexander and I did what was expected. It was a different time. In the long term, I don't think marriage would have suited either of us. And now, I think we've had enough of an old lady's sad stories. Thank you for indulging me." She picked up the picture and walked over to the bookshelf. Ben and Beau exchanged a quick glance while her back was turned. Millicent said over her shoulder, "Tell me about your rooftop garden, Ben, and we'll see if we can come up with something bright for this winter."

She resumed her seat and we carried on from there, talking about gardening and other things. Ben was interested in the antiques Millicent had and in local history. Beau asked a couple of questions, but for the most part sat quietly, a thoughtful expression on his face. When we'd finished eating, Millicent offered a tour of her garden, which was readily accepted. We put on coats and set out.

"Now let's see if we can find some things that will work for you in the city," Millicent said. She and Ben led the way. We'd made it through the first couple of flower beds when I reached into my pockets and found that I'd left my gloves inside. It was a brisk day, so I told the others I was going to run in and get them.

"Go through the greenhouse, Greer, and then through the office. Everything is unlocked. And bring my walking stick, please. It should be right inside the office door," Millicent said.

I went up the flagstone path and into the greenhouse. Though not as warm as the house, the sun coming through the glass panes made it feel cozy. It smelled of earth and green things. There was a long table with trays on top and bags of soil beneath. I knew this was where Millicent started her tomatoes every year. Along the other side were rows of potted plants, all neatly labeled. I looked at the names as I went by—some I recognized, some I didn't. I thought most were local and would end up in the flower beds, but I wasn't sure.

I passed through the office and into the house. Once I'd retrieved my gloves, I returned the same way. I paused in Dr. Ames's office. It really was amazing. There were wooden file cabinets and an old medicine cabinet, and a magnificent manual typewriter. I took a closer look—it was an Olivetti, and probably as old as Millicent. I decided that as long as I was having a quick snoop, I'd do a thorough job of it, and had a peek in the medicine cabinet. It was more of a cupboard, with a glass door that locked. It still held bottles of various ages, the older ones with handwritten labels.

Mindful of the fact that Walters had been poisoned with something plant based, I tried to open the door. It was locked. The key might be nearby, or Millicent might have it elsewhere. I didn't have time to look for it. Instead, I squinted through the glass to see what I could see. Nearly all the bottles were empty. I didn't recognize the names on most of them, but one of the hand-labeled ones looked like it said digitalin. That was for cardiac use, or had been back in the day. A couple of yellowing labels had the classic skull and crossbones on them. Those were empty. Still, not something I'd want to keep next to the cough syrup—too much potential for a tragic middle-of-the-night mistake.

I couldn't see anything else. There was a row of old books on the bottom shelf, some outdated standard medical formulary, a couple of old home remedy books, and one incredibly old volume titled *The Physic Garden*. I glanced into the greenhouse. My guess was that Dr. Ames was more interested in traditional healing herbs than he was in heirloom tomatoes. And what about Millicent? I didn't have time to figure that out—I'd been gone long enough.

I spotted Millicent's walking stick where she said it would be and went back outside. I was a little out of breath when I caught up to everyone at the edge of the orchard. I handed Millicent her stick.

"Did you have trouble finding it?" she asked.

"No, it was right where you said it was," I replied. "I stopped to admire your father's typewriter. An Olivetti! My gran had one. I learned to type on it."

"I'll bet you developed very strong hands," said Millicent. "It is a classic, but I'm happy to use a computer. I don't think I could manage a manual typewriter now." She turned back to Ben and pointed out a plant that looked dead to me but was apparently dormant. We set off again, with Beau and I behind the other two. My friend was quiet, the hint of a frown on his face.

"What's up?" I said, elbowing him. "You're thinking too much. I can smell the smoke."

Beau sighed. "My mother," he said.

"Is she okay?" I asked.

"Feeling her age, I think, but otherwise fine," Beau said. Then he changed the subject. "You know, it really is nice up here. Very pretty. And it seems like a friendly community. Apart from the odd murder," he added.

"I like it. More than I expected, actually. The people *are* nice, though I'll be the 'new librarian' until I'm replaced, for whatever reason." I thought of Peg Emerson and had a sudden vision of a body bag being rolled away from the reference desk. Not a productive thought. "And I don't think Raven Hill is any more murderous than the next small town."

"Good to know," Beau said. Then he shifted gears again. "We thought we'd stop by your place tonight, if that's okay. We can catch up, just the three of us. We'll bring wine and snacks. Or dinner if you'd like."

"I couldn't eat a big meal tonight, not after all those little sandwiches and pastries. Something light would be fine. Around seven?"

Beau agreed. We caught up with Millicent and Ben near a small pond at the back of Millicent's property. I'd seen it in the summer, with the trees in full leaf and flowers all around. It still had a stark beauty to it.

"Is this a spirea?" Beau asked, pointing to a nearby shrub. Millicent turned to him, and Ben wandered toward an old barn at the edge of the orchard.

"It is, indeed. You have a good eye," Millicent said.

"My mother has one in her yard. It's been there forever. Still very pretty in the spring," he said. The two of them chatted about different varieties of spirea for a couple of minutes. Then Millicent looked up and saw Ben peeking into the barn.

"Oh, Ben, no! Please don't," she said, waving her walking stick. "It's falling down."

Ben jogged back to us. "Sorry!" he said.

"That's all right. I just don't want to end your wonderful visit with a trip to the emergency room for a tetanus shot.

That thing hasn't been used in years. And we're losing the light. We should start back."

With that we turned toward the house, taking a more direct route. Millicent pointed out one or two more things to Ben, but she seemed tired and out of breath. I wasn't the only one who noticed, because when we got back, Beau declared that he and Ben would clean up while Millicent and I took it easy.

"We promise not to break anything. We were visiting my mother last month, and she had us washing all her good china and polishing the silver. The two of us are still in good form," Beau said, flourishing a dish towel. We retreated to the sunroom, and I lit the fire Millicent had laid before we arrived.

"This really is a very pleasant room," I said, looking around.

"I spend most of my time here in the colder months," Millicent said. "When my father retired, we turned what used to be the waiting room into a library. It's cool and quiet in there during the warm weather, and of course closer to the greenhouse, but fall and winter I'm usually in here."

"Did you have to open up walls or do any rewiring? Henri said the renovation of the carriage house was a much bigger job than he'd thought it would be. And I noticed a new electrical panel near the greenhouse."

"It wasn't too bad. There was already access to the office from the house. I added the new panel recently so that I could have more light in the greenhouse. The old one needed to be upgraded as well. It really wasn't up to current standards. Richard Hunzeker did the work. He heard me talking to

Mary Alice one day after a big storm had caused most of the village to lose power. His family's company had always done our electrical work. He gave me a good price too. It was right before he sold the business. I think it was his way of making up for Anita's behavior."

There was a sudden crash in the kitchen. Ben stuck his head around the door frame. "Nothing broke, I just knocked a couple of things off the pot rack. We'll wash them too." He popped out of sight. Millicent and I exchanged a look.

"I'm sure it's fine," she said.

"Me too. Thank you so much for having us. We've had a wonderful time."

"My pleasure, Greer. I've thought lately I'm getting too set in my solitary ways. I've enjoyed the company."

Ten minutes later, Ben and Beau declared victory over the cleanup and said it was time for them to go. I told them I'd see them later, and Millicent walked them out. While she said goodbye to her guests, I went to the bookshelf and studied the photos. I could see her mother in Millicent, but the resemblance wasn't strong. I'd thought the picture must have been taken in the office here, but when I looked more closely, I could see the distinctive woodwork of the manor. It must have been taken while Elizabeth was working for the Ravenscrofts. The picture of Millicent and Horatio certainly was. It was charming—it looked like the two were sharing a joke. And then Millicent as a young woman with those handsome boys. These were the college friends that Ben and Beau had reminded her of.

I heard Millicent coming down the hall and went back to my chair. I was curious about this favor she needed. Perhaps she really wasn't well. I studied her as she came back into the room. She looked a little tired, but there was a sparkle in her eye, and she was breathing easily. She moved carefully, but I knew she had arthritis, so that wasn't unusual. She sat and folded her hands in her lap.

"I'll come right to the point, Greer, and as I said, feel free to say no."

I nodded, and Millicent continued.

"I'm sure I've mentioned that I have no close relatives left. There may be a couple of distant cousins on the Ames side, but we've had no contact in decades. I'm leaving everything to various nonprofits, including the library. There are bequests of money and also of books. I have a couple of valuable collections passed down to me from my father. There are other—unusual disbursements. I need an executor with a certain knowledge of what's involved, as well as one of discretion and good judgment. I'm hoping you'll be willing to take on the job. If not, my attorney will oversee it."

I was flattered and touched that she trusted me. And also surprised, though I guess I shouldn't have been. I knew Millicent had no family.

"Of course I will, Millicent. I appreciate your faith in me. I'll see that your wishes are carried out."

She gave me a grim smile. "It's going to be a bigger job than you think. The estate isn't small. The law specifies a percentage as an executor's fee, and I expect you to take it. You'll have earned it, trust me. Anyone who has to spend that many hours in a lawyer's office deserves a reward. And as I said, there are unusual circumstances. I'll get everything sorted out as well as I can, and I'll leave a letter with specific instructions. Now—you're sure?"

"I'm sure," I said. "I did have to sort things out after Dan died. That wasn't exactly straightforward either, given the circumstances. I'll deal with whatever comes up."

"I know that wasn't easy, what you went through. I appreciate your willingness to take this on. I'm seeing my attorney early tomorrow. I'll try to make things as simple as possible for you. Thank you."

"Millicent. Tomorrow? I hope you're not planning on leaving us any time soon. I can't face those genealogists without you." I kept my tone light, but I was concerned.

"I have no immediate plans to depart this earth—or the library, for that matter—but nothing is promised. I'll feel better knowing it's taken care of. And before you go, I'm going to give you a key and the alarm code."

Once that was taken care of, I said goodnight. Millicent was looking tired, and I wanted a little time to think before Beau and Ben arrived.

Chapter Seventeen

"Guess what we discovered?" Ben said as he and Beau unloaded a grocery bag of goodies in my kitchen.

"What?" I said, getting out plates.

"Well, we stopped at the wine store off Main to pick up something for tonight," he said, gesturing to the Adventure Wine and Spirits bag on the table. "And there was a very tired police officer in there—silver hair, casually dressed, glasses—asking questions."

"Sounds like Sam O'Donnell, Jennie's boss," I said. "What did he want to know?"

"He was asking about a certain brand and variety of wine. He came in while we were browsing near the back, so we tried to keep a low profile. We couldn't hear everything. But we did hear that the wine that poisoned the Walters guy was only sold to four customers. The owner said it was a small shipment because he's testing out this new vineyard, or something like that. Anyway, the only four people who bought it were you, the Hunzekers—Anita the first time, and then her husband, and someone named Baker."

"Baker? Are you sure?" I said.

Ben nodded. Beau added, "The police officer said exactly what you did. He seemed surprised and spoke more loudly than he intended, I think, because then he looked around and lowered his voice. We couldn't hear much after that."

"Did he mention a first name?" I asked.

Both shook their heads.

"But we did see them huddled over a bottle from the same place. They seemed to be looking at the cork. The owner, Eric, was explaining something. We couldn't hear them too well. We tried to get closer, but the police officer left."

"Hmm. Jennie said the bottle didn't look like it had been tampered with, but they couldn't really tell. That's why she took mine. It sounds like they're still having trouble figuring it out. I took a couple of pictures of the bottle before I gave it to her. Maybe that will help."

"We can go you one better. We got a couple bottles from the same vineyard. We can do a little detecting while we eat," Ben said.

"You're too good to me," I said. "Are you sure you're willing to drink it? You sounded a little put off last night."

"We also got a bottle of the red you bought for Henri," Beau said. "It was wonderful. We'll have that with dinner."

"I'm sure the other is perfectly safe to drink," I said.

"So are we," Beau replied, "but the poor guy who owns the store is worried. We felt bad, so we bought a mixed case to bring back to the city. He has a great selection."

"Yeah, I thought so too," I said, pulling the wine bottle out of the bag. "Here you go." I handed Beau the wine he'd purchased for dinner, and then took one of the same brand used to poison Walters into the living room, where the light was better. I turned a lamp up to high and turned the bottle in my hands, studying the cork.

"I guess we'll take care of the food," Beau called after me.

"Thanks," I said, without looking up. "Silverware and a corkscrew are in the drawer under the toaster. Did you get anything for dessert?"

"Sweets for my sweet. Of course. When you are involved, there is always dessert. I didn't think you hit your quota of little cream puffs at Millicent's."

"I love those things. I was trying to show restraint," I said.

"It was nice of you to leave a couple for us," Ben said. "And speaking of Millicent—why does she keep that classic Cadillac locked away in a barn?"

"What?" I said.

"Vintage Caddy. I'm not sure what year. I didn't get a good look. But it's all grill and fins, so probably from the fifties sometime."

"Grill and fins?" I said. Something about that was ringing a bell. I shook my head. "I don't know, Ben. Millicent has a Subaru. She's had it for a while. I've never heard her mention anything else. It must belong to whoever owns the orchard. I'm sure it's their barn."

Ben looked doubtful. "I don't know. The barn was outside the orchard fence line, but then, it seemed to be beyond the edge of Millicent's garden. There's an old dirt road leading away from it around that grove, so maybe you're right. But who'd leave a beauty like that in a decrepit old barn?"

"You'd be surprised what people have in old barns around here," I said, thinking of the items that had been donated to the last jumble sale. "It doesn't sound like Millicent's style, though."

"Could have belonged to a relative and she's attached to it. That happens a lot," Ben said, setting down a plate and taking a seat.

"Since when do you know so much about classic cars?" I said.

"He's actually more of a muscle car guy," Beau said. "I think it's a New Jersey thing."

"I'd like to argue with that, but all my friends were into old cars. For them it was more about the horsepower. I was more into the design. But I still know my way around an engine. Try not to look so shocked, will you?"

"Sorry, Ben. It's just that I never even suspected . . ."

Beau laughed. "Now that you know, let me see that wine bottle. Do you think someone opened it and then shaved down the cork to get it back in?"

"I think the police would have been able to tell if someone did that," I said. "Unless it were broken, but even then . . ."

"Didn't we see something on TV about wine bottles being tampered with? A mystery series in New Zealand, I think," Beau said to Ben.

"*The Brokenwood Mysteries*," I said. "I saw that episode." I'd seen all of them. I often thought that if Raven Hill were in New Zealand, it would be the next town over from Broken-wood. "But those bottles were sealed with tin or something. You know, the heavy foil? That's done by a machine."

"That's right," Beau said. "Let me see."

I handed him the bottle. "I think it probably does have to do with the cork. There's no other way."

I got my cell phone and pulled up the pictures I'd taken of the bottle I'd handed over to Jennie. I found the best one of the cork and enlarged it.

"The logo stamped on this almost looks like a bullseye, don't you think?" I asked. The other two nodded.

"It would certainly help you aim the corkscrew, especially if you were a few bottles into the evening," Ben said.

"Yes, it would," I agreed. "If you were going to mess with the cork, to try to get something into the bottle, I'd do it there. You wouldn't be able to tell afterward because you'd have screwed through it. But could you disguise it well enough that no one would notice, and also keep the bottle from leaking?"

"Well, the stamp makes the top of the cork uneven," Ben said, running his fingertip over it. "So it would be harder to tell if it had been tampered with. Besides, cork is porous, and it'll expand to fill the space it's in. No obvious hole, and no leaking. As long as you didn't break it. My niece did an experiment like that for a science fair project. As long as the hole was small, you'd be in the clear."

"Maybe if you injected it?" I asked. "Do they track sales of needles and syringes?"

"I don't know, but you can get some that aren't medical grade. You can just buy those online," Ben said. He shrugged. "Same science fair project."

"So it could work," I said. We all studied the cork. Finally, I leaned back, took a sip of my wine, and said, "The more important question is—was the wine meant for Walters, or was it meant for Anita?"

"You know the players. What do you think?" Beau asked.

"It seems more likely it was meant for Anita."

"A backup plan in case the car accident didn't work?"

"Maybe, but then why go bash her on the head? Whoever it was would have to know she'd handed off the wine to someone else."

"Unless more than one bottle was poisoned," Ben said. "Didn't she have another one in her car?"

I nodded. "I'm sure the police are checking it." My late-night question popped back into my brain. "Jennie said that there were only two sets of prints on the wine bottle at Walters's house. How is that possible? *Is* it possible?"

The other two were silent for a minute.

"I would think that whoever sold it would have left prints," Beau said. "Although—we picked up a couple of the same vintage, and Eric only touched one when he rang them up."

"Or if they were for a gift, maybe Anita wiped them down? If there was a visible smudge or something. Would she do that?" Ben said. "I mean, I would eyeball it and make sure it looked nice, but then I add ribbon or use a nice gift bag. But a lot of people will just show up with a nice-looking bottle."

"She might wipe it down, or tell Richard to. Anita wasn't a festive ribbon kind of person."

"So does that kill the theory that the wine was meant for her?" Ben asked, frowning.

"Not necessarily," I said, "because we don't know exactly where that particular bottle was from the time it was sold until it ended up at Walters's house. She only had to handle it between the time the poisoner wiped it clean of prints and when Walters opened it. And it's not strange to see people wearing gloves this time of year."

"There's a certain amount of precision involved in all this. And invention. Could all of your suspects pull that off?" Beau asked.

"Millicent has the brains. Physically, doubtful, because of getting down the bank to whack Anita on the head, though adrenaline can carry you through a lot. Cynthia Baker—I don't know. She's no dummy, but I see her as too nervous."

"She had a bottle of the wine. What if she thought out the poisoning but saw her chance on the road and took it?" Ben asked.

"Again, maybe. And as for Jilly—I just can't see it. The crash, yes, if she felt threatened enough, but the wine, no. And Anita's daughter and son-in-law are wild cards. And if the wine wasn't intended for Anita, they have a connection to Walters. So does Cynthia Baker," I said.

"It looks like it all comes down to whether there was one intended victim or two," Beau said.

"Exactly. Maybe the police have come up with something. I'll talk to Jennie tomorrow."

And then we talked about Danny. The things that didn't make sense to me. The things that Beau and Ben had noticed and thought odd, separately and together, and never discussed until last spring, when I had told them that I thought something wasn't right.

"It's not just you, Greer, and not just us," Beau said. "I told you the Ginsburgs want to talk to you. Goldie said that something funny happened, but she won't tell me. She wants to check with you. She did say the police didn't take her seriously."

"And Suleiman too. He said he saw someone else, but the police didn't take a statement," Ben said.

"Suleiman? But I thought they talked to the doormen," I said.

"So did I, but according to Sule, it was only the daytime guy. He went down to the police station when no one contacted him, but they'd already made an arrest. He'd seen someone else but didn't get a good look, so the police told him to go home."

"Hmph. You two are turning into fine detectives," I said.

"We're writing everything down. So when you come—Christmastime?—we can go over it. Unless you want to do it sooner?" Ben said.

"No, I have things to look into. Like I said, there's some information I got at the wedding, and Ian Cameron has something for me to look at once he finds it. Even Millicent has been helping. She's asked some good questions."

"She's a smart woman. And Henri is looking at the police file, right? And your friend Jennie will help you with the police, I'll bet. We'll all help," Beau said.

"Thank you. I'm a lucky woman. I'm going to make the two of you honorary Raven Hill Irregulars," I said, raising my wine glass.

"Ooh, do we get a secret decoder ring?" Ben asked.

We laughed and went on to other subjects. Still, part of my mind kept turning over everything I'd learned. That only led to more questions. Was this really about a new building or some grant money or someone's job at a university? Or did it go back decades to some secret reaching out of the past? I sipped my wine and thought of Millicent's comment about things in the manor needing to see the light of day. There were plenty of secrets there, I was sure. And then the kids at the book sale and their rhyme. Six for a secret, or was it seven? And the classic from Ben Franklin—*"Three can keep a secret if two of them are dead."* Something like that.

I shivered. Two people were dead.

So far.

Chapter Eighteen

Halloween morning dawned bright and crisp. It was a beautiful day for the afternoon cemetery tour. I wouldn't be leaving until after lunch, so I had time in the morning to do a little investigating. Cheryl had picked up this morning's shift but was running a little late, so I went to the reading room to do the preopening tasks. Mary Alice walked in right behind me, and once I was done with my list, I went to help her with the book drop. We chatted about how the book sale had gone and about the get-together at Millicent's the day before.

"I had to find Millicent's walking stick, so I got to look around the greenhouse and her father's office. Very interesting. I heard he would sometimes create his own herbal remedies," I said.

"Yes, he did do some of that for his older patients," Mary Alice said. "He told my husband once that many of the older local people had greater faith in what was grown in the ground than what was manufactured in a lab. He would prescribe what he thought was needed but also give them the kind of tonic they'd always had. It was sometimes the easiest way to get his patients to take the prescription medicine. Dr. Ames spent a lot of time studying the interaction between herbal remedies and prescription drugs, even after he retired."

"His version of 'a spoonful of sugar helps the medicine go down'?" I asked.

"Exactly," Mary Alice said. "Some of the old farm families were set in their ways, but he was a smart man, and they trusted him. He was shrewd about people. It was really interesting—he grew his own medicinal plants and would distill them himself."

"What they call a physic garden? I've heard of those."

"That's right. He was in many ways ahead of his time, though there are those who would have said behind, what with the tonics and the fact that he still made house calls. He used to drive around town in a big old Cadillac. Kept it for decades. Millicent finally sold it, I think. Anyway, there's been a resurgence of interest in herbal remedies. Millicent is knowledgeable about those kinds of plants as well. She used to help him. She gave a talk about it at the garden club once. She still has a small collection."

"Did she ever consider going into medicine? I remember her once saying something about wanting to continue her father's work," I said.

Mary Alice frowned. "I don't think so, no. She's always been more interested in history and literature. She's a born researcher."

"That's true, and her options would have been limited. I can't see her as a nurse."

"No, not as a career. Though she did help care for her mother after the leukemia diagnosis. They got a professional nurse in at the end, but for a while it was Millicent and her father. Then when he was ill, it was just her, though he went quickly. That was cancer too. Millicent has lived quite a bit longer than both her parents, but I've been concerned once or twice lately."

"So have I," I said. "She was in good form yesterday, though. Pulled out her mother's china and gave us a tour of the grounds. We had fun, and I'm sure she did too."

"That's nice. And what did your friends think of Raven Hill? First visit, wasn't it?"

We chatted a bit. Once I saw Cheryl slide into her chair at Reference, I went back to my office and looked up Sister Mary Josephine's phone number. I always enjoyed talking her—she had a great sense of humor and a thorough knowledge of local library collections. She'd told me the first time we met that she'd been given a temporary assignment to assist the elderly nun in charge of the diocesan archives and library when she first arrived at St. Catherine's. "That was over forty years ago," she said. "When Sister Scholastica died eight months later, they told me to carry on until they found a replacement. I've been the interim archives librarian ever since. There is nothing so permanent as a temporary position—nothing!" And then she had laughed. She confessed that she liked not only her work but also the unusual amount of autonomy she had, and that working with the students kept her young.

Sister Mary Josephine picked up after several rings. She sounded a little out of breath. Though she was nearly as wide as she was tall—she barely topped five feet—she was light on her feet and always moved at high speed, habit trailing behind her. I greeted her and asked if she had time to talk.

"Of course. Bit too early for the students to be in. Let me just put the kettle on," she said. "It's time for my midmorning cuppa. There. Now, what can I do for you?"

I got straight to the point. "I'm looking for any information you have on one of your faculty members, J. P. Walters, including, or maybe especially, any gossip you've heard about him."

"No beating around the bush, then? None of this 'can't speak ill of the dead'?"

"Nope," I said.

"Well, in that case, he was a pompous twit. Thought quite a bit of himself. Didn't have the brains or the skills to back that up, from what I could see. Got the job because of a wealthy relative who'd gotten her degree here—his aunt or grandmother, I forget which—and left a lot of money to the school. I heard it was predicated on lifelong employment for Walters. Now that last bit may be gossip, but I've heard it in enough different places that I think it must be true."

"Probably. He did inherit a nice cabin over here near Raven Hill from an aunt. And I didn't find anything about him that suggested he was hired for his scholarly abilities."

Sister snorted. "Hardly surprising. Not sure he's ever set foot in the library. Sends a graduate student to pick things up for him on the rare occasions he's doing research. Come to think—he's had a problem with one or two people he's advised. I'm not sure, but I don't think he's what you'd call *in demand* for thesis advising anymore."

"What sort of problem, do you know?"

"He was leaning on them a bit heavily for his own research, something like that. Nothing that would inspire anyone to poison him, though."

"Ah, you've heard that too," I said.

"Hard to miss. That assistant of his was telling anyone who would listen about finding the body. Sheila Thompson. An anxious sort to begin with, and she didn't like him, but seeing him dead—literally—wasn't what she was after. She was in here the other day, talking about how he looked just like an animal on her uncle's farm who ate cowbane when she was a kid. Chewed his own tongue to bits, or something. She wasn't too clear."

"Ick," I said. "Cowbane? I've never heard of it. But I'm a city girl."

"Same," Sister said. "But one of our science librarians said it's a form of hemlock. Grows wild. Poisonous from bloom to root. It's a convulsant."

That would explain why Jennie said that the murder scene wasn't pretty and that it was unlikely Waters had committed suicide.

"Anyway, you're not the only one asking about him lately."

"Oh, really? Do you feel free to tell me who?" I asked.

"I don't see why not. It was more of a casual inquiry than a patron request, and she wasn't one of ours anyway. One of yours, actually. Can't remember the name. The woman who went off the road. I recognized her picture in the news. Something to do with your library, wasn't she?"

"Anita Hunzeker. She chaired the board. But she was probably working on something for the historical society."

"Hmm, I'm not sure about that. She had questions about adoption records. Who could get access, that sort of thing. She didn't just want to know about New York—she wanted to know about Massachusetts too."

Well, well, well. Anita had gotten ahold of something. Probably not as much as Peg, who had eyewitness source material, but something that made her wonder.

"That *is* interesting. I'm not sure what she was after there," I said.

"I don't think she was either. Her questions were general, though she seemed to know that all we have here are records of adoptions overseen by organizations related to the Catholic Church. It wasn't so much that she was looking for something in particular as that she was trying to figure what she might be able to turn up."

"Casting a wide net and hoping she would catch something?"

"I'd say so. She didn't look too happy with what I told her—laws vary by jurisdiction, the location of records varies, and so on. She accepted it, though. That's when she moved on to Walters. Seemed like an afterthought, actually. Said the main reference desk was busy when she went by, and could I help her."

"Could you?" I asked.

"Yes and no," Sister Mary Josephine replied. "She wanted to know if we had copies of any scholarly work he had produced. We usually do. Even if it's something they've published before they get hired here, we like to have it. Their department is supposed to ask for a list of work, and copies of it, once they've started. But in his case, we don't have anything except for articles that are in a database we subscribe to. And there are precious few of those. Not a prolific publisher, that one."

"Did Anita look annoyed?"

"Now that's the funny thing. She didn't look annoyed or even surprised. If anything, I'd say she looked satisfied. She smiled, but not in a nice way. Got quite pleasant and chatty after that."

"Huh. That is interesting. I wonder what she was really after?" I said. "I thought she was working on something for the historical society, some research to do with a grant."

"What kind of grant?"

"I'm not sure, but I know they'd recently gotten some family papers related to the Revolutionary War."

"Is that his time period? Maybe she turned up something that contradicted his dissertation. If she didn't like him, and most people didn't, she might have enjoyed pointing that out."

"An academic mystery," I said, more to myself than her. Something was niggling again. A stolen document? A missing letter? What book was that? Something set at Oxford, maybe. The thought drifted away as Sister Mary Josephine started to speak.

"Love those, even more than the ones set in convents and monasteries. Laypeople always get the details wrong unless it's historical and the author is keen on research. Your board chair seemed pretty keen on research herself. I'd say she was a sharp lady. Came across as a real stickler."

"She was," I said. "No more popular than Walters, but it sounds like she was smarter. Listen, if you hear or remember anything else, will you give me a call? I'll give you my cell number."

Sister Mary Josephine said she'd be happy to help and offered her number as well. I promised to drop in for tea and a chat the next time I was over her way, and we hung up. I sat, tapping my pencil and staring at the notes I'd scribbled while we talked. I added thoughts and questions, then folded the paper and tucked it away in my bag. I sent Jennie a text saying I'd spoken to my contact but hadn't come up with much, but that I'd fill her in when she had time. Then I sighed and went back to my actual job. Five minutes later, I picked up my phone and texted Jennie again.

Old car in barn behind Millicent's house. Something feels odd. Don't know if it's important. Described as all grill and fins? Familiar? I paused, and then, feeling disloyal, added, *She'll be out all afternoon.*

She responded almost immediately.

Thnx. Will check. TTYL.

Then, a few minutes later—*Yes. Familiar. Doesn't really fit.*

And that was it. I sighed again and turned to my computer. After all my investigating, I was sure of only one thing.

I was missing something.

Chapter Nineteen

Millicent's Halloween cemetery tour was a highlight of the season. It was the most successful of the collaborations between the library and the historical society, not that there were many. I thought that might change now that Anita wasn't around to aggravate our local historians. The tour started and ended at the library, with a representative from both organizations taking part. I was this year's "library lady," as I heard one of the tour group refer to me. Helene saw it as a good opportunity to drum up new card holders, so we advertised it heavily and provided information for the tour handout, pointing people to library resources that would provide more information on the sites visited. I skimmed the brochure as the bus loaded. I could see Anita's point about having both the archives and the historical society collections in the same building—they were complementary and, together, provided a more comprehensive look at Raven Hill and the surrounding area.

The woman in charge of the cemetery tour was younger than the usual historical society member, and I said as much to Millicent as we waited to get on the bus.

"She's interested in cemeteries, especially old ones," Millicent said. "She's trying to draw in a new crop of volunteers—people interested in local landmarks and preservation, something beyond the family history crowd. I think it's wise. There's a lot of new development in the area—and new residents. If we want to keep what brings them here to begin with, they need to feel attached to it."

We boarded the bus and set off. Millicent did a wonderful job of pointing out interesting landmarks as we drove, connecting them to the graves and monuments we were about to see. It was a nice change from an afternoon at the reference desk. The group members asked questions and pointed things out to one another. Several had been on a similar tour of Civil War–related locations, and all of them had signed up for an upcoming outing about the Schuyler family. It would coincide with a touring production of *Hamilton* at one of the area's bigger theaters. Millicent was right—I could tell from the questions and conversations that many of these people hadn't lived in the area all their lives, but they were quickly becoming invested in local history.

The tour went smoothly, and the weather cooperated. The only snag was snarled traffic that put us behind schedule on the way to the last stop. It was an old private cemetery in Raven Hill, where the Ravenscroft family and other notable locals were interred. No one had been buried there for decades, according to the handout provided by the historical society, though it was maintained by a trust set up by the village's founding families.

We pulled into the turnaround near the path that led to the cemetery. The area was well maintained, but the light was fading. I didn't fancy a walk in the woods after sundown, but Millicent was confident she would get though the material before it got too dark to find our way back to the bus.

"Don't worry," she said. "I know what I can skip and where I can speed it up. We'll have time."

We exited the bus and walked single file down the path. We emerged in a sizable clearing, its perimeter delineated by a low stone wall interrupted only by a wrought iron gate that stood open before us. The surrounding trees were tall and sturdy, their branches arching overhead, tips touching and creating a perpetual twilight beneath. Millicent, walking stick in hand, led the way confidently to the center of the graveyard. I paused at the entrance, running a finger over the scrollwork on the gate.

"Pretty cool, isn't it?" said Judy, the tour leader. She'd been helping a straggler navigate the path. Mission accomplished, she stopped next to me and gestured to the gate.

"It is," I said. "The whole place is. I've never been here before."

"I came on a tour a couple of years ago. It's what inspired me to get involved with the historical society. You should look around. I come a few times a year with my dogs." She grinned. "None of the residents seem to mind."

"I wouldn't think so," I said. "Millicent seems to have things well in hand. I think I will take a look around."

Judy waved and headed toward the group. I set off toward what appeared to be the oldest part of the cemetery. The stones were small and weathered, still upright but most at odd angles. As I meandered toward the back, the headstones became larger, and it was clear that certain families had good-sized plots. A number of village residents had died during various wars, others in the flu epidemic. Many had died young. Others had lived to a ripe old age, even by current standards. Those monuments tended to be larger and more ornate.

I had reached the back and was turning around when a name caught my eye. Ames. Solid and respectable markers, with minimal ornamentation. Based on the engraving, Millicent's parents. Jonathon Ames had a Rod of Asclepius, with its single snake beneath his name and dates, appropriate for the local doctor. Elizabeth Ames was next to him, with her own headstone. She was younger than her husband by a decade but had died well before him. Beneath her dates was engraved a flower, one stem with several blossoms. Perhaps Elizabeth had enjoyed gardening as much as her husband. Under that, at the very bottom of the stone, was a pattern that ran around the edge. Birds. But grouped, three and then seven, with a mark between. Hard to see clearly because the grass had grown up over it. I looked around, but I didn't see any other Ames family members.

There was a small empty patch and then a row of dark, polished stones. I went around to see them from the front. Each had a bird, or birds, above the name Ravenscroft. Not surprising—from what I knew of them, the Ravenscrofts were not a weeping angel kind of family. Individual names, and sometimes more engraved images, were below that. These people were represented by pictures in the main hall at the manor, but the names were hard to read in the twilight. I found Harriet and then Hieronymus, whose stone also featured birds and plants and the phrase "A friend to all." And Horatio, the library's chief benefactor, had to be here somewhere. There he was. His stone had a bird motif similar to that of Elizabeth Ames. I was bending to take a closer look when Millicent called my name. I turned to see her waving to me as the tour group started to file toward the entrance. Mindful of how easily she fatigued lately, I went to her immediately.

She was leaning heavily on her walking stick when I reached her. "Everything okay?" I asked.

"Fine, Greer, really. I'm just a little tired and want to avoid tripping on anything on the way out. Your eyesight is better than mine. Would you mind leading the way?"

"Sure," I said. "It's getting dark, isn't it? And windy," I said as a cold breeze prompted me to zip up my jacket. "I lost track of time. Let's go."

I started down the path to the gate, and Millicent fell in behind me. I pointed out one or two tree roots, but otherwise we didn't speak. Judy was waiting for us at the entrance and congratulated Millicent on a wonderful tour. I stopped for one last look, and the wind set the trees swaying and whispering. For a moment, I glimpsed the manor through a break in the branches, and then it was gone. Could we be that close? I turned back to ask Millicent, but she and Judy were already into the woods. I hurried after them. Halloween in an old cemetery was fine with a crowd, but I had no wish to be left there on my own.

When we got back to the library parking lot, I waited with Judy and Millicent to say goodbye to the group members. I directed a couple who wanted library cards into the manor and told them how to find the circulation desk. Once everyone had dispersed, Judy told Millicent she'd be in touch and got into her own SUV.

"If you want to go straight home, I'll let Helene know how it went. She's closing tonight, and I need to go in anyway," I said to Millicent.

"Thank you, Greer—I think I will go home. It's been a long day. I did take care of those things with my attorney, but I was there longer than expected. Tell Helene I'll speak to her tomorrow when I'm in. And if you wouldn't mind, please make sure the archives are locked. The new page forgets if she goes to put something away after I've left."

"Sure, I'll run up and check before I leave," I told her. I stowed her walking stick in the back of her car and waved as she drove off. Once she was down the drive and onto the road, I took a quick look around the lot. Helene was here, as expected. I was pleased to see that Dory's Cadillac was in its usual spot. I needed information, and it was quicker to ask her than look it up. I checked the time—with any luck, I'd be able to catch her on her dinner break.

I went in the back door and down the stairs to the staff room. Dory was at the table with a bowl of soup and a magazine.

"Oh, hi, Greer," she said. "Back from the tour? How was it? Packed as usual, I'll bet. What did you think of the new girl from the historical society? You're not working tonight, are you? I though Helene was closing."

Dory stopped for breath and put aside her magazine. As always, she'd much prefer a chat. I'd counted on that and planned my approach on the way in. I wanted information from Dory, but I didn't want to tell her why. Mostly because I wasn't sure myself, but I sensed I was on the edge of something important.

"It was great," I said as I put the electric kettle on and grabbed a mug and a package of cocoa mix. "I'm glad I got to go. Yes, it was full. Judy seems to be doing a fine job. I stopped in to pick up my tote bag and tell Helene how it went. I got chilled, though, so I decided to have hot chocolate first. I'll catch Helene when she gets to the reference desk."

"Probably a good plan—I think Helene's on a call with the board," Dory said. No matter what was going on, Dory always seemed to know who was doing what when she was in the building. She was one of the world's great observers. Also nosy, but that was to my advantage. Most days.

I sat down with my drink and gave Dory my impressions of the tour. I finished up with "And then we went to an old cemetery off Orchard Road. It's where all the Ravenscrofts are buried. And Millicent's parents, I think."

"Oh yes, that's the oldest cemetery around here. One of the oldest in the Capital District, actually. Hasn't been used in a long time, though I think if you have a family plot and can prove the connection, you can still be buried there. I'd forgotten that's where Millicent's parents are. The rest of the family are in Schenectady, I think, at least on her father's side. Her mother came from downstate somewhere."

"How did they end up out in the woods by the Ravenscrofts?"

"I'm not sure," Dory said. "If I had to guess, I'd say it was because Millicent's mother—what was her name?" Dory paused, frowning.

"Elizabeth?" I said.

"That's right, Elizabeth. She worked as a secretary to old Horatio for years. Helped him with his research, paid the bills, typed up letters—that sort of thing. I think he might have gifted the plot to Dr. Ames when Elizabeth died. He was the last of the family, so he could do what he wanted. The Ravenscrofts were an odd bunch," Dory said.

"So I've heard. I was surprised that the family burial ground was so far from the manor, but then I thought I could see the tower through a break in the trees. It didn't seem like it was that far off, but it was hard to tell. The light was already fading."

"It's not that far, actually. There was an old trail that led to it, but I'm not sure where it starts. By the back parking lot, maybe. Years ago there was a brochure, 'Historic Hikes' or something like that. There's probably one in the archives. But once all the new development started, a lot of those trails disappeared. And Orchard Road used to continue, but they stopped paving at that little turnaround. Those old farm roads were just dirt tracks, and most of them are gone now. Oh, look at the time! I'd better get to the circ desk. David will be wanting to get home to dinner."

With that, she was off. I rinsed and dried my cup, mentally sorting through what Dory had told me. That Elizabeth Ames had worked for Horatio Ravenscroft was common knowledge. That she'd started out as Harriet's secretary back when Hieronymus was still alive seemed to have been forgotten. The burial plot was an odd gift, but then the Ravenscrofts were an odd family. Maybe that's how they'd always rewarded faithful staff who died while employed. Had Elizabeth Ames died while she was working for Horatio? I thought so but wanted to get another look at the dates. Those gravestones felt important; I just wasn't sure why. Meanwhile, I had to find my boss and check the archives before I left.

I got my tote bag from my office, then stopped by the reading room to talk to Helene. The dinnertime lull had begun, so I was able to tell her about the tour without interruption. I finished up by saying, "Millicent went home right after. She said she was tired. She wanted me to check the archives, though. She's worried the new page is forgetting to lock up."

Helene opened the desk drawer and handed me the keys. "I think Rachel is finally starting to get the drill down, but it doesn't hurt to check."

I took the keys and went upstairs. The second floor was quiet—no meetings going on. The initial excitement about Anita's death had faded, and all the committees she was on were regrouping. The community room was unused every night this week.

I checked the door of the archives and found it locked. I paused, keys in hand. Could the old hiking trails brochure be in there somewhere? If it was, I had a good idea where it might be. This would only take a minute. I unlocked the door, stepped in, flipped the light switch on, and then closed the door behind me. What I was after would be in an old wooden filing cabinet near Millicent's desk. Vertical files were an anachronism in modern libraries. So much of what they used to hold was readily available online now—maps, for example. One of the projects Helene had asked me to help with was going through this cabinet and seeing what was available elsewhere, what was worth keeping, what might be digitized, and so on. But every time I started, either Millicent found something else for me to do, or I came across a bit of ephemera so strange even she couldn't figure out why we'd kept it. But I'd been able to create some order, so I knew where to start.

I opened a center drawer and pulled out a file. It was full of brochures from local attractions, most long gone. I knew they were in no particular order, so I dumped them out on a table and did a quick sort. There were a couple with maps, most hand drawn, so I took a closer look at those. Nothing. I put everything back and tried one more file. This one had to do with local flora. Most of the papers in it had to do with gardens, but there were maps detailing how to find speci-men trees and rare plants. I thought maybe the hiking map was mixed in, but was disappointed. I put everything back, turned off the light, and locked up.

I dropped the keys back at the desk and left for home. I could always go back to the cemetery the long way, via Orchard Road. It would be quicker to find the path through the woods, though, presuming it wasn't overgrown. Raven Hill was full of forgotten trails and shortcuts. I'd found one or two myself. I'd been all over the place, physically and mentally, for a week. It was time to get a bird's-eye view of things.

Chapter Twenty

I picked up something for dinner on my way home and booted up my computer as soon as I got to my apartment. I set up my usual command center on the coffee table in my living room and got to work. Maps and directions relating to the two crime scenes were in one pile, copies of pages from Walters's thesis were in another, and everything I'd pulled out from behind Harriet's picture was in a third. Mindful of the eggplant parm sandwich in my hand, I left those for last and began studying the printouts I'd made of the roads around the crime scenes. I laid them out as though they were a map for the bird's-eye view. Nothing jumped out at me, but it occurred to me that I didn't have the complete picture.

I finished my sandwich, wiped sauce off my fingers, and searched Jilly's address. I mapped her route home from the library and then zoomed out to see if I could figure out what she meant by "the back way." There was only one real possibility, and while it took her near the road to Walters's cabin, it wasn't close to where Anita had died. It would have taken time to kill them both—she'd have had to double back to avoid all the traffic cameras. I printed it out anyway, since while it was likely the same person *had* killed them both, that hadn't yet been proven.

Next up—Millicent. I pulled up her address and mapped her route home from the library and then to both crime scenes. I didn't see how she could do it without running into a traffic camera or another motorist. Agnes and her friend had seen two cars—the one they'd passed on the way home and the one that had scared them and then disappeared. Based on her description, the first one could have been Cynthia Baker. The second was still a question mark. Neither could be Millicent. Agnes knew her car.

Out of curiosity, I zoomed in on Millicent's house, then panned outward. The old barn was visible, as were the rows of trees left in the old orchard. Many of them had died, leaving bare patches. These images had been taken in spring or summer, when everything was in full leaf. If it had been winter, it would have been harder to tell. Odd to have a barn out there unless it was for equipment storage. Could you drive something between the rows of apple trees? I kept scrolling around and found a bare stretch of uniform width that lead away from the barn. It also led away from the road Millicent lived on. It wound back in the direction of the manor and split. One part disappeared into trees near the intersection where Main met the road to the library. I'd only gone to the far end of Main Street once. As I recalled, it didn't so much end as turn into a dirt road that disappeared into the woods. At one point, the two must have met, and perhaps still did.

The other veered off and tapered out not far from a cul-de-sac at the end of paved road.

What had Dory said? Something about Orchard Road continuing and old farm roads disappearing. This was the cul-de-sac near the cemetery. The trees obscured the old burial ground and any footpath to the manor.

"As the raven flies, none of these are very far apart," I said, looking at Millicent's house, the barn, the manor, and the cemetery. "But none of them provide quick access to Winding Ridge Road either. Hmph."

When you came right down to it, none of the places I was studying were far from each other when viewed from above. It just wasn't easy to get from one to the other quickly or without being seen by human eyes or electronic ones.

Time to try another tactic. I put the maps away and brought my plate into the kitchen. Thinking how nice it would be to relax with a martini, I poured myself a glass of sparkling water and got back to work. I tackled Peg's list next. From what Sister Mary Josephine had said, Anita had been following a similar line of inquiry. I copied the questions onto my notepad. The dates that Hieronymus was abroad and the fact that he died away from home weren't things I could follow up on. I had one newspaper article on his trip and a reference in a letter, and that was it. The attractive young widow, her child, and her conveniently dead husband were suggestive, but without last names, dates of birth and death, and many hours of research, I wasn't going to learn anything.

The other three questions interested me more. *What did Harriet mean?* There were two statements attributed to Harriet that made me wonder. The first was when she said that Margaret had got hold of the wrong end of the stick. That was related to Margaret's theory that Hieronymus was the father of Aileen's child. Harriet's phrasing implied that Margaret was on to something but hadn't quite nailed it. Later she had referred to "both children" when discussing Hieronymus's will. I thought that she meant Aileen's son and Millicent, two children of whom he was fond. He was also fond of both mothers, from what I'd read in the letters. How fond? His epithet was "A friend to all." Perhaps he was friendlier with some. Margaret certainly thought so. Elizabeth Ames?

That brought me to the next question. *Why not Dr. Ames?* Why indeed? Perhaps the good doctor simply realized that his patient needed someone with greater expertise in heart ailments than his own. Alternatively, if he suspected his wife of an affair with his patient, he would be disinclined to treat that patient. Something about that didn't feel right, though. I'd have to read through the letters and journal pages again.

Where is the missing will? I had no idea. I wasn't even sure there was one. But—there had always been whispers about something like that when Horatio died. I'd heard it last spring when Joanna Goodhue was murdered. According to Dory, Mary Alice, and even Millicent, those rumors had been around for decades. They'd started with something and, perhaps like a game of telephone, had become something else.

"Maybe it's with the purloined letter," I said, putting down my notebook. Poe's Dupin had found his client's missing letter. Christie's Poirot had found his client's missing will. Both had the advantage of knowing that the item they were looking for actually existed. Not to mention that they weren't decades removed from the document's disappearance. If any of the Ravenscrofts had stashed away a will, it had been done before I was born.

It was time to fuel up for what was looking like a long evening of detecting. I pulled out the cherry-red air fryer my sister had sent me for my birthday. It was still in the box when she called to see how I liked it. I was giving her a big story about how I'd been so busy I hadn't had time to try it, when a message popped up from my nephew. *I can hear my mom on the phone. You know you can make s'mores in that, right?* He'd included links to YouTube videos. The fryer had since become my favorite appliance. In addition to s'mores, I'd added frozen French fries and onion rings to my repertoire. I could tell my sister with a clear conscience that while I hadn't attempted any proteins, I often used it for veggies. I counted the eggplant I'd had for dinner as my daily vegetable quota, so I assembled a few s'mores, fired up the fryer, and went back to my notes while it worked its magic.

I eyed the pile of copies I'd made from Walters's thesis, and decided I couldn't face anything academic after such a long day. I had tomorrow off—better to look at it when I was fresh. Instead, I started my own list of questions beneath Peg's.

Why kill Anita?

I left plenty of space under that one.

Why kill J. P. Walters?

One murderer or two?

Was the wine actually meant for Anita?

Those last two were related. If the wine was meant for Anita, maybe as a backup plan if the car accident didn't work, there was only one killer. But if so, how did the wine get to Walters? The most logical answer was that Anita took it there. She had mentioned having to take care of something unexpected when she left the library that night. And if the wine wasn't meant for Anita, who would want to kill them both? I added that question to the list because if I couldn't come up with an answer to that, I'd need to find a second murderer.

Or two people working together. Sloane and her husband? I scribbled down that thought. And then, hearing Jennie Webber's voice in my head, added the question, *Who could physically have done it?* I'd have to answer that for each of the victims. I looked at the list of questions and the pile of maps and decided I needed some kind of chart. The very thought exhausted me.

The air fryer beeped. Saved by the bell. All of this would have to wait—I was too tired to think it through. I'd let my subconscious work on it. Meanwhile, I'd have dessert while consulting with one of my favorite detectives. I queued up Christie's *Halloween Party*. I'd seen it years ago but decided it would be fun to watch it again tonight. Poirot fueled his little gray cells with more sophisticated fare, but I was happy to settle in on the couch with my s'mores and see what wisdom he would impart. The book was not considered one of the author's better efforts, but it had been revised for the television series and was more straightforward. A nice change from what I was currently dealing with.

An hour and a half later, the s'mores and the distraction had done the trick. My mind had stopped spinning, and I was yawning. One thing stuck with me, though: Poirot focused on the murder victim, not just the murderer. I had scribbled down what he said.

"The victim. One must always return to the victim. For their personality, their nature, it, it is the key."

That spoke more to character than to behavior or likeability. No one liked Anita, but she had qualities that people respected. It was often the way she went about things rather than her goals themselves that people objected to. Walters was more of an enigma—no major accomplishments, but no major scandals either. From what I could tell, not liked, but not hated either. A moderately successful career achieved by using *who* he knew rather than *what* he knew, and by a willingness to deal with administrative tasks.

Was character key? Maybe. I finished washing my dishes and went back to my list of questions. Across the top I wrote, *The character of the victim?* Would that explain why someone would kill one or both? I yawned again. Perhaps after a good night's sleep it would all become clear.

Sleep proved elusive. I tossed and turned, running through everything I'd learned, convinced I'd missed something. If I could only figure out what that was, I might have the answer, or part of it. I still had too many unknowns. I also had a headache. I sat up and checked the time. Not too late. I texted Jennie and asked to meet for breakfast. My phone pinged seconds later.

Sure. 7?

I grimaced. Not if she wanted me to be coherent.

It's my day off. 8?

I got back an eye-roll emoji, followed a second later by:

Make it 9. I'll stop by the station first.

I sent her a thumbs-up and got up to take something for my headache. Thinking I should cut down on sugar and admitting that I wouldn't, I went back to bed.

The dream began the way it usually did. I was opening the door to my apartment in New York, uneasy because I had found it ajar. This time, I didn't walk in to find my husband on the floor. Instead, I was in the upstairs hallway at the manor. Danny stood at the other end, a letter in his hand. Next to him was my friend Joanna. She opened her mouth, but it was her husband, Vince, that I heard.

"I know it's here somewhere in all these papers."

A low, hissing voice responded. *"Blackmail."*

I looked around, but there was no one else there. I tried to get to Danny, who was smiling at me and holding out the envelope in his hand. But I couldn't move, and then Danny and Joanna dissolved into a cloud of large, black birds. Ravens. The birds flew off and I was standing in the old cemetery. Millicent was there too. She was standing with her back to me, in the empty space next to her mother's grave. I called her name, but she didn't turn. She started to walk away. A path appeared at the back of the cemetery, leading into the woods.

The trees swayed and I could see the manor through them. I called again, and this time Millicent turned.

"It's long past time some of the things buried in this house saw the light of day," she said, and then she turned and disappeared on to the path leading to the manor.

I heard the deep, gurgling croak of a raven. I looked up and saw three of them perched on top of Horatio Ravenscroft's gravestone. Four more landed next to them. Seven. They kept launching themselves up and resettling. They'd open their beaks, and I'd hear children's voices, far away, reciting a rhyme. Then all the ravens took off toward me. I stumbled and caught myself on Jonathon Ames's desk, an old-fashioned key between my hand and the Olivetti. I reached for it, but a noise stopped me. Hinges creaking. I looked up and saw Richard Hunzeker standing near the cabinet, his hands in his pockets.

"I'm worried about those fuses," he said. He turned and opened the door into the greenhouse. I followed and walked into Horatio Ravenscroft's study. There was a woman leaning on the desk, looking out the window and smoking a pipe. Harriet. She turned to me and smiled, the light from the window catching on her eyeglasses.

"Poor Margaret had the wrong end of the stick. You'll fig-ure it out, and faster than Peggy did, I'll wager. You're a clever girl. I've been watching you. They'll help." She gestured out the window, where the manor ravens were swooping and circling. When I looked back at her, she faded out of sight, leaving nothing but a curl of pipe smoke hanging in the air. I smelled a hint of cherry.

"Smoke," I said aloud, sitting up in bed. I sniffed the air—nothing. I stared into the darkness, seeing fragments of the dream. Once again, I heard the croak of a raven. I looked out the window. It was the middle of the night, but I could swear I saw dark shapes flitting past. The birds, the gravestones, the children chanting a rhyme.

The book sale. The kids on the lawn, chanting the counting rhyme.

I grabbed my phone, opened the browser, and started to search. It wasn't hard to find. There were different versions—it was an old rhyme—but I thought it was the more modern one that mattered.

> One for sorrow,
> Two for joy,
> Three for a girl,
> Four for a boy,
> Five for silver,
> Six for gold,
> Seven for a secret, never to be told.

The repeating pattern—three and seven. The birds in my dream and on the gravestones. I went into the living room, flipped on the light, and picked up Harriet's letters. There it was, the detail I'd noticed and then forgotten. It was why Harriet said Margaret had gotten the wrong end of the stick. She hadn't realized, but Peg had. Of course, she would have seen the gravestones.

Hieronymus had nearly died when he had the mumps as an adolescent. The mumps. While it wasn't a sure thing, it was likely that a severe case of the mumps would have rendered him sterile. Hieronymus had not fathered any children, legitimate or otherwise.

I read the rhyme again, picturing the gravestones. Three birds—ravens—then seven, in a repeating pattern. Horatio and Elizabeth had left a message.

Three for a girl, and seven for a secret, never to be told.

Millicent.

Chapter
Twenty-One

❧

I beat Jennie to the Java Joint the next morning and snagged a table near the back, where we wouldn't be overheard. I'd brought all my notes and questions, as well as the copies Anita had made of Horatio Ravenscroft's will and the family trust papers. After my brainstorm about Millicent the night before, I'd looked everything over, gotten it in order, and then slept the sleep of the righteous until my alarm went off. I woke up ready for action and ravenous. Jennie arrived at the same time as my breakfast sandwich and ordered one for herself. She still had dark circles under her eyes, but she seemed more upbeat. Maybe we'd both had a breakthrough.

"What've you got?" she said.

"The missing heir to the Ravenscroft family trust, which is a motive for getting rid of Anita; a couple of theories about the Walters murder; and a whole lot of questions. But I think we're close to a solution."

"Based on?"

"A feeling," I said. Also a dream, but she was even less likely to go for that. As it was, she quirked an eyebrow and asked, "What kind of evidence do you have?"

I pushed my folder across the table to her and ran through everything I'd discovered. She followed along, occasionally asking questions. When I finished, I gave her time to look it over and ate my sandwich. She went back through the notes and papers I'd brought. When she sat back and picked up her own sandwich, I could see her wheels turning.

"I know I've made a few leaps," I said, "but I'm sure I'm on to something. Anita was following this same line. I think she was close to proving that there was another Ravenscroft— that Horatio wasn't the last one."

"Millicent Ames."

"Yes," I said. "Elizabeth and Jonathon Ames were married for a while before she got pregnant. That was after she started working for Harriet. It's possible she just wanted a child—her relationship with her husband seemed solid. Or perhaps she and Horatio formed a real attachment. The whole family was very fond of her. Hieronymus seemed more likely at first, and I suppose he could be Millicent's father, but he was never in good health, and then there's the mumps."

"I'm following all that, but does it explain Anita? Why would it make a difference to her if Millicent were an illegitimate Ravenscroft? And after all this time, would Millicent kill to keep that secret?"

Never to be told.

"I don't know." I sighed and slumped back in my chair. I didn't like to think it of her—I'd grown to like Millicent in the last few months. But she'd said things that made me won-der. And then there was Peg, and the cup of tea right before she died. My mind flashed to Millicent rooting around in the staff room and producing a red tin, rooibos, though she had nothing like that at home. Anita, with her usual mug of tea at the board meeting, and then Millicent again, asking if there would be a toxicology screen.

"Did you do a tox screen?" I asked Jennie.

"Results pending. That stuff takes time. We need to rely on the state labs, remember, and we're not high on the priority list. Why?"

"Millicent asked about it. I just hate to think . . ."

"I know you do. To be honest, so do I. But there's some-thing you should know. It's just a theory, but it explains some odd things."

"What?"

Jennie sighed. "You know that 'grill and fins' comment that you thought was familiar?"

I nodded.

"It rang a bell with me too, but I couldn't think of why until I was in that old barn looking at the car Ben found. The way the sun hit the front when I looked in the door—the grill looked like teeth, like the car was grinning at me. And then I remembered. Teeth and fins. It's what Agnes kept saying when she made the 911 call the night you thought someone tried to run you over."

I was stunned. "You think Millicent tried to kill me last spring?"

"I think it's more likely she was trying to scare you, and it may have been spur of the moment. You were nosing around after Joanna died. If your theory about her parents is right, she probably got nervous about what you'd find. Maybe she thought it was you roaming around the manor at night. Or it was her, and she used her father's old car to throw people off if anyone saw her. The registration expired years ago, but it looks like she kept it running."

"Mary Alice said Dr. Ames used to make house calls in it and that Millicent kept it for a while, but said she'd sold it years ago. But wouldn't Agnes recognize it?"

"It was foggy, remember? And she only got a glimpse as the car went under the streetlight," Jennie said. "She was still drinking then too. And Agnes is not a car person. She notices anything unusual, but that's about it. If Cynthia Baker didn't have that metallic finish on her car, Agnes wouldn't have noticed. It would have looked like any other SUV."

"Do you know it was Cynthia's car?"

"We do. We know when she went through the traffic camera, and the time lines up pretty well with when she was at the Hunzekers'. She still could have run Anita off the road, though."

"So could Millicent," I said, and told her what I'd found on the maps. "She could have gotten from the barn onto Main and then out of the village."

Jennie shook her head. "It's a good theory, but that old car hasn't seen action for a while. All the tires were flat, and enough debris had blown in that it was clear it hadn't been moved recently. But I think we can eliminate Millicent for other reasons. I finally got her to come clean with me last night."

"Really? About?"

"About why she was in Agnes Jenner's driveway after the board meeting. It *was* her that Jilly saw. Millicent did leave the building when you saw her going out the front. She said she wasn't feeling well. Apparently, she's been getting short of breath and having dizzy spells. She thought she could make it home, but figured out she shouldn't be driving. She expected Agnes would be home, but then realized she wasn't, so she turned the car around and gave herself time to catch her breath. She saw Jilly drive by, and Anita. Then she felt better and decided she could make it home. I told her to call 911 next time."

"She's been getting short of breath lately—we've all noticed it. I didn't know about the dizziness. You're right about 911, but I can't see her doing that. Too much fuss."

Jennie nodded. "I think that's true, but I also think she's afraid she'll have to retire. She didn't say it outright, but I got a feeling that's what was worrying her. She tried to downplay it—said everyone in her family had heart issues and she knew what to look out for, but I think she's concerned."

"Jonathon and Elizabeth Ames both died of different kinds of cancer. The Ravenscrofts had cardiac problems. So that's consistent with my theory." I said.

"But what was in all of this for Anita?" Jennie asked. "Did she think she could blackmail Millicent into supporting her vision? Or changing the terms of the bequest somehow? Can she even do that?"

"I—" I stopped, a voice from my dream replaying in my head. Vince Goodhue, whose wife, my friend Joanna, had been killed in the manor. And Millicent. But it was a conversation I'd overheard months ago, right after Joanna's death. Millicent had mentioned blackmail. What had Vince said? *"I know it's here somewhere in all these papers."* Something like that.

"Greer?"

"I think maybe Millicent could have made changes, but she'd need proof. And I've always heard that papers went missing when Horatio died. A will, a letter, a codicil—something like that. No one's clear on exactly what."

"That's true," Jennie said. "Every time something happened at the manor, rumors would start. I heard them when I was a kid staying here with my grandparents. My sister asked about it once, if there really was another Ravenscroft that no one knew about, and another will. My grandmother told her it was nonsense and not to spread gossip. I remember that because once my sister turned away, my grandparents kind of looked at each other, and then my grandfather shrugged and shook his head. They didn't realize I was there. As the years went by, you still heard about the will, but not so much about another Ravenscroft."

"Well, we have the other Ravenscroft. At least I think we do. And as for a missing will—I'm sure it's somewhere in the manor, probably in the archives." I told her about the overheard conversation between Vince and Millicent.

"But we don't know that whatever it is, it's still there. And it doesn't tell us who killed Anita. I agree it gives Millicent motive if your theory holds up, and I think it makes sense. But Millicent couldn't have killed Anita. I believe what she said about the dizziness. She could have run Anita off the road, but no way is she in good enough shape to climb down there and hit her in the head. Maybe once, as recently as a year or so ago, but not now."

"You're right. I'm glad to hear she's off your list. I don't see how she could have poisoned the wine either. But I still think this ties in somehow. Cynthia?"

"It's possible. Agnes and her friend both identified the car from a picture, so that puts her on the road. We already knew she was driving around. She had purchased the same wine, and she had a history with Anita."

"But what about Walters?" I said. "How does it tie together? Was the wine meant for Anita, and he was collateral damage?"

"That's looking more likely. We got Anita's phone records late yesterday. There was a call from her cell to his after the meeting. It was a brief conversation, but enough to arrange to meet. We don't have an exact time for the accident, so it's possible."

"You don't sound convinced."

Jennie made a face. "It's possible, but the timing is tricky. And it's just too neat."

"I agree. There are too many connections between Walters and other people involved." I ticked them off on my fingers. "Cynthia Baker has an unusual interest in his work, which she says is related to the historical society. Anita—same, but she was doing an awful lot of digging into his past. I can't see her bringing him a bottle of wine for any reason. Sean Harris worked for him, and there's some debate about tenure there. I'm not sure exactly. But that also gives Sloane an interest. On the upside, it leaves out Jilly and Millicent."

"Millicent we've pretty much ruled out for the reasons we discussed. Jilly's neighbor saw her come home while he was out with his dog, and she went through a traffic camera a distance from the accident scene. The time stamp would make it tricky, though not impossible, for her to pull off either murder, never mind both. So she's not out, but we're not looking at her seriously."

"That's a relief. So it's down to Cynthia, Sloane, or Sean Harris, or some combination. With Anita accidentally poisoning Walters with wine meant for her?"

"In some scenarios."

"And if Anita didn't accidentally poison Walters, who would want to kill them both?"

"And who could have physically done it?" Jennie added.

"I know, I know, you're not a big fan of motive," I said, waving my hand at her.

"Because it's not enough to take to court," she replied. "I've got to go, but I'll let Sam know what you figured out about Millicent and the Ravenscrofts. He may see an angle we don't—he's lived here longer. I'm taking another look at the Harris alibis. We can place both of them on roads near the crime scenes that night."

"Wow, that's news. How'd you manage that?"

"Sam said his nose was still twitching every time he thought about them, so he called in a favor from the police in the next county. We've got traffic cam shots of them leaving home separately, going through Albany, and then into Raven Hill. I'm going to talk to them again. Call me if you come up with anything else. I feel like we're missing an important link—something that will seem obvious after the fact, you know?"

"Me too," I said.

I sat drumming my fingers on the table after Jennie left. If Anita had been hunting down information on the Raven-scroft family, to the point of going downtown and making copies of all the trust-related documents, it was important. It had to be related. All the legalese was beyond me, but at least I knew someone who could help.

I pulled out my phone and called Felicity James. I explained what I had and what I suspected. She was famil-iar with the bequest of the building and the issues with the trust, from volunteering with the Friends of the Library for years, but had never examined the original documents. She said she'd be happy to take a look, and I promised to drop everything at her office fifteen minutes later.

I decided that after that, I'd focus on the mechanics of both crimes. Maybe that would give me the who and thus the why. I was trying to come up with a plan of action when Jack came by with the coffeepot.

"You and Officer Webber making any progress on the case?" he said, refilling my cup.

"I am not an official part of any investigation," I said. "You know that."

Jack chuckled and pushed the creamer toward me. "Of course, but unofficially, Sam doesn't have the budget for the kind of research you can do, and he could certainly use the help. Your friend Jennie is sharp, but she's not going to hear things, the way you and I do, because she's a cop."

"True," I said as I stirred my coffee. Then what he'd just said sunk in. "What have you heard?"

"Not a lot," he said.

I narrowed my eyes. Jack grinned.

"Not a lot that's new, anyway. There's the usual talk about the Ravenscroft bequest and missing papers—that's among the older crowd. Then there's the group that can list a million reasons someone would want to do in Anita Hunzeker. They're a little younger and have been on a committee with her at some point. Then there's the college kids. A couple of our regulars go to Saint Catherine's, and they're more interested in the other guy that got killed."

"J. P. Walters," I said. "He worked there—department head."

"The kids don't think much of him," Jack said. "One complained that he has graduate students handling most of his teaching—just shows up to give the lecture. Another says that he spends all his time sucking up to donors and local bigwigs. He sounds like a petty bureaucrat that likes the trappings of the office, but not the work."

"I got that impression too. I don't know if that's enough to make someone want to kill him, though."

Jack shrugged. "Maybe he's fiddling with the finances or stole someone's work. That's the kind of thing that gets you in trouble in academia, right? But what I'd really like to know is if the same person set out to kill both of them or if it was a coincidence, or just an unlucky break for Walters."

"Nobody knows," I said. "Did Sam share any theories with you?"

"He doesn't like coincidences, but that's all he said when he stopped in for coffee this morning. Me, I think it was well planned."

"It would have to be. Tough to get from the accident scene to Walters's cabin and then away without being seen." I pictured the satellite images I'd looked at and remembered Dory's comment about the old farm roads. "You know, none of these places are that far apart. Can you think of a way to get from one to the other without using any main roads? Dory mentioned something about old farm roads, and I've found paths through the woods in odd spots."

Jack considered that for a moment. "A lot of the farms were broken up and sold decades ago. When I first moved here, we used to ride dirt bikes on the old fields. Most became housing, but others, the ones with barns in decent shape, were bought for equipment storage or renovated into something else. Still a few around, but almost everything's either paved over or grown over."

"Hmm. Well, it was a thought. Thanks, Jack."

He moved on to another table. I left and went straight to Felicity's office to drop off the documents I wanted her to review. She promised to take a look that day. Then I sat in my car and tried to figure out my next move. I wasn't ready to go home and face the pile of papers on my coffee table. Maybe a look at a bigger, older map of the area? We didn't have anything at the library or in the archives, but the historical society might. Someone had been looking at old maps the last time I was there. And maybe Cynthia would be in and would let something slip. I checked the time—they would have just opened. Off I went.

There were only four cars in the lot when I pulled in. One I recognized as Cynthia's. Perfect. If I didn't run into her, I'd pop back to her office to say hello. I walked into the front room. There were two women paging through old ledgers at a table. A trim, fiftyish man was straightening a rack of brochures. He turned and I could see he was wearing a badge that proclaimed him a volunteer whose name was Brian Simon. He greeted me with a smile and asked if I needed research help or just wanted to look around. With his glasses, button-down shirt, and khakis, he had the reassuring air of one of my college professors. I decided to save myself some time and put my research needs in his hands.

I explained that I wanted to look at maps of Raven Hill, both current and historical, and make comparisons. Keeping in mind what Jack had said about old roads being either paved or overgrown, I thought it might help to see what had changed. I'd discovered shortcuts down nameless roads, though admittedly that usually happened when I was lost. The mapping program I'd been using only gave me current routes, and I couldn't get satellite photos to order—I had to use whatever year and season they were taken. Besides, I liked old maps. I'd never found one that led me to a treasure, or even dragons, but hope springs eternal.

Within minutes, Brian had me set up at a table with maps of Raven Hill from different decades. I worked backward from the present, watching housing developments and strip malls disappear and parking lots revert to green space. The bulk of the building in the area had occurred in the last ten to twenty years, as the universities grew, and research centers and businesses expanded. Before that, it had been older neighborhoods that housed people who worked in Albany, and family farms or orchards.

The area near the center of the village had always been densely populated—for a small town. Nothing unusual there. People liked to live close to businesses and services. The manor was set a little apart from the central business district, which had expanded over time. Harriet had sold off the Ravenscroft land in chunks at intervals. What was closer to town became new neighborhoods, and what was farther out was a mixed bag of residential, agricultural, and light industry. You couldn't have paid me enough to go to those zoning board meetings.

I shifted the maps around and focused on the area around Winding Ridge Road. This hadn't changed much over time. The terrain was varied, with lots of streams that fed into the Ravens Kill. It also got hilly as it wound its way into the Helderbergs. There were not a lot of houses because there were not a lot of level places to build, and there was a lot of water. The lower part of Winding Ridge, where the Hunzekers lived, was a combination of woods and fields. Farther up, which was where Cynthia lived, was all woods and streams, punctuated by rocky outcroppings, based on the terrain map that Brian had helpfully provided.

I was tracing my finger along an unnamed road on one of the older maps when Cynthia appeared. She startled me—I'd been so focused on the faint lines in front of me that I hadn't heard her coming.

"Hello, Greer. What brings you here today?"

"Oh, just doing a little research. You have a much better map collection here than we do at the library."

Cynthia looked pleased. She came around the table and looked at the maps. She frowned.

"What are you researching?" she asked.

I scrambled for a reasonable response. Being honest and saying, *"Trying to figure out if you could have killed two people,"* was a bad plan. It not only lacked diplomacy, but it also put me on the wrong side of Lieutenant Sam O'Donnell's directive to keep my mouth shut and stay out of trouble.

"Er, well, you see, I—I have friends who are thinking of moving to the area, or rather, coming for the weekends. A weekend house is what they're after, and . . ."

"Oh, are those the friends who were helping at the book sale?"

"Um, yes, yes, that's right, Beau and Ben."

"How nice. So charming, both of them." Cynthia smiled. "The taller one told me he was dressed as the Marquis de Lafayette. Does he have an interest in history?" In her eyes appeared the predatory gleam of a volunteer coordinator who has spotted a potential recruit. Perhaps I could use this.

"He does, actually, but really has no time to indulge it. So busy. That's why they're looking for a weekend place, somewhere to get away and spend time on hobbies."

Cynthia was now invested in the imaginary house hunt.

"Hmm, where are you looking? Well, this is out by me—a bit off the beaten path. Although if they enjoy the outdoors?"

About as much as I did, which meant I'd walk to brunch as long as it was less than a mile away and there were sidewalks. But I could give her a somewhat honest answer.

"Ben is very interested in gardening," I said.

"I see. Some of these maps are quite out of date, though."

"Oh, I think it's always good to get the history of a place. You want to know what's been there before. And of course, with all the development, you need to worry about where water has been diverted and that kind of thing, don't you?"

Cynthia considered that. "I don't think you need to worry much about that here, though it's a fair point. Did they want something turnkey? Most of the houses in my neighborhood could use updating."

"I'm sure that would be fine. Renovation is not an issue. In fact, they thought the converted carriage house I live in was lovely. They'd be happy to repurpose something. Perhaps a barn? Like the one Felicity James lives in."

I was well into fantasy land here. Beau would be aghast at the thought. I should have had my story straight before I showed up.

"That's a lot of work, and there aren't many left standing. The only one I know of belongs to Richard Hunzeker. He used to keep supplies and old work vans there. Though he may have sold it along with the business. Well, I need to make some calls. Would you like me to give you a ring if any of my neighbors are thinking of selling?"

"Sure, that would be great. Oh, by the way, Cynthia, did you ever find what you needed for that grant? That was what Anita was looking for, wasn't it?"

Cynthia waved a hand. "Oh, that. Well, that's not a problem. There have been changes on the committee, and I think what we have will be sufficient." She gave me a big smile and headed for her office.

That was an about-face. I wondered if the "changes on the committee" were the result of someone killing off J. P. Walters. My bet was yes. I wondered how that had helped and if it gave Cynthia an even stronger motive. But—grant money? How much? Though it never paid to underestimate people who were truly passionate about something. There was a fine line between that and fanaticism.

I was about to go back to my maps when Brian approached me with an oversized bound volume in his hands.

"I couldn't help but overhear your conversation with Cynthia just now," he said. "I thought you might find this helpful. It's a collection of old surveys of the area. I'm sure Richard Hunzeker still owns that old barn, and I don't think it's ever been used for anything else. But these should help you out." He paused, then tsked. "It's too bad about Anita. Not an easy person, but not afraid to make an unpopular decision. She had backbone."

I thanked him and took the book. He told me he was going to lunch, but that if I finished before he got back, I could leave everything on the table, and he'd put it back where it belonged. Then he went on his way, and I took a look at the book of old surveys. The title page explained that it was the collection compiled by a resident of Raven Hill who had worked as a surveyor. Small libraries and historical societies often ended up with this kind of thing, and some of those bequests proved useful.

I found the surveys that matched the area I was looking at. There wasn't a survey for every property, but there was one for the Hunzeker land and adjacent acres, and several more around Winding Ridge Road. The barn Brian and Cynthia had mentioned was marked on one of the surveys. It wasn't far from the Hunzeker house, but was accessed from another road. It had originally been part of a different property. I went back to the map I'd been looking at when Cynthia interrupted me. There was a line that ran along the edge of the Hunzeker lot—was that a stream or a road? It wasn't named, so hard to tell. I compared it to the survey—same line, but it swung out to meet Winding Ridge. The survey indicated it was an access road. The lot it was on had no buildings other than the barn and a shed, and was wedge shaped, like a piece of pie. There were clusters of trees sketched in as well. Winding Ridge ran along one side, and Hilltop Road along the other. The two didn't intersect.

I followed Hilltop. In one direction, it went southeast and met the main road toward Albany. In the other it went up into the Helderbergs, where it met some smaller roads. One of those was where the Walters cabin was located. If you cut across that pie-shaped lot, you could get from Anita's accident scene to J. P. Walters's cabin without using a main road and passing a traffic camera. At least, you could if the terrain allowed. I thought of Agnes and her friend, and the vehicle that had raced toward them and then disappeared into nothing. There must be a way.

"By the pricking of my thumbs," I whispered, "someone murderous this way comes."

Chapter
Twenty-Two

Before I left the historical society, I took pictures of the map and the survey. I wanted to be able to send them to Jennie once I'd worked out more details of my theory. I zipped home and printed them out, then added them to the collection I had. I took all the various pieces and put them together as well as I could. I sketched in the old access road and the barn, and marked where all the traffic lights and cameras were. I was no artist, but it was good enough. I traced the route from where Anita went off the road, across the Hunzeker lot, and onto the road leading to J. P. Walters's place. Once you were within that triangle of cameras, you could move between locations without going through one and, at that time of night, in the dark, without much risk of being seen. As long as you could get across that lot, anyway. The terrain map suggested you could.

I went online and into the mapping program I'd used before. Pulling up the satellite images, I panned around until I found the area I wanted, and then zoomed in.

"It could work," I said.

I grabbed my phone and texted Jennie.

Can you talk? Found something.

A minute later the phone pinged.

Couple minutes.

I popped up and paced. If that shortcut worked, the most obvious suspect was Cynthia. Her comment this morning added weight to that. But it also put Sloane and Sean Harris back in the picture. They'd come in from different directions, but once in the area could move between locations and then leave the way they'd come. They could have worked together, though this way they didn't have to. But why?

My phone rang. Jennie.

"What've you got?" she said.

"A back way between crime scenes," I said. "Listen to this." I ran through what I'd found, told her I could send pictures of the various maps, and then repeated Cynthia's comment and my theory about passion and fanaticism.

"And from what you said this morning, either of the Harrises could be back in the picture," I added.

"They're definitely back in the picture," she said, her tone grim. "I just left Sean. When I confronted him with the traffic camera shot, he panicked. Told me he'd driven up to talk to Walters about his job. He'd heard that he might be shown the door—said it was departmental politics, though he stumbled over that—and wanted to plead his case. He told Sloane

265

he was going back to the office and that he might be late. He did stop at the office but then went to Walters's place. He said when he got there, the back door was open, and Walters was dead on the floor."

"Do you believe him?"

"I don't know. He said he checked for a pulse, and there was none, but the body was still warm. He bolted—said the scene was horrific and he got scared. He thought somebody must have killed Walters and could still be in the house, so he ran back to his car and took off. The timing of him coming and going supports a short visit."

"And you didn't find his prints, right?"

"He said he wore gloves except for when he checked for a pulse. It was a cold night, so that tracks."

"And Sloane lied to cover for him," I said. "That must be what Sam picked up on."

"Not exactly, and here's where it gets interesting. He said when he got home, Sloane wasn't there. She came in ten minutes later and said she'd gone to try to talk to her mother. They'd had an argument earlier and she wanted to clear the air. She had Caleb with her. He believed her because the kid was half asleep and said, "Went to Grandpa's" or something like that."

"But Anita wasn't there, and Richard didn't mention seeing her."

"Sloane said she saw her father in his workshop, but Caleb was asleep, and since her mother's car wasn't there, she turned around and came home. I'm going to see what she says, but right now she's not answering her phone, and her husband doesn't know where she is. She's been gone a couple of hours. At least she doesn't have the kid with her."

"Uh-oh. That doesn't sound good."

"No. But send me those pictures. I'll send them on to Sam. Someone needs to check your theory. Not you," she added quickly.

"I know. My car couldn't handle it or I already would have. I thought a nice, sturdy police SUV would be a better choice."

"True. You can stay put and try to figure out a motive for one of the Harrises to kill two people. I can't see a job teaching history being the reason."

I thought of the academics I knew and the heated departmental politics they described. Jennie might be underestimating the situation, but time would tell.

"Maybe." I couldn't resist a dig. "And I thought motive was overrated."

I heard a snorting noise and could picture her eye roll.

"It is, as a starting point. But if you've figured out the how, we're going to need a why. Juries like that."

"Right," I said. "I'll see what I can come up with."

We hung up and I sent pictures of everything I thought would be useful. She'd be able to follow, and so would Sam. Then I paced some more.

Motive. If one or both of the Harrises had done it, it wasn't about the manor and Anita's obsession with the new building, or the Ravenscroft family. If Cynthia was our murderer, the new building angle came back in. With both Walters and Anita gone, so was the pressure to merge collections and absorb the historical society into the library. At least for now. Cynthia seemed to think the removal of Walters from the equation would make for smooth sailing on the grant front, if there really was a grant. Getting rid of Anita as well would make her life easier on many counts. She had a bottle of the wine. And she knew the area.

Still, it didn't feel right. It was possible she'd just snapped, but I didn't think she had the nerve to pull off a double murder. With Millicent and Jilly out of it, and Richard with an alibi, that left Sean and Sloane Harris. Or both of them together. Probably not. It sounded like Sean had freaked out at the sight of his boss's body. We had only his word for that, though. And hadn't his work bio said he enjoyed gardening? Perhaps he was growing and distilling poisonous plants in his backyard and had actually gone to drop off a poisoned bottle of wine that night. With his mother-in-law's fingerprints on it? No, too much of a stretch.

Sloane. She was the more likely of the two, in my opinion. Nervy she might be, but that made her tightly wound enough to snap. She'd already threatened her mother—it would help to know what that was about. But then again, it sounded like the two had always been at odds. And as for her husband's boss—well, maybe she was fed up with him too. His death certainly made it unlikely that Sean would have to start looking for another job anytime soon. But that was more like two motives unless Sloane had gone right round the bend and started a killing spree. That didn't work even for me, never mind trying to sell it to a jury. I couldn't see her doing that and then pulling herself together enough afterward to keep everyone guessing for a week.

I plopped down onto the couch and rifled through my notes again. What angle hadn't I covered? Who could have done it? I'd done pretty well with that, though we still had three viable suspects. What was the motive? There were a few, but none of them worked for me for both murders. What was the common thread?

I looked at the words of wisdom from my old friend Poirot. *"The victim. One must always return to the victim."* In the absence of a better idea, I flipped to a fresh page. I wrote "Anita" on one side, and "Walters" on the other, and drew a line between them. I knew Anita better, so I'd start with her.

I started with the obvious: driven, efficient, energetic, abrupt, inconsiderate, ambitious, bull-in-china-shop approach. Also underhanded, manipulative, obsessive, and a possible blackmailer, though all that appeared to be more recent. Then I added the comments people had made since she died: good researcher, a stickler, a snob about her principles, a snob in general, not afraid to make an unpopular decision. Delightful. I reviewed my list and marveled that no one had killed her sooner.

Now Walters. He was trickier—I had only other people's impressions to go by. From what I'd inferred, he was ambitious, political, lazy, arrogant, and of reasonable intelligence, but not scholarly. A bit backhanded in the way he dealt with things, per his assistant, and someone who liked to hobnob with big donors and dump grunt work on people with less clout. So also a snob. Described as very fond of himself and very fond of his comfortable existence.

I reviewed my list to see what I had. Answer—two unlike-able people that someone had disliked enough to murder.

"Well, that's certainly helpful," I muttered.

There must be something else. I read through the list again. What connections were there other than Cynthia Baker and Sean and Sloane Harris?

Both Walters and Anita were historians. Walters had the PhD, but by all reports, Anita was as good or better with research. Walters was lazy on that count. He liked the trap-pings of the position, but not the work. Anita, on the other hand, was all about the work. And she had recently shown an unusual interest in *his* work. So I would as well.

I got my laptop and while that booted up, found all the printouts from Walters's thesis. I sighed. It looked just as riv-eting as the first time I'd seen it. Which is to say—not at all. I might still need the whole thing, but for the moment I was grateful I'd handed that off to Helene. I read through the table of contents and turned to the bibliography. It looked like Walters was illuminating the role of a minor player in the run-up to the Revolutionary War, a presumed loyalist who'd secretly provided aid to the patriots. It built on earlier research done by another scholar who'd used letters and diaries kept by the loyalist's spinster sister, who was herself sympathetic to the cause of freedom for the colonies.

Nothing wrong there. Walters had used the previous work as a jumping-off point to pursue his interest in the clandestine activities of the brother. He had also gone to original source material, in this case a cache of documents held by a local family. The name was familiar—I thought there was a small park in their honor somewhere in the capital district.

So what was the issue? Anita had either found one or thought she had. Having gleaned as much as I could from what I had, I opened up the union catalog I used to search for items from outside the system. Walters did not have a large body of research—it shouldn't take long to run it down. He might not have provided it for St. Catherine's, but it would be somewhere, and if it were cataloged anywhere, I would find it here.

After an hour of searching, I'd concluded that Walters was indeed lazy. He'd taken his thesis topic and refashioned it into a dissertation, with some additional material, and every bit of scholarly writing he'd done related back to the same topic. Nothing ground-breaking, but enough to pass muster at the schools he'd attended and worked for, especially if he was willing to take on administrative tasks. Not one for a mental stretch, our J. P., but mediocrity was not a crime. Plagiarism was, but I hadn't found or heard any evidence of that. Maybe Anita had.

I went into the resource sharing interface and took another look at every request Anita had placed. I recognized the ones I'd done for her, but there were several she'd placed herself, like the thesis. They all related somehow to the Walters thesis. She'd gotten a few articles and a book. What she'd requested and hadn't gotten was more interesting. The dissertation that Walters had used when researching his own was held in only one library, and the request had come back unfilled. The reason—missing. The author, Rebecca Griswold, had gotten her degree at a university in Vermont, about an hour and a half away. They owned the only copy of the dissertation. As far as I could tell, it had never been digitized.

I did a quick internet search. Dr. Rebecca Griswold was now a professor at another small college in New England. According to her bio on the school's website, she still taught one class a semester but was no longer serving as advisor to any students. Sounded like semiretirement, however that worked in academia. She'd have a copy of her own work. She also had office hours starting shortly. I decided to try calling her. If I could reach her, it would be faster than email. I got voicemail and left a message, saying I was a librarian helping a local historian with some research and wasn't having any luck finding what I needed through the usual channels. Worth a try.

I tapped my pen against the notepad. What else? What had I missed? I ran through all the conversations I'd had about Anita and Walters. Sister Mary Josephine had dealt with them both. She'd called Anita a stickler and Walters lazy and pompous, and theorized that we had an academic mystery on our hands. It was looking that way. I went to my bookshelves and surveyed my collection. I'd read quite a few mysteries set in universities, but not many of those scholarly crimes had made it into my permanent collection. I pulled *Gaudy Night* by Dorothy L. Sayers off the shelf—that was one of my favorites. Alan Bradley's *The Sweetness at the Bottom of the Pie* wasn't academic, but featured characters driven by their obsessions, and Flavia de Luce, the brilliant young detective and chemist, had a passion for poisons.

A passion for poisons. Anything could be poisonous in large quantities. A doctor had once told me that the most dangerous substance in most households was a large bottle of acetaminophen. But that wasn't what had killed Walters. What had Jennie said? Something vegetal? Who could make or get their hands on something like that?

My phone rang. It was the number I'd just dialed—Dr. Griswold. I answered with my work greeting, "Hello, this is Greer." Dr. Griswold introduced herself. Before I had the chance to ask her anything, she began to apologize.

"I'm so sorry about the delayed response. I only just got the message last week and haven't had a chance to call back. I've been out—hip replacement—so inconvenient, and right at the beginning of the semester. Now, you're with the Raven Hill Historical Society, is that right?"

"Actually, I'm with the library, but—"

"Really? I could have sworn the message said historical society, but I could be mistaken."

"Oh no, I think you may have heard from them. The library and historical society work together on certain projects. That's why I'm calling—it's a joint project, and one of their people was in an accident, and another is tied up with a grant deadline, so—"

"Ah, here it is. Yes, she did say she needed information for a grant. On the Valkenburg family. Subject of my dissertation."

"Yes, that sounds right. I'm trying to figure out—"

"Now, let me see. She also mentioned something about some letters, I think."

Deciding that attempting another question was pointless, I waited. I heard the rustling of papers. Her desk must look like mine. Possibly worse, I thought as the noise continued.

"Ah! Here it is," she said. "Are you still there?"

"Yes, I was wondering who—"

"Excellent! So many dropped calls these days. Makes you appreciate the landline. Your colleague was interested in my dissertation and the correspondence I used for my research. Of course, I also had personal journals and household ledgers. Scholars so often overlook the domestic sphere, and it can be so revealing, don't you think?"

"Yes, certainly," I said.

"Anyway, she wanted a copy of the dissertation, preferably in digital form. That's not available, but I do have an extra bound copy somewhere that I could dig out if necessary. Now what really interested me about her message was that she mentioned a local professor who had published on a related subject. She wanted to know if he'd ever contacted me."

"J. P. Walters?" I asked.

"Yes, that's right."

"Had he?" I asked.

"No," she said. "*I* contacted *him*. Must have been about thirty years ago. I'd read an article he published. It was going to be part of his dissertation. I got in touch because in the course of further research on the Valkenburg family, I'd come across something that contradicted one of his key points. He wouldn't have seen it—I found it in a collection of letters that were still held by the family of the writer. I wanted to let him know before he went much further with his work."

"What did he say?" I asked.

"I don't think I ever got a reply. It was right before I was leaving for a sabbatical, and I'd completely forgotten about it. It only came to mind when I heard the name of the town. Raven Hill. That's where the family lived—Raven Hill. Now what was their name? Stevenson, that's it. Now, do you happen to know if Ms. Hunzeker will still be needing the dissertation?"

Hunzeker. Bingo.

"I don't think so. You've given me enough to go on with the family names. It's been helpful—thank you."

Dr. Griswold said to get back in touch if I needed anything else, and hung up. I jotted down some quick notes on what she'd said, and then sat back and thought. What did I have here? Anita had followed up on the missing dissertation by contacting the author but hadn't gotten anywhere because Dr. Griswold had been off having her hip replaced. She'd also wanted to know if Walters had been in touch. Why? It sounded like she suspected that there was something not entirely kosher about his research. But how had she figured that out?

Then it hit me. *Gaudy Night.* One scholar had found something that disproved another's work. She could also prove he must have known about it. Anita had found something and was trying to determine if Walters had known his work was flawed. Cynthia had mentioned something when I spoke to her, something about receiving a collection of letters. At least that's what I thought she'd said. Since she was still on the suspect list, I didn't want to call and ask.

I checked the time. The historical society should still be open. Perhaps I could get the helpful Brian on the phone. I was in luck. I explained that I was helping a patron with his research and that Cynthia had mentioned the donation of some family letters, and could he tell me the name of the family?

He could. He was helping to organize them.

"It was the Post family that donated them," he said.

"Oh," I said, "No, that's not who he's researching."

"Wait, I'm sorry. They came down through the wife's family. Her maiden name was Stevenson. Does that help?"

"Yes, it does. Thank you. Oh, one more thing. This patron mentioned a lecture he attended that was given by J. P. Walters. He thought it was at the historical society, then thought it might have been another library. Do you happen to know?"

"That was here, maybe three weeks ago? Very interesting— he talked about the Valkenburg family. I think he's been researching them since graduate school."

"And when were the letters donated?" I asked.

"I think we've had those a couple of months. Most are from the time of the Revolutionary War. That's why Dr. Walters was invited to lecture—the board thought it would be a nice tie-in."

I thanked Brian for his help, and we hung up. The pieces were coming together.

Anita must have found the same letter Dr. Griswold had, either before or after the lecture. She'd probably mentioned it to Walters, just as Dr. Griswold had. Something about his reaction made her suspicious, so she'd started tracking down his publications.

I looked at the dates of those and the years his various degrees had been granted. Dr. Griswold had said she contacted him thirty years ago. That would have been when he was finishing his PhD program. If his dissertation had been almost complete, that would have set him back a bit. I couldn't guess how much. A true scholar would have done the work necessary to correct the record.

Anita would have. Walters—no. If it came out that he'd known his work was flawed, he might have been out of a job, especially since he'd continued to build on that work. It sounded like Anita suspected that he *had* known. What would she have done with that?

If recent history was a guide, she might have tried a little discreet blackmail. For grant money? No, Cynthia wouldn't have been so wound up about that once Anita was dead. She was worried when she thought he was still alive, but not after. Of course, Anita could have used the leverage to secure her son-in-law's position. Was that something that was important to her?

Maybe, but I didn't think it was enough. *The personality of the victim.* Anita was passionate about history. She had always been very principled about doing good research and getting it right, even Millicent had said so. What would have mattered to her was correcting the record. If Walters wouldn't do it, she would do it for him.

Which gave him a great reason to murder Anita. Except that someone was murdering him at around the same time, so that wouldn't work. Who else had a stake in this? Sean Harris, who didn't want to start looking for another job and maybe start again as an adjunct somewhere else? Sloane, who didn't want to uproot her family? But it wouldn't have been that bad—Caleb wasn't even in school yet.

Caleb. The light of his grandfather's existence. That's who would suffer the most if the Harris family had to move away—Richard Hunzeker. He'd sold his business and devoted himself to his grandson, his little "mini-me." There was not much affection between Richard and Anita, and he wasn't close to his daughter, from what I could see. He'd led a pretty lonely existence. But he loved Caleb, and Caleb loved him. Richard had told me he'd be lost without him. Agnes had said the same thing, almost—that she was lost when her husband died right after they sold their business. She'd started to drink to fill her empty days. What would Richard do? He'd taken a fair amount of abuse because of, and probably from, Anita, at least in my opinion. He faded into the background and went about his business. He didn't have the same kind of zeal and passion about anything that his wife did. Until Caleb came along. And now Caleb might be taken away. And why? Because Anita put her principles above all and felt a minor academic should be taught a lesson.

Richard Hunzeker had the motive, but he also had the alibi.

Didn't he? The neighbor had seen him come home and go into the house. Cynthia had seen his car and heard activity in the workshop. Richard was mechanical—he could have rigged something up. Only Sloane had claimed to see him there. She could be protecting him. She'd been afraid about something since the accident. I'd thought it was because she was worried about what might be in her mother's file about Sean Harris, and maybe that was part of it. Come to think of it, the missing files on Harris and Walters made sense—Richard didn't want any attention drawn to them. Grabbing the Ravenscroft deeds file might have been an accident. Either way, Sloane suspected her father was involved.

I checked the maps again. Richard could have come home, gone to the workshop, started up whatever gizmo he wanted to have running, and made it to the old barn he used to store work vans in. Were they all gone? Or did he have another vehicle there he could use?

I called Agnes Jenner. When she picked up, I asked her to describe the vehicle she'd seen race at them and disappear the night of Anita's murder.

"Well, I've never been very good with cars, you know. I can tell you that it was big."

"Like a truck? A pickup?"

"No, different shape. It was more like a square, and taller. I'd say it was gray, but it was hard to tell in the dark."

"Have you ever seen anything like it before?" I asked.

"Well, my plumber has something like it. He carries parts in the back. But his is white with blue lettering."

"Thanks, Agnes. You've been a big help."

A plumber needed to carry parts and tools. So did an electrician. If Millicent could have an unregistered car in an old barn, so could Richard Hunzeker. He could have run his wife off the road, then cut across the field and gone to the Walters' cabin. With a bottle of poisoned wine that he just happened to have? And with Anita gone, would he need to kill Walters?

That depended on how far things had progressed. Maybe Richard thought that if he could convince Walters that Anita wouldn't be a problem, he could save Sean's job. Sean had already heard departmental gossip that he was getting the axe, but Richard wouldn't know that. So Richard had appeared with a pretend peace offering? Walters would drink it eventually, even if he didn't open it that night. Richard had the wine, and if I could figure out how to get the poison in, so could he.

The fingerprints were an issue. I ran through some possibilities, but only one seemed likely. He had poisoned the bottle they had at home, wiped it down, and then gotten Anita to handle it. If he were careful, he could keep his prints off it. If not, well, he was the one who had picked it up from the store. He *had* just picked up the one in her car, which may have been a decoy. It probably was, I thought, running through the time line. If my theory held, he'd run his wife off the road, parked out of sight, and made sure she was dead. He'd called Walters, using Anita's phone to make sure where he was—that's why her phone was on the floor and not zipped into the pocket of her bag. Maybe she'd moved or made a noise, and that's when he'd grabbed the flashlight and bashed her. Jennie thought it had been a panicky move, not part of the original plan.

But where had the poison come from? When I thought it might be Millicent, that was easy. She had all kinds of plants, and her father's office held old bottles of who knew what plant-based remedies. And in sufficient quantities, some of them could be lethal.

I sat up. Millicent's house had been rewired by Richard Hunzeker, and not too long ago. He'd certainly worked unsupervised some of the time. He might have the alarm code. He could have taken anything. Millicent might not have noticed. He could have pocketed the stuff and kept it until he saw his chance. I felt a little sick at the thought—he must have hated his wife for a long time.

I called the library. Jilly picked up, told me Millicent was in the staff room, and connected me.

"It's Greer. I have a question. It has to do with Anita's death. I know you didn't have anything to do with it, but I'm trying to figure something out. It has to do with plant-based medicines."

There was a brief silence. "All right. What is it you need to know?"

"I know your father was truly knowledgeable about them. I've been told that, and I saw his books and that case where he kept bottles of tonics, things like that. What I was wondering is if you know of anything he might have had that would act as a convulsant, especially if too much were taken."

"A convulsant?" Millicent sounded surprised. "That's not at all what I expected." Now she sounded relieved. "No, I can't think of anything . . ." She trailed off, and there was another brief silence. "At least, I don't think so. To be honest, I never looked in that cabinet after he died. I only walked through his office to go to the greenhouse. It's possible. I'd have to look something up. Why do you ask?"

"I think someone took something from the office or the greenhouse and used it to poison a bottle of wine."

"But no one's been in there."

"Richard Hunzeker?"

"Richard? Yes, when he did the wiring. He was there on his own most of the time. And the cabinet is locked, but the key is right in the desk. But I thought the police had ruled him out."

"I'm not sure his alibi will hold up. Once you've checked, can you call me back? Can you do it from there, or do you need to go home?"

"I can do it from here," Millicent said. "It'll be easy to find. There are certain local varieties of hemlock—never mind, I'll call you as soon as I've narrowed things down."

"Thanks, and be careful. Jilly and David are both there tonight, aren't they?"

"Yes, and yes, I'll be careful."

I called Jennie. She picked up right away.

"Did you find Sloane? Because I think she's lying about seeing her father that night. And find out from whoever was checking that field if there's an old van in that barn."

"We're there now. That's where Sam found Sloane. He came to check the terrain. On his motorbike."

"Sam has a—"

"Yep. And he found her in the barn. Searching an old van that used to belong to her father's company. He's talking to her now. She's not saying much, but I think she's terrified."

"I think I know why," I said, and gave her an abbreviated version of what I'd found out. I ended with, "So she either didn't see him, or she's an accessory."

"Let me put it to her that way and see what she says." Jennie's tone was grim. I heard a brief conversation and recognized Sam's voice. Then I heard a wail. Sloane.

"I'll call you right back," Jennie said.

Chapter
Twenty-Three

~

I hung up and paced. This had to be right. If Millicent could verify that something had been stolen from her father's old medicine cabinet, it had to be Richard. I checked the time. It hadn't been long since I had hung up with Millicent. Calling her now would only slow things down. I waited, willing either Millicent or Jennie to call me back. I paced some more, running through everything again. Then I checked the time—the library would be closing soon. I picked up my phone and dialed the number that went straight to the archives. It rang and rang. Maybe she was helping someone. I'd try Reference.

As I was about to dial, my phone rang—Jennie.

"You were right. Sloane didn't see her father. She wanted his help talking her mother out of blowing the whistle on Walters. She didn't want to move, and she knew her father would be devastated. She checked the house when he wasn't in his workshop, thinking he had gone inside for something. Then she decided to check the barn because he still keeps supplies in there. She didn't go in, but she could see that it was empty—the door was partway open—no lights and no van. So she drove home."

"Are you going to arrest him?"

"We'll bring him in for questioning when we find him. He's not at home. I just left there. I saw the neighbor—he was out with his dog when Richard left. According to him, that was a while ago. He said something about fuses."

"The library," I said. "He's at the library. And Millicent's there, checking on the poison. I asked her about them. She should be in the archives, but she's not answering."

"I'm on my way," Jennie said.

So was I. I grabbed my keys and flew down to my car. Fortunately, there was no traffic on Main. Dusk was falling, and few people were out. I pulled into the library lot and saw Jennie's SUV stopped right in front of the door. As I got out of my car, the lights started going out in the building.

I ran inside. I smelled something like burning rubber, and more lights went out. David and the page were herding people toward the door, and I could hear Jilly yelling instructions from the front part of the hall. I ducked into my office and pulled my little headlamp out of my drawer. I turned it on and stuck it on my head and used the light to find my flashlight. When I got back to the hall, I saw Jilly up front, guiding people out the big double door.

"That's everyone, I think," she said as she heard me come up behind her. "Greer, what are you doing here? I thought you were David."

"He's getting people out the back. Rachel is helping. Where's Millicent?"

"I think she's upstairs. I saw her talking to Richard Hunzeker in the Local History section—she had one of those big, illustrated books on plants in her hands. The next time I looked, she was gone, but he was paging through it. I was surprised—when he got here, he told me he'd be in the basement, because he'd finally figured out the problem with the wiring between the fuse box and—oh my God!"

I turned and saw black smoke billowing out from the back stairwell. It seemed to be coming from the basement. Or the boiler room. This was a disaster.

"Go," I said to Jilly. "Hit all the alarms on your way out. Something's got to be working. I'll look for Millicent."

"But—"

"Jennie Webber is here. She was going to the archives. We'll get Millicent and get out. Now go."

I turned and ran up the main stairs as the last of the lights went out. The alarms started going off. I got to the door of the archives and stopped. Jennie was grappling with Richard Hunzeker, hampered by the fact that he was holding one of the antique pewter candlesticks from Millicent's desk and was swinging at her wildly. He connected. Jennie dropped to the floor. He turned and raced for the door, not hesitating when he saw me. I gripped my flashlight, stepped aside, and took a swing. I caught him a glancing blow in the shoulder, but he kept going, around the corner and down the stairs into the thickening smoke.

I went into the archives, shutting the door behind me in the hope of keeping the smoke out. I went to Jennie. Her head was bleeding, but she opened her eyes when I called her name.

She was dazed but conscious. I looked up at Millicent. She was pale and silent. I thought she might be in shock.

"I'm not sure what's burning, or where, but the halls are full of smoke. Help is coming, but we need to get out. I've always suspected there was a way down from here, another way no one knew about. Is there? Millicent!"

Millicent focused on me then. After a second, she nodded. "It comes out in Horatio's study. Can she walk? The passage is narrow."

"I'll drag her if I have to. Open it. We don't have much time."

Smoke was starting to seep in under the door. I hoped it wasn't too bad in the study and that any fire was far away. A passage might function as a chimney otherwise. Then we'd have to brave the hall and the main stairs. Richard Hunzeker could be anywhere, and I didn't want to gamble on his state of mind.

Millicent turned and opened the door to the attic stairwell. It was in the far corner of the room. You wouldn't notice it unless you were looking for it. She came back and tried to help me with Jennie, but I could tell she was having trouble breathing. I handed Millicent the flashlight and said, "I've got her. Lead the way."

Jennie struggled upright and leaned on me. She was more coherent but still wobbly. "I can do it," she said. "Let's go."

We followed Millicent into the stairwell. She pushed at part of the wall, and I heard a click. The wall swung open, and she disappeared into the rectangle of darkness it left. She pointed the flashlight downward, and I could see steps. I followed her in, grateful that for the moment the air was clear. That would end when she opened the door at the bottom. I gave her a head start. I didn't want to stumble with Jennie and send all three of us tumbling down the stairs.

The passage was steep but narrow. I wedged Jennie between me and the wall, and we slithered downward. Millicent was pressed against what looked like a solid wall at the bottom. I heard another click, and it opened. Smoke rushed in, but we could still see. We came out under the ledge with the stuffed raven on it. Jennie stumbled, and Millicent took her other arm. We staggered out into the hall and made our way onto the porch. I propped Jennie on the rail. I needed to catch my breath now that there was clean air to breath. Millicent was gasping too. I could hear sirens, but I knew we weren't in the clear yet.

"We've got to get away from the manor," I said. "We don't know what's burning. It could be the boiler."

Jennie started to shake her head and groaned.

"Electrical," she said. "The smell."

"Okay, good to know. But we've still got to move."

"Can you manage her without me?" Millicent asked.

"Yes, I think so. Come on, Jennie." I put her arm over my shoulder and turned us toward the stairs.

"I'm sorry," I heard Millicent gasp. "I must—I forgot—" The rest was lost in the sound of sirens.

"What? Millicent! No!" I turned my head enough to see her stagger back into the manor. I couldn't stop her. Jennie started to turn. It threw me off balance, and we both tumbled down the steps.

The wind knocked out of me, I lay on the ground until I saw an ambulance skid around the corner of the building. It caught us in the headlights and drove straight across the lawn. A man on a motorcycle followed close behind. Within seconds, an EMT was checking me over, asking questions and carefully helping me up.

"What happened?" The man in the motorcycle took off his helmet. It was Sam O'Donnell. I gaped for a minute.

"Did you hit your head?" he asked.

"No, but Jennie's hurt." I explained what had happened as best I could. Sam got on his radio. Jennie and I were moved to the back of the ambulance. We sat side by side, wrapped in blankets, trying to see what was happening amid the smoke and flashing lights. I watched the door, hoping to see Millicent. An EMT bandaged Jennie's head. I heard a radio squawking.

"They're taking someone out the back on a stretcher," Jennie said to me. "That's all I caught." She moved her head and winced.

There was activity at the front door. We both leaned forward, trying to see. It was two uniformed officers, a handcuffed Richard Hunzeker between them. He was talking nonstop. It sounded like he was weeping.

"I didn't do it. I didn't start a fire. I was trying to fix it. I finally figured it out. I came to fix it, and then I saw her with that book, and I knew she knew. I had to stop her. But I would never hurt the library. Caleb loves the library."

The sound faded away. I believed him about the library— he came to try and fix something in a place important to his grandson. It was bad timing that he had run into Millicent, looking up local varieties of hemlock. I closed my eyes, trying not to cry myself. If I started, I didn't know if I'd ever stop. I sat like that until I felt someone touch my shoulder.

"Greer?"

It was Helene. "Are you alright?" she asked.

I nodded. "I think Jilly and David got everyone out," I said. "But Millicent went back in. Do you know if she's okay?"

"I don't. I just got here. I've seen Jilly and David. Rachel too. They said everyone got out but that you and Jennie might be in the front. So I came around. Just take it easy. I'll find out what's going on."

We didn't have to wait long. Sam appeared on the porch, spotted us, and walked over.

"Helene. I'm glad you're here," he said. "Most of the staff and patrons made it out without injury."

"Millicent?" I asked.

"We found her in the study," he said.

"And?"

He looked down for a second before he met my eyes.

"I'm sorry," he said.

Chapter
Twenty-Four

Millicent's house had the feel of a place long abandoned, though it had been only days since she locked the door and left for work for the last time. I had met with the lawyer that morning—a brisk, no-nonsense woman about ten years my senior, named Patricia Burke. I was invited to call her Patricia. She was not a Pat. We spent a couple of hours going over everything.

"She said there were a couple of documents she wanted you to have, to make it easier to sort things out, but that she'd left them in the desk in the study. She didn't get a chance to drop them off here, so you'll probably find them in her desk at home. She also wanted to make sure you got these."

She handed me an accordion file, neatly tied, and a sealed letter. My name was written in Millicent's elegant handwriting, with the words "Personal and Confidential" beneath. The envelope was made of quality paper, the kind now so rarely used it seemed almost exotic.

"Now," Patricia continued, "I don't know what's in either of those. Millicent said you'd understand, but if you need help with anything, don't hesitate to call. I'm not interested in running up a bill, but I'd rather get things right the first time. She warned you there were some complex elements to this, yes?"

"Yes."

Patricia nodded. "Good. You know where to find me." She'd handed me her card and walked me out. I had spent a few minutes sitting in my car, deciding on my next steps. Patricia had given me a list of tasks, to which I had added notes as we talked. I would have to spend time in Millicent's house, doing everything from finding the aforementioned documents to clearing out her belongings and prepping the place for sale. The thought made me sad. The first visit would be the worst, so I decided to get it over with. The library was closed while the manor was being evaluated for safety. That gave me a few days off, but I might have to start pitching in with planning and inventories soon. I'd pick up lunch at the Market on Main—I wasn't up for chatting with anyone at the Java Joint—and spend the rest of the day at Millicent's. It was as good a time as any. I glanced at the sky—there was a storm rolling in.

So here I was. The house was chilly. I checked the thermostat and found it was set to lower the temperature during the day. I overrode it and went into the sunroom. This would be my base of operations. I noticed that Millicent had laid a fire, perhaps in anticipation of a cool night spent in her comfortable chair with a book. I felt tears prickle in my eyes. Too much had happened, but this was no time to fall apart. There was a lot to do.

"Get a grip, Greer," I said aloud. There was no one to hear me talking to myself, but the sound of my voice pushed back against the emptiness of the house. I picked up my list, notepad, and pen, and got to work. Per Patricia, Millicent said that she'd cleaned out a lot of her belongings in the past several months. This was true. The upstairs closets were mostly empty, holding only spare bedding. Millicent's room was tidy, the bed made and some items in the hamper. Her closet held a moderate number of the classic styles she preferred—if she'd set out to create a capsule wardrobe, she couldn't have done better. There were some well-worn sweaters within easy reach, and others that were dressier or in better shape stacked on a shelf, with bars of cedar between the piles. Millicent had left nothing to chance. Vowing to clean out my own closet and dresser, I made a note to get cedar bars myself, to discourage moths in the warmer months.

The bathroom was equally tidy. I bagged the prescription drugs to bring to a drop-off location. There weren't many, and those were related to cardiac issues. No painkillers—she'd managed the arthritis with over-the-counter products. I decided to get rid of the lot. Tomorrow was trash day according to the schedule I'd seen on the fridge. I filled up the wastebasket next to the vanity, added notes to my list of things to toss and to donate, and went downstairs to have lunch.

I cleaned out the fridge while my soup heated, and hauled the bag into the garage where Millicent kept her trash can. I'd roll it out before I left. The recycling can was half empty. I'd take a look at the blue bin I saw in the pantry, but I thought it could wait another week. I checked the soup, decided it needed more time, and went into the pantry to take stock. I'd be able to get the unopened nonperishables to the food pantry with a couple of boxes. I'd bring those next time. I grabbed an armload of open items to put in the trash and used my foot to pull out the recycle bin for the empty packaging. It had more in it than I'd anticipated. When I returned with some cereal boxes, I spotted something shiny and red in one corner. Shoving aside the week's local newspapers and recent catalogs, I fished out a tin. It was from Tea Total, and the label read "Autumn Falls Rooibos."

I paused, then took it out and put it aside. I sorted through the rest. Other than the papers and catalogs, I found a couple of newsletters, several advertisements, and a colorful box that had held a bottle of CBD oil tablets. But no bottle. There hadn't been one upstairs. She might have had them with her or kept them at work. I paused, bits of conversation coming back, images of an unusually chatty Anita, and Millicent saying she was looking for her tea. I pulled the box out and put it with the tin, then put everything else back, hauled the bin to the garage, and emptied it. When I came back, I put my lunch on a tray, added the tin and the box, and carried it into the sunroom.

Since I planned to tackle the desk in the corner that afternoon, I lit the fire. The skies outside were steel gray, and the temperature was dropping, along with my mood. The warmth and light from the flames could only help. I settled into Millicent's chair, studied the tea tin and the box, ate my lunch, and thought. The wind had picked up, and sudden squalls of rain were hitting the windows by the time I carried the tray back into the kitchen. Wanting something hot, but not in the mood for tea, I found a packet of cocoa and made that instead.

Back in my chair, I poked the fire and pulled the accordion file and letter toward me. Letter first. It would explain what the file was about and hopefully what documents it was Millicent had meant to leave with Patricia. I opened the envelope and unfolded a letter several pages in length, written on the same heavy cream paper.

Greer,

I have instructed Patricia Burke to give you this letter upon my death. What you do with the information it contains is up to you. Perhaps it is cowardly of me to abdicate this responsibility—I think so—but I am so very tired. I believe that the time I have left is short, and I am not equal to the task. I trust in both your judgment and your integrity.

Well. I was both touched and apprehensive. Though I had my suspicions, I was uncertain of what I might find. I read through the rest of the letter quickly. I was at times surprised, but not shocked. When I finished it, I sat for a minute, then began it again, lingering over certain sections. I still had questions.

The documents I have left with Patricia will validate a suspicion I believe you hold: I am the daughter of Horatio Ravenscroft.

The story was roughly what I'd pieced together. Elizabeth had wanted a child and been unable to conceive. Her husband was consumed with his research and didn't see her pain. Horatio, who had always admired her, did.

In my mother's defense, she loved and respected them both, though she could not forgive herself for the deceit.

I couldn't see why not —neither man had placed Elizabeth's needs above his own. They were of a type, each engrossed in his own interests, and Elizabeth got what was left. She'd used what agency she had to achieve her goal.

I don't know that my legal father ever knew. If so, he never revealed it through action or word. We had a strong relationship. Horatio obviously knew but acted in all ways as the doting uncle. It would not surprise me if his sister Harriet knew as well. Little got past her, and I suspect that certain loopholes were left in the wording of the trust for that reason.

I was unaware of all of this until I nursed my mother through her final illness. She wanted me to hear the story from her, as she wasn't sure what Horatio would do after her death. His brother and sister were both gone, and he was very much alone. He took my mother's diagnosis badly, though she made him agree to say nothing while Jonathon Ames was alive. She made me promise never to tell anyone, to do whatever was necessary to keep her secret. And so I have, until now.

"Never to be told." Nothing like a deathbed confession to rock your world, and this one was a doozy. Today, nobody would blink. At the time, it would have been a major scandal. And Millicent had been about twenty-five. That the illness and death of her mother, the responsibility to two fathers, and the weight of the secret had warped her life became clear as I read on.

There were always rumors, but after a time they faded. Talk of a missing will or codicil would resurface periodically. It took me a long time to figure out why. Once I did, I realized how stupid I'd been. Margaret Emerson was Harriet's closest friend, and she and her husband were the obvious choice to serve as witnesses to a will. Both Harriet and Horatio would trust their discretion. Margaret, as I recall, kept both a calendar and a diary. Peg must have found something when she was going through her parent's papers.

Yes, she had.

I regret Peg's death, so public and undignified. I had no idea how ill she was, how little time she had left. I lashed out when she came to me with what she had found (and what I suspect you have since found). We had been friends all our lives. I apologized when I brought her that last cup of tea. She was gracious enough, but I knew that she wouldn't let it go.

Right on both counts. Peg hadn't let it go, and I had found her evidence.

Dr. Jonathon Ames taught me many useful things. He was a healer in the ancient sense of the word—one who made the sick well and did his best to alleviate suffering. I was heartbroken when he told me about the cancer. He wanted to die at home— he had no wish to linger and end his days in a hospital, so I did my best to care for him. I followed his instructions to the letter. His wish was granted. His illness was brief. Death came before the pain became unbearable.

So I had been told. Millicent went on to say that she grieved both her parents deeply, and in retrospect, held on to her mother's secret and her father's memory in an unhealthy way. Her father's office, Horatio's study, all the ephemera related to the Ravenscroft family—she needed those vignettes of happier, more normal times and had become obsessive about maintaining them

It's no excuse—I could have, should have—sought help.

"Give yourself a break, Millicent. At the time, that wasn't really done." I shook my head, unable to envision Millicent in therapy. I read on.

Millicent had taken over her mother's position as secretary to Horatio Ravenscroft. She described their relationship as cordial and warm. She enjoyed the research element, and Horatio split time between his proposed monograph on Poe and his desire to collect as much material as possible to populate a library and archive. He purchased the morgues of small, local papers as they went out of business or were acquired. He did the same with collections from historical societies and weeded materials from libraries. The two of them had done a good job, I thought, since I was sure Millicent had a hand in the selection process. She'd worked in a private library before coming back to Raven Hill. She'd mentioned that to me before and included more information in this letter.

Horatio, like the rest of his family, suffered from a heart ailment. He knew when he was nearing the end of his life, and it

was then that he told me what he had done. The documentation was very thorough, as you can see. He left it to me to decide. I chose to keep the secret.

But she kept the documents. Why? Was that the archivist in her? Or did she need that connection to her parents, to all the people who had raised her?

As time went on, I could see the limitations of the trust. The needs of the community grew along with the population and advances in technology. I was not a dinosaur—I knew something would have to give. But then Anita Hunzeker joined the board and became obsessed with a new building. While I agreed with her on many counts, some were out of the question, and her approach made me dig in. Childish, I know, but there was no compromise with her. I started to become paranoid, believing any number of people were looking for evidence of the truth. I behaved badly, attempting to frighten both you and Vince Goodhue, and for that I apologize.

Looks like Jennie's theory was right. Millicent *had* tried to scare me and had nearly run me over.

It was then that I started to come to my senses. I knew the truth would have to come out, but I wanted to do it on my terms. If only Anita had let it rest for a bit, but no. That woman brought out the worst in me.

No kidding. Anita had the same effect on almost everyone.

I confess I wanted her out of commission for a short time, so I could consult with my attorney and come to terms with what I needed to do. I did not anticipate the car accident and was relieved to learn that it was through the actions of another that my reprieve had come.

If I had wondered before, I wondered more now. But that was all she said on that subject. Instead, she moved on to me. She apologized again for laying her burden, her secret, on me, and then referenced the conversations we'd had over the past months.

I know that you have your own burdens, your own ghosts. Please, learn from my mistakes. Bring the truth, no matter how unflattering, how painful to yourself or others, into the light of day. Taking the easy road will not bring you peace. You must discover what really happened the night of your husband's death and in the time leading up to it. I wish I could be of greater help, but I have done what I can. I've followed a line of inquiry suggested by your comments and a story I've been following in the news. I believe it has merit, but I leave it to you to decide. If it does, I have saved you doing this research yourself. If not, I know you will appreciate the thought behind it.

I looked at the thick accordion folder Millicent had left for me. She had asked some questions over the summer that started me thinking. If we were on the same track, she had saved me a great deal of time. I'd dig into that file shortly. But that wasn't all she'd done.

You will need to go back to the city to sort this out. I have taken the liberty of giving your name to a colleague at a specialty library in Manhattan. Because of the bequest of a large private collection, they will be in need of additional help for several months next spring. The contact information is below. It will not only put you where you need to be, I believe you will enjoy the work. Your ability to keep secrets will serve you well there.

That had raised my eyebrows, but when I saw the name of the library, I could see her point. She had gone above and beyond, and with the future of library operations in limbo, this opportunity could work out well. Millicent had left me with a few moral dilemmas, but I was grateful for this.

There were other things—she had left me a list of books from her personal collection that I was to take for myself, because I might find them useful in the course of my investigation into Dan's death. The list was esoteric, to say the least. Some of these must have been her father's. She also instructed me to take whatever mementos I wished from her home or her desk at work, and she mentioned the Olivetti specifically. Done. Then she wrapped it up.

> *I thank you again for taking on this task. Please know that whatever you decide, I support.*
> *I am glad to have gotten to know you, and I value our friendship, however brief it has been.*
> *I wish you every good thing, Greer.*
>
> *With much fondness,*
> *Millicent*

There was a lot to digest here. Even after a third reading, I wasn't sure I'd taken it all in.

"Oh, Millicent. What did you do?" I asked. What would I have done? And if I found Danny's killer—what would I do? I shook my head. That was for another time. I had things to do now.

One thing was clear: I needed to find the documents she referred to. Felicity had determined that the trust wording allowed for some changes in the disposition of assets. If there was a later will, or a codicil, or another legal document signed by a Ravenscroft and duly witnessed, those wishes would be honored. There would be jumping through legal hoops, but that was the gist of it.

I got up and went to the desk in the corner. It was an antique drop front with drawers and cubby holes. There was a wooden file cabinet beneath. I opened it up and went through every inch of it. Nothing. I checked the file cabinet. Nope. I tried the desk again, making sure I pulled out the drawers and felt behind the wooden slats that formed the cubbies. She'd said the study—perhaps she'd meant her father's office. I gave that a thorough search and came up empty again. I didn't think there were any other desks in the house, but I checked anyway. There were not. Just in case she'd taken them out of the desk in preparation for bringing them to her lawyer, I went through her bedroom and closet. Still nothing.

Frustrated, I went back downstairs. Maybe she'd tucked them into the other file she'd left me. I sat and opened it up. It was well organized—handwritten notes, printouts of news stories, legal precedents, and financial regulations. A prospectus, IPO information—things related to Danny's company. There were marginal notes containing cross-references and questions. Following all these different threads was a lot of work, even for a trained researcher. Millicent was good. Then I remembered that Harriet had planned to teach her about the stock market as soon as she was old enough. Looks like she had. Harriet probably could have pulled this off too, though it would have taken longer without the internet. But there were no legal documents, and nothing relating to the Ravenscrofts.

I sighed and sat back. Maybe her desk at work? I'd check whenever I could get back into the manor. Tired and uncertain what to do next, I started flipping through the file again. Millicent had started her notes with "Follow the money!" I smiled. Good advice. Dan had been a finance guy. That was my theory too. I read through a couple newspaper articles. Millicent thought she had found a parallel to another company, one that had gone south in a spectacular way. As I read more, I thought maybe she was onto something. It was an angle I hadn't considered. A picture began to form. I was missing information, but I had a workable theory. Follow the money, indeed. If I was right, it was a small fortune. Enough for someone to kill for, at least once and maybe twice. That I knew of, anyway. Which meant they wouldn't hesitate to get rid of me if I showed up asking inconvenient questions. I had known I needed to be careful, but it would take more than that. Self-defense training? Not my thing, but I had no choice. A geyser of rage bubbled up within me, as it had increasingly often in the last few months.

A gust of wind hit the window. I jumped and realized the fire had gone out. It was late afternoon, and I was chilly. There was nothing else I could do here today. I put everything back in the file, including Millicent's letter. I cleaned up from lunch, made sure some lights were on timers, and double-checked the fire. After a long look at the empty tea tin and box, I picked them up and pushed them deep into the bag of trash. All that was left to do was take it out before I drove off.

I picked up my coat, then put it down. I drifted around the room, restless, irritated that I hadn't found what I was looking for. After examining the art on the walls and pulling a couple of books off the shelves, I came to the pictures I'd seen on Sunday afternoon. I picked one up. Millicent had said to take what I wanted, and I wanted this—the photo of Millicent and her beautiful boys.

I was turning to put it in my bag when something struck me. I turned back to the remaining photos. Elizabeth Ames at her typewriter, in the office with Horatio, who was standing near his desk. Then there was the one of Millicent with Horatio, the two of them laughing. What had she said? He'd taught her a magic trick—he loved tricks and puzzles of all kinds. And there it was on the desk, visible in both photos. The puzzle box. It was still on the desk—a part of the permanent display. I'd tried to open it once, thinking it held fountain pens or some such, and then realized what it was. But it was barely larger than an envelope, and not more than an inch deep. The papers I was looking for wouldn't all fit. Somewhere else in the desk? And then I had it.

"'The Purloined Letter,'" I said. The Poe detective story I'd read last week held the answer. The missing letter was hidden in plain sight, among other letters. On Horatio's desk was a wooden tray, more of an in-box/out-box set up on two levels. I'd seen it every time I was in there—nothing ever changed. On the top was opened correspondence; on the bottom, sealed envelopes with typed addresses. I'd looked through them once. All of them were business related, addressed locally. I'd thought they were props, but if I remembered correctly, at least one was addressed to "law offices of." It was possible.

What had Patricia said? "In the desk in the study?" I'd thought the phrasing was odd—why no pronoun? "Her desk" would have made more sense, but at the time I thought Patricia had misspoken. But if she was quoting Millicent exactly, this would make sense.

I'd need permission to go into the manor. It was both a crime scene and still being inspected for safety. I'd start with Jennie, but I wanted to be as sure as I could before I asked for that favor. I found Patricia's card and called. Once I got her on the phone, I explained what Millicent had written in her letter, and told her about my fruitless search of her home. Then I asked her if she remembered exactly what Millicent had said about the location of the documents.

"I do. She said, 'the desk in the study.' I thought it was oddly phrased, but then decided that either she had desks in more than one room or that she was just tired."

"I think she meant the desk in the study at the manor," I said.

"Horatio Ravenscroft's old office? Yes, that would make sense. No one's allowed in there, are they?"

"Um, no," I said. "But as a staff member, I check it when we're closing. But no one touches anything."

"I think it's worth a look. I haven't seen the original trust documents, but I don't think this one's going to be easy to untangle."

"I can get you copies of those. Felicity James has a set. I can ask her to drop them off."

"That would be helpful. I'll be here until six, and back at nine tomorrow. Do you need any help getting access to the building? The sooner we have them, if they're there, the better I'll feel."

"No, I think I can get in. I'm calling a friend on the police force now."

"Good luck. I'll wait to hear from you."

I hung up and dialed Jennie. She picked up on the first ring. I could tell by the background noise that she was at the station.

"I need a favor. Two actually," I added, looking at the folder Millicent had left for me.

"What's up?" she asked.

I explained what was going on as quickly as I could. "So I need to get into Horatio Ravenscroft's study. The fire was nowhere near there, and it's right inside the front door. Can we do that? It's urgent."

"Give me a minute," she said. I heard muffled conversation. Then she came back.

"Sam said the safety inspection is done, though not all the paperwork is signed off. Our people are going in tomorrow. If we limit our visit to that area, I can take you in."

"I'll meet you there in ten," I said. "Park in the old lot. It's closer to the front door."

We hung up. I wrapped the three photos in my scarf and put them in my tote, then gathered the rest of my things, set the alarm, rolled the trash to the curb, and left for the manor. Jennie pulled into the lot right behind me. I grabbed my flashlight—we had a little daylight left, but the interior would be dark, and the electricity was off.

I stood next to Jennie on the porch as she removed the crime scene tape and unlocked the door. I never came in this way. I looked over my shoulder. The trees were swaying in the wind. For a moment, I thought I spotted the path to the old cemetery. Then it was gone. Thunder rumbled in the distance. I heard the croak of a raven but couldn't spot him.

When the door swung open, I was hit with the smell of acrid smoke. I coughed, transported back to Tuesday night.

"Are you ready?" Jennie said.

I nodded. We turned on our flashlights and went in. There was light coming in through the peacock glass above the door, but it was gray and flickering because of the storm. The rest of the main hall, the reading room, and the stairway were dark. Our flashlights barely made a dent. It didn't matter—we'd lost power so often I could find my way around with no light, and I led the way into the study.

The desk was pushed back, the items on top jumbled. That must have happened when the EMTs were working on Millicent. I shoved the thought aside and searched the piles on the blotter. I spotted the puzzle box and picked it up. Something moved inside when I gave it a shake.

"We'll need to take this," I said, handing it to Jennie. "I'm not sure how to open it." She took it from me and moved closer to the window for better light. I went back to searching the desk. The bottom of the letter tray still held all the sealed envelopes. I pulled them out and sorted through them. Two were addressed to a local law firm, the others to various businesses. I opened the ones to the lawyer. Bingo. Last will and testament of Horatio Ravenscroft, signed and witnessed by Peter and Margaret Emerson. There was a letter as well, also signed by Horatio, stating that Millicent Ames was his natural daughter with Elizabeth Ames and that he was therefore leaving her all his worldly goods and complete discretion over the disposition of the trust and the assets held therein. This matched what was in the will, and there was more legal language in both, but if it held up, it looked like Millicent scooped the lot. Would it hold up, though, if she were already dead before this was probated? Or would the trust take care of that? And what about Millicent's will? How did all these interact? My head started to throb.

I heard a click. I turned to find Jennie, her flashlight tucked under her chin, sliding open the puzzle box. She looked up.

"I used to have a bunch of these as a kid. My dad would get them for me when he was stationed overseas. Here, I think you're going to need this too."

She held out an envelope. It had my name on the front, followed by the usual "Personal and Confidential." On the back, Tuesday's date was written across the flap where it sealed. I opened it and found another letter. This one was from Millicent and stated that I was to act as her representative in the disposition of the assets from the family trust. This, too, was signed and witnessed, in this case by Mary Alice Quinn and Cheryl Studebaker.

"Quite a story," said Jennie, who had walked over and was reading Horatio's letter. "Makes me kind of glad my family has never had money."

I blew out a breath. "I'm not sure everything is legal. But then, I'm not sure how trusts work. I think you can do a lot with those that you can't with a will." Since my family had never had money either, I had no idea.

Jennie shrugged. "That's why lawyers make so much money. They make things impossible for the rest of us to understand. But the Ravenscroft family could afford the best. It may be knotty, but I bet it'll hold up."

"Yeah, I guess," I said. I looked through the papers again, making sure I had everything. I was thrilled to have finally found these, and sad for everyone involved. "I can do this," I muttered.

"Of course. You're a clever girl."

The voice seemed to come from behind me. I spun around. Jennie was in the doorway, looking out.

"Did you say something?" I asked. "Or—hear anything?"

"No, but it's starting to rain," she said. "We better go. I promised Sam we'd be quick."

"Okay," I said. I tucked the papers under my coat and walked toward the hall. Jennie was a few feet ahead of me. It was when I reached the door that I smelled it, the same smell I'd noticed before in this room. Cherry pipe smoke. I turned and looked back. There was a faint shimmer in the air, and then flitting shadows as the manor ravens rose off the lawn in a flurry of black wings. Then the smell and the shimmer were gone.

I joined Jennie and we walked out, locking up and replacing the crime scene tape. Thunder rumbled, closer this time. There was a flash of lightning, and the rain started coming down harder. I looked up, and spotted ravens in the trees. They looked down at us, silent and watchful. I started for the steps. Jennie reached out and touched my arm.

"What's the other favor?" she asked.

I paused. The image of Danny, dead on our living room floor, floated through my mind. I turned and faced her.

"I need to learn how to shoot."

She raised an eyebrow, then studied my face. She only asked one question.

"Tomorrow?"

I felt a flutter in my middle. I was going to do this.

"Tomorrow," I said.

She nodded, and then we walked down the steps and into the storm.

Acknowledgments

Many thanks to all who provided support and encouragement while I was writing this book, chief among them my husband, Mark, who kept our lives running, and my family—always my biggest fans. For their unwavering positive reinforcement and excitement about my writing career, I thank the staff of the Lee County Library System, particularly Angela Ortiz and the Technical Services team, and the members of the Reading Festival Committee. The fictional Eric, proprietor of Raven Hill's Adventure Wine & Spirits, has a real-life counterpart, and for sharing his extensive knowledge of all things wine related, I thank Eric Tuverson, owner of Adventure Wine•Beer•Spirits in Middletown, Delaware. Any errors on the subject are mine and not his. As always, thanks are due to Julie Gwinn and the Seymour Agency, who make sure the whole process keeps humming along.